TUESDAY NIGHT AT THE KASBAH

When Judy Blackwell joins a belly dancing class, she is only looking for a distraction from her empty marriage and emptying nest. She doesn't expect to get caught up in the lives and loves of other women in the group. As the women make exotic costumes and learn to undulate and shimmy, their menfolk are drawn into the circle. Judy, who has always believed in not rocking the boat, finds herself drawn towards Naz's widowed father, Trevor. Maybe it's the sinuous Middle Eastern music, maybe it's all that wine they keep drinking, but soon everyone finds themselves behaving in unexpected ways.

Tuesday Night At The Kasbah

by

Patricia Kitchin

Magna Large Print Books
Long Preston, North Yorkshire,
BD23 4ND, England.

British Library Cataloguing in Publication Data.

Kitchin, Patricia
    Tuesday night at the Kasbah.

    A catalogue record of this book is
    available from the British Library

    ISBN   978-0-7505-2651-7

First published in Great Britain in 2005 by Transita

Copyright © 2005 Patricia Kitchin

Cover illustration © John Hancock by arrangement with
P.W.A. International Ltd.

Published in Large Print 2007 by arrangement with Transita

Magna Large Print is an imprint of Library Magna Books Ltd.

Printed and bound in Great Britain by
T.J. (International) Ltd., Cornwall, PL28 8RW

ACKNOWLEDGEMENTS

Thanks to Dorothy Lumley, for all her hard work on my behalf.

And to the ladies of the Spirit of the Nile dance group, for fun, friendship and Eastern promise.

DEDICATION

To Albert,
who proved that there can be
second chances,
with love

CHAPTER 1

'Oh Mum, you're not!'

'That is so gross.'

Judy Blackwell's sons stared at her with identical eyes. Their father's eyes. Judy wondered if their father would look as horrified when he found out. Intrigued or delighted was too much to hope for. But even horrified would be all right. She'd settle for that. It was better than indifference.

'And what is so gross about it, exactly?' she asked.

Not that she didn't know. Parents dancing was excruciating at the best of times.

Oliver and Toby looked at each other, their faces mirroring despair. Even now, at seventeen, they looked ludicrously alike. They had different hairstyles, Oliver's cropped and Toby's shaggy, and Toby had rings all round his right ear. But there was no disguising that they were twins, especially as they were similarly dressed in the uniform of the young, Toby in combats, Oliver in jeans, both in dark tee-shirts splashed with slogans. The strain of being her sons was visibly weighing them down. Judy felt a smile tugging at the corners of her mouth.

'That sort of thing, it's for–'

'I mean, like, you're too–'

'Old?' Judy suggested. 'Fat?'

The boys had the grace to look embarrassed.

'Well–'

'Fat women are admired in the Middle East,' Judy told them.

'For real?' said Toby sceptically.

'But this isn't the Middle East, it's Mellingford,' Oliver pointed out.

'It's Middle Eastern dancing,' Judy told him.

The boys looked at each other again.

'But Mum, I mean, it's like–' Oliver began.

'Gross!' Toby finished for him.

Judy knew just what they meant. Having your mother doing belly-dancing was like finding out that your parents still had sex. Not that there was any danger of them suffering from that discovery, since Alan was 'too tired' these days. She tried to close her mind to what that meant.

'Tough,' Judy said. 'I'm going and that's that. Don't worry, your friends don't have to know. I'm not going to go out and perform in public. It's just an evening class.'

'Why can't you do pottery or flower arranging or something?' Oliver grumbled.

Well yes, she was beginning to ask herself that. She'd been thinking about going out and doing something different in the evenings, something to fill in the spaces now that summer was nearly over. All the usual possibilities had crossed her mind. Improve her shaky French. Find out if she had a talent for painting. Get to grips with the computer. But somehow, none of them had really grabbed her. Then she'd seen a poster in a shop window. It was a bright pink one with a picture on it of a long-haired dancer in harem pants and a little waistcoat, her arms raised above her head. *Learn to Belly-dance. Come and try the ancient art of Eastern dancing. All ages and abilities, everyone welcome.*

And something in her had responded. Something or someone. A different someone from the middle-aged wife and mother-of-four. Someone who wanted to escape from the daily home-work-shopping-home-television round. At the time, it had sounded far more interesting than pottery or flower arranging. Daring. It was years and years since she'd been daring.

'Because I don't want to, all right?' she said to the boys. 'Now shove off and watch *Neighbours* or something, I want to get the dinner on early.'

She wanted to make sure she had digested it before she went wobbling her belly about. There was plenty to wobble, God knows. She glanced down at it, bulging beneath her sensible tunic top. What if all the people at this class were young slender girls? All ages,

13

the poster had said, but supposing she was the oldest by twenty years? It didn't bear thinking about.

'When's Dad going to be in?' Toby asked. 'He said he'd take us for a practice run in the car some time this week.'

'He's working late,' Judy told them, and had to stop herself from joining in with their groans.

She watched them as they slouched out of the kitchen and slumped down one each end of the living room sofa, their long arms and legs overflowing in all directions. Her babies. What on earth was she going to do next year when they went to university? The thought of it made her feel oddly breathless. She held on to the kitchen table, waiting for the panic to recede. It left her shaky in the legs and slightly nauseous. Bloody menopause. Or rather, she supposed, non-bloody menopause. The *Neighbours* theme belted out. Judy took several steadying breaths.

It had been bad enough when their older brother and sister had left, for at least then she still had the twins at home to care for. But when they went it would be just herself and Alan rattling round in this big family house. There would be nothing then to deflect her attention from the excuses, the working-late-at-the-office, the weekend conferences, the mysterious wrong numbers. The being too tired.

She set to work in the spacious farmhouse-style kitchen, peeling potatoes, shredding cabbage. Her knife sliced viciously into the vegetables. Who was she this time? A new secretary? Some IT whizz kid? Whoever she was, why couldn't she stick to boyfriends her own age, men who weren't married?

Judy looked at the backs of her hands. Practical hands, with short unpolished nails. Her fingers bulged round her rings. Her skin looked like the bottom of a reservoir in a drought. Ageing hands. She put down the knife and felt her face. The sagging flesh along the jaw, the threatening double chin, the odd stiff hair she'd forgotten to tweeze out. Ageing face.

So – Alan was ageing too. He wasn't the handsome sports hunk she'd married. His hair was greying and thinning. His waist was thickening. But the stark truth was that he was still a good-looking older man, while she was a middle-aged has-been.

Was that why she was going belly-dancing? Not because of a sense of adventure, but because she hoped she would magically morph into a sinuous seductress who would take Alan's mind off the latest young thing at the office? At the doctor's surgery where she worked as a part time receptionist, they'd all hooted.

'Oo, Judy, you dark horse you.'

'Putting some oomph back into the

marriage, eh? Watch out, Alan!'

And she had laughed with them and played up to it. 'Oh yes – it'll be dance of the seven veils if he's lucky.'

She imagined the scene. Alan is slumped on the sofa watching the sexy WPCs in *The Bill,* whisky glass in hand. Then the sound fades and in its place is mysterious Middle Eastern music. Alan looks up, annoyed, about to ask what the hell is happening when his attention is riveted by a seductive figure emerging round the door. Her head and body are draped with coloured veils just transparent enough to hint at the luscious body beneath. Slowly, she dances round the room, shedding layers as she does so. Alan is mesmerised. Can this really be his wife? But she is the sexiest thing he has ever seen. Why has he not realised this before? As the last layer falls to the floor he catches her in his arms and flings her on the sofa. They make mad passionate love...

The knife slipped, nicking her finger. Blood dripped over the cabbage.

'Bugger!' So much for dreams.

Judy tore off a strip of kitchen towel and wrapped it round her finger but still the blood oozed out. The mild pain was welcome, distracting her. She reached in a drawer for the plasters. How long had she been putting plasters on her marriage? For ever, it seemed. But at least she was still married. That was what counted. They were still together, in spite of everything. That was an achievement, something to be proud of, when so many of her friends' marriages seemed to be falling apart.

Women who appeared to have far less to complain about than she did were making a break for freedom, buying places of their own, taking lovers. But in the end, what did it add up to? The lovers didn't always stick around, and if they did, they just turned into husbands mark two, with all the same problems as husbands mark one, plus the huge additional difficulties of who has the house, who has the children, trying to get on with stepchildren, coping with a whole new set of relations, coping with all the relations you already had ... the list was endless. She'd seen it happen, listened to friends wailing about the escalating nightmare.

Judy washed the blood off the cabbage, dumped it into the boiling water. That was that done. She would leave a nice dinner plated up for Alan – steak and kidney pie with lots of lovely gravy. Good home-cooked food that not many people bothered with these days. Whoever she was that he was seeing wouldn't know how to do a decent steak and kidney pie. He would come back when the shine had worn off.

He always did.

Maggie Stafford threw her heavy bag onto the back seat, started the car up and shot out of the staff car park, scattering a bunch of teenagers on bikes. Just down the road, a mother with a buggy and a toddler stepped out in front of her onto a zebra crossing. She stamped on the brakes.

'Stupid cow. Could have caused an accident!' she yelled.

The woman just stared at her vacantly and ambled to the other side.

Maggie felt a pounding in her head, a tightening of her chest. Just one more thing, one more, and she was going to lose it. Lose it and enjoy losing it. Especially with a man. If any man as much as looked at her he was going to get it.

On autopilot, she headed for home, until she passed the scruffy parade of shops at the edge of the rundown estate that always depressed her, even on good days. All of them except the off licence had metal shutters up, either because they were closed for the day or for good. The offie had bars over the windows even when it was open. Graffiti were scrawled over every building. *Kosovan scum go home. Wayne is a wanker.* Litter blew round in a miniature whirlwind.

Her own house, across the town, was a different world from this, but somehow its civilised quiet and order didn't beckon. She wanted company. She wanted a sympathetic

18

ear. She wanted a drink, and she made it a rule never to drink alone.

She reached behind her for her bag and scrabbled around for her mobile. Several calls later, she was heading for the Chequers in the centre of Mellingford. It wasn't a pub she liked especially, but it was convenient for Jan, the friend she was going to meet. As usual, the car park was full and she had to use the church hall one up the road, which didn't make her mood any better. She marched into the lounge bar, glared at any men who looked as if they might even glance at her and ordered two vodka and tonics. She had practically finished her one by the time Jan appeared.

'What's that? Oh no – I'm on a diet. I'll just have a slimline bitter lemon. Whatever's the matter, Mags? You sounded in a right old strop.'

Where to start? Maggie drained her own vodka, picked up the one she'd bought for Jan and poured out all the horrors of the start of term.

'Then he had the cheek to say that he had to change the bloody timetable again. He's had all summer to do it! And I'm the Head of Department, he should have consulted me before he made any more changes...'

Jan nodded and agreed until she ran out of words and drink. 'Another?'

Maggie sighed. 'No, best not. I've got to

drive home. Honestly, though, don't you think he's just the end?'

'Infuriating.'

Maggie lit a cigarette and took a long, satisfying drag. But even that didn't really work, any more than the vodka or Jan's sympathy. 'Do you know, there are times when I think I should just get out of teaching.'

Jan laughed. 'Oh come on, you know you don't mean that.'

Maybe she didn't. It wasn't the teaching, although Christ knew it wasn't getting any easier. It was the ever-changing goalposts. And the other teachers. 'There must be easier jobs.'

'Of course there are, but you're good at teaching. You know very well you'd never give it up. It's just John Lang that's winding you up.'

She was right, of course. 'I can't stand bloody perceptive friends,' Maggie grumbled.

'You shouldn't rise to him all the time.'

'I don't.'

Jan just looked at her.

'I can't help it.' It was the truth. Here she was, a competent woman, holding down a difficult job, responsible for the future prospects of several hundred young people, and she let a creep like John Lang get under her skin.

'You can't still fancy him, surely?' Jan said.

'Of course not!' Except that she did.

They had met just over a year ago, when she first came to work at Watfield Comprehensive. John Lang was the Deputy Head, attractive, and about her age. He also turned out to be that rarest of beings, an available man. He had been divorced four years and his children were grown up. Maggie instantly saw him as her property.

She had thought that her careful siege of him was working. He was friendly, he was helpful, his response to her jokes and remarks was becoming almost flirtatious. He was always willing to come out for drinks at her suggestion, though somehow other people always seemed to be included in the invitations as well. Then she noticed that those other people always included that little tart from the Languages Department, Emma Drew. Maggie disliked Languages on principle. Her ex was a Languages teacher. He'd left her for a younger colleague.

'I just can't forgive him for the way he humiliated me,' she said.

'Bastard,' Jan agreed.

'He strung me along all that time—'

And then, last term, to announce it like that. The two of them had stood in the middle of the staff room, holding hands, all pink with self-satisfaction.

'Emma and I are getting married.'

It was like a kick in the stomach. She had

just sat, speechless, breathless with pain and shock, while the rest of the staff offered congratulations, made jokes, admired the ring. And that tart stood there, young enough to be his daughter, smiling. Well might she smile. She had his arm round her shoulder and his diamond on her finger. Maggie had wanted to smash them both to a pulp. They had married in the summer break. No doubt that was why he hadn't had time to make a decent job of the timetables.

'Do you know what he said to me today?' she said.

'No, what?'

'He said, "Maggie, you are such a typical scientist."'

She avoided him if she could, but at lunch time she had got into a discussion about holidays and he had come to join it. All she had said was that she wouldn't like the sort of holiday where you went over the Channel and started driving and didn't know where you would get to by the end of each day, and he'd looked at her and made that remark

'What exactly do you mean by that?' she had asked. Too tartly.

'You wouldn't do anything that wasn't analysed and planned down to the last detail, would you?'

She couldn't see anything wrong in that. 'You have to plan things, otherwise you get into a terrible mess,' she said, meaning the timetables, amongst other things.

'A planned life is a controlled life?'

'Yes.'

She could see small smiles on the faces of some of her colleagues. They were well aware of what her plans had been for her life a year ago. And of how badly off-target those plans had been.

John Lang wasn't looking at them. His eyes were on Maggie. 'How about, a planned life is a boring life? Don't you think that it's the chance happenings that give it real meaning?'

Chance happenings generally gave you grief, in her opinion. 'No.'

John shook his head sadly. 'Poor Maggie. You don't know what you're missing. I bet you never acted on impulse in your entire life.'

'No, and I don't intend to.'

Now, sitting in the smoky bar with Jan, she felt the injustice of it all over again.

'He was so patronising,' she complained.

'Well, you can't help how you're made.'

Maggie stared at her. 'You're not saying that you agree with him are you?'

Jan shrugged. 'Perhaps it wouldn't hurt if you loosened up a bit sometimes.'

All the simmering anger of the day came to a boil. Maggie stood up. 'And I thought you were my friend!'

Jan blinked, horrified. 'Of course I am. I just said–'

'I heard what you said. You were siding with him. That really is the end.' And she marched out.

Which was, had she thought about it, an entirely unplanned action.

The evening air was cool on her flaming cheeks as she stumped up Church Lane towards the St Aidan's hall car park. Snatches of conversation ran round her head. *Such a typical scientist. You don't know what you're missing.* She reached the church hall before she took any real notice of where she was. It was the music that did it. Sinuous and seductive, it wound itself round her clashing thoughts. Middle Eastern music, incongruous and fascinating. Maggie found her footsteps slowing. It appeared to be coming from the church hall. She walked towards it.

There was lots of information on the notice board. Times of the Cubs and Guides, the Bridge Club and the Townswomen's Guild. A big yellow poster saying 'Save Our Playgroup'. And a bright pink one with a picture of a dancer in harem pants and a little waistcoat, her arms raised above her head.

Learn to Belly-dance. Come and try the ancient art of Eastern dancing. All ages and abilities, everyone welcome.

Never acted on impulse in her life, indeed. She would show him, the patronising bastard. She stubbed out her cigarette, opened the door and walked in.

24

CHAPTER 2

The first thing that struck Judy was the music. It was playing as she came in through the door, a quick hand-tapped drum beat overlaid with a sensuous winding melody on wind and strings, played on the Eastern scale. It caught at Judy immediately, making her heart beat faster, inviting her to move and sway. It seemed so out of place here, in an English church hall, yet as she listened to it, it invaded her body and shivered over her mind until the music was natural and the hall and the gaggle of chattering white women in their jeans and sweatshirts and styled hair were slightly odd.

She moved into the hall and put her bag down on one of the plastic chairs that lined the walls. Everyone seemed to know each other. They were all talking away as they changed.

'Hi. You new as well? Crappy place this, innit?'

A tall, stunning looking redhead in her twenties had dumped her bag down on the next chair and was looking round the room.

'Oh – yes – it's my first time–' Judy admitted.

'Virgins, eh?'

The girl shrieked with laughter at her own joke. Judy found herself smiling. 'Bit late for that.'

'Too right. I'm Shauna.'

'Judy.'

'Pleased to meet you.'

Shauna kicked her shoes off and peeled off her skin-tight jeans. Underneath she was wearing a dancer's leotard in bright red. She produced a gold crochet fringed shawl and tied it round her hips.

'This do, d'you think? It's my Mum's. God knows why she kept it, it's like Seventies stuff, innit? Not very belly-dance, but this is only classes, after all.'

It wasn't at all belly-dance, but it looked amazing on Shauna. Judy pulled her scarf out of her bag. A souvenir from a long-ago Spanish holiday, it was pink silk with long white fringes, and embroidered with flowers. Shauna pounced on it.

'Let's have a look. Oh, flamenco – Olé!'

She flung it round her shoulders and struck an attitude, head back, knee forward, arms raised as if holding castanets. Judy stared at her. She was a Spanish dancer.

'Do you do flamenco?'

'Nah – done practically everything else, though – ballet, jazz, tap, modern, salsa, ceroc – hey!' Shauna broke off and nodded towards a group of the other women. 'Fuck me, will you look at what some of those old biddies are wearing?'

Judy looked.

It was like dressing up time at infant school. Middle-aged women, some just as flabby if not flabbier than herself and even one or two real permed grannies, had on long full skirts of silk and gauze and shiny stuff. One even wore a fantastic silver fabric with a hologram effect on it, so that it shimmered all the colours of the rainbow as it reflected those around it. Some women wore toning tee-shirts or tops with the skirts, and wonderful beaded and sequinned scarves round their hips, others had long semi-transparent tunics with sequinned trims, others still had bare midriffs and sparkly matching bras and belts.

'Amazing–' Judy breathed.

'I didn't know we had to dress like something out of a harem,' someone else said.

Judy and Shauna turned round. A slender brown-skinned girl with black straightened hair was staring at the women and their costumes.

'All I've got is trackie bottoms and a scarf,' she said.

'I don't think us new girls are expected to have all the gear,' Judy told her. She introduced herself and Shauna. The girl gave a guarded smile.

'Naz.'

Other women came in. There was a small dumpy one with glasses in a tie-dyed skirt, and a beautiful thirty-something blonde dripping with designer labels, the sort who always made Judy feel inadequate. Then a woman of about her own age in a business suit with sharp-cut hair marched in. She walked straight up to the front of the hall and looked round.

'Right, who's in charge round here? Where do we sign in?'

The chatter died away. Naz looked at Shauna. 'Are we supposed to sign in?' she muttered.

Shauna shrugged. 'No idea.'

A dark-haired woman in her thirties came forward. 'Er – I don't have a book or any-thing. You just turn up and pay at the end. Five pounds.'

'You're the instructor?' Suit Woman asked.

Naz caught Shauna's eye. They both pulled faces. 'Bossy cow,' Naz muttered.

Judy had to agree.

'Sounds like a fucking teacher,' said Shauna.

'Er – yes. I'm Cheryl,' the instructor said. She had a high-pitched, rather girlie voice.

'I see.' Suit Woman didn't sound very impressed. 'Well, I'm not exactly dressed for this. I might just observe this week.'

'Oh – no – there's no need for that. I'll lend you something,' Cheryl scrabbled around in a suitcase and pushed a colourful bundle of clothes into Suit Woman's arms. A hubbub of talking burst out.

Cheryl stood in the middle of the floor. She was simply dressed, compared with some of her class members, in a black top and long green skirt with a green and gold beaded hip-scarf. She raised her voice.

'Er – everybody – hello!' Gradually, the chattering died down. Cheryl was slightly flushed. 'Thanks – er – well, it's nice to see everyone again after the summer holidays. And we've got some new people here today. Hello new people! Nice to see you. Hope you're going to enjoy it. We're going to start with a warm up as usual, and I think what'd be best is if all you new ones be ever so brave and come to the front, and then you can see what's going on.'

'Oh dear,' said Judy. 'I really don't want to go to the front. I'll feel all exposed.'

'Don't be such a div,' said Shauna, and strode confidently to stand right in front of Cheryl.

The rest of the new contingent followed her like sheep.

Cheryl put on a slow, gentle piece of music and put them through a warm up routine. Then she changed it to a faster piece and showed them a hip drop.

'Both knees slightly bent, now drop – and up – and drop–'

The class followed, one hip, then the other, fast then slow, two right, two left, forwards and backwards, travelling... Cheryl turned her back to them so they could copy more easily. Judy saw how the simple step became a dance. The heavy beaded fringes on Cheryl's scarf underlined her movements, and the lift and fall of her hips became something mesmerising and beautiful. Judy knew her own attempts were clumsy and exaggerated, and concentrated fiercely, trying, and failing, to achieve grace.

'Great! Terrific! You're doing really well!'

Cheryl went along the line, correcting posture, loosening stiff limbs. She stopped by Shauna. 'You're a dancer, aren't you?'

'Yeah.'

'Thought so. It shows. You've got to remember that this is a grounded dance, earthy. Not like ballet, where you're flying up into the air all the time.'

'Yeah, earthy. That'll do me,' Shauna grinned.

Judy felt a flash of jealousy. She wanted very much be able to do this, but she felt like a hippo.

They learnt a slow sinuous movement of the hips. They combined the smooth and the sharp movements. Then Cheryl formed them into a circle and got them all moving round slowly while she called one or other of the last year's class in to improvise to the music. Judy watched, amazed. Some of the women were wonderful dancers. Age didn't come into it. Their hips flashed and dipped and shimmied, their backs curved and undulated. They seemed to be able to move different parts of their bodies independently. Laughing, they reacted and interplayed with each other, throwing the emphasis of the dance back and forth, leading, following, mirroring each other.

'It's great, isn't it?'

It was one of the other new ones, the young woman with the glasses and the tie-dye skirt. They were taking a breather. She held out her water bottle to Judy.

'Like a drink? I haven't got anything catching.'

'Thanks, it didn't occur to me to bring water,' Judy admitted.

The young woman's face was bright red with effort. 'It's more tiring than you'd think, isn't it? And not what I was expecting. I don't know quite what I *was* expecting, but this is really great. I'm definitely coming back next week. Oh – I'm Cathy.'

'Judy. Yes, I'll be back, too. I'm really enjoying it, though I don't know if I'll ever be as good as some of them.'

Naz joined them. 'I've just got to have one of those costumes,' she said. 'I'm going to look for fabric tomorrow.'

'They're so beautiful, aren't they?' Cathy

sighed. 'Just like something out of a fairy tale. *The Arabian Nights.* I adored those stories. I read them over and over. And I used to love dressing up when I was little.'

They danced some more, then did cooling-down exercises. Judy couldn't believe how quickly the time had gone.

'Bye everybody,' Cheryl was calling. 'See you next week. Don't forget to put your fivers in the box.'

And there they were, changing back into their outdoor clothes.

'It's only half past nine,' Shauna said. 'I'm not going home yet. Who's coming for a drink?'

'Oh yes, good idea,' cried Cathy, much to Judy's surprise. She didn't look like the sort that hung out in pubs.

'I'm not sure,' Naz said. 'I ought to get back.'

'Bloody hell, what's the matter with you? Your mum not know you're out or something?' Shauna asked.

Naz went stony faced. 'I've left my little girl at home.'

'Who's babysitting?'

This was the blonde in the designer label clothes. She was pulling on her Armani jeans.

'My dad.'

The blonde smiled. She had perfect bone structure and wide blue eyes. Just the type that Judy always imagined Alan falling for.

32

'My husband's looking after mine. I think they can be left for a bit longer, don't you?'

'Well, yeah, I s'pose,' Naz said.

Judy held back, not sure if she was included. They were all younger than her.

Shauna looked at her. 'You coming, Jude?'

It would be nice not to have to go home to an empty house. 'Yes. Thanks.'

'Right, we're on,' said Shauna. 'Mine's a Red Bull and vodka.'

'The Chequers is the nearest, and it's not a bad place,' said Suit Woman.

Shauna looked at her. Her face was a picture. Judy was afraid she was going to tell her to get lost, or worse. In a rush of sisterly support, she got in before Shauna could open her mouth.

'Is it? Oh good. That'll do nicely, as they say.'

So the six of them ended up squeezed round a table in The Chequers.

'Fiver in the kitty,' said Shauna, producing hers and slapping it down on the table. 'What are we all having?'

They were all driving home except Shauna, so they ordered cokes or fruit juices.

'Bloody hell, it's like going out with a kids' party,' Shauna complained.

Introductions were made. The elegant blonde was called Fiona. The bossy woman in the suit was Maggie.

'I never intended coming to the class this

evening. I didn't even know it existed. I just happened to be passing and heard the music and decided to go in. On impulse,' she told them. She said it defiantly, as if she had done something out of the ordinary.

'And are you glad you did?' Judy asked.

'I think so. It's certainly different. But it's a bit of a shambles, isn't it? No records of who's attending or what they've paid. And really there ought to be two classes, one for us beginners and another for those who've been going for a while. I mean, it doesn't work at all well at the moment, does it? The advanced people must be bored going over the basic steps that we're doing, and we certainly couldn't follow the advanced stuff she was doing later in the session. That's the trouble when untrained people start running things like this.'

Judy could sense the irritation in the others.

'I thought it was good. I enjoyed it,' Naz said.

'That Cheryl's an ace dancer,' Shauna said. 'I can tell.'

'A wonderful dancer,' Cathy agreed. 'And very nice too, don't you think? The way she went round encouraging everybody.'

'Yes, it was a good evening,' Judy chimed in.

Maggie was unfazed. 'I'm not saying that it wasn't an enjoyable evening, or that this

Cheryl person isn't a good dancer. What I'm saying is that the organisation is virtually non-existent. If she can't cope, then somebody ought to step in and help her to get her act together.'

'You volunteering?' asked Shauna, voicing everyone's thoughts.

'If necessary, yes.'

Fiona spoke. She had a low, quiet voice, so everyone had to listen attentively to catch what she said. 'Don't you think that this is a case of, if it ain't broke don't mend it?'

'Yeah! Good on you, Fiona,' Naz cheered.

'I must say, I rather agree with you. It seems quite all right as it is,' Judy said.

'After all, we only started this evening,' said Cathy.

It was getting to Maggie. You could see that. And she wasn't going to let it drop. 'What I'm saying is–' she began.

'For Chrissakes, why don't–?' Shauna interrupted.

'Weren't some of those costumes lovely?' Judy said loudly. 'I must say, I felt quite underdressed.'

To her surprise, Naz came in on her side. 'Yeah, I'm going out tomorrow to find some fabric.'

'Can you sew? I didn't think you young girls knew one end of a needle from the other. They don't seem to teach needlework in schools these days,' said Judy.

'The National Curriculum—' began Maggie.

But nobody was listening to her.

'My mum taught me,' Naz explained. 'I make things for friends – clothes, soft furnishings, that sort of thing. It's a business, almost. It fits in with looking after my little girl.'

'That's very enterprising of you,' Judy said.

'What sort of design were you thinking of making? The full belly-dance costume with the bra and belt or the more ethnic look?' Fiona asked.

'I liked those tunic things,' Cathy said.

'Oh yes. I can't see me showing too much flesh.'

'I thought a little cropped waistcoat and harem pants.'

They all had ideas. Fiona fished in her Hermès bag and took out a notebook and gold pencil. 'Something like this?'

She began drawing with swift, sure strokes and beneath her fingers a design emerged – a tight bodice, sheer full sleeves, V-shaped band on the hips and baggy trousers. 'Square or scoop neck, do you think?'

'Scoop. And you could catch the sleeves up here and here.' Naz indicated on her arms.

Fiona altered the design. 'What about something on the head?'

'A pillbox hat with a veil. And a yashmak,'

suggested Cathy.

'I like the yashmak,' said Judy.

'That's really good,' Naz said, looking at the finished effect. 'Like a proper fashion sketch. Are you a designer?'

'Oh no, nothing like that. I'm just interested in art.'

Talented as well as rich and beautiful. How sick making.

'I fancy one of them proper belly-dance efforts, but God knows how I'm going to get it 'cause I can't thread a needle,' said Shauna.

Fiona drew more designs. They all threw in suggestions. Naz explained how to cut a basic circular skirt. Time was called. Fiona offered to run Shauna home. They all agreed that they were looking forward to next Tuesday. Judy got into her car feeling more cheerful and carefree than she had done for ages.

Naz drove home in her father's Mondeo and ran it into the driveway of the house they shared. Once it had been the family house where they had all lived, her mum Sadie and dad Trevor, her brothers Billy and Joe and herself. Now Joe was married and Billy was living in a flatshare in London and her mum – her mum was dead. Now the house was two flats, and Naz and her six-year-old daughter Karis lived downstairs so that Karis could have the run of the garden and her dad lived upstairs and they all looked out for each other.

She let herself in. The television was on and her dad was sleeping on the sofa in front of *Newsnight*. He woke up as she came into the room.

'What? Oh – I wasn't asleep,' he said.

'No, of course you weren't,' Naz said, dropping a kiss on the balding bit on top of his head. 'Everything all right?'

'Yes, yes, we had a story or two and then she went to sleep like a lamb.'

'Chocolate?'

'Please.'

She peeped in at Karis. She was lying on her back with one arm spread out and the other cuddling her favourite rabbit. Her dark hair was fizzed out over the pillow. Naz bent and kissed her round brown cheek, then stood gazing at her. Her baby. Her wonderful, beautiful baby. Sometimes, she was almost glad that Dominic had walked out on them. It meant that she didn't have to share her with anyone.

Her dad was sitting up and looking more alert when she brought in the mugs of chocolate. 'How was the dance class?'

'Great.' Yes, it had been great. She had really enjoyed it

'That's good. You ought to get out more, love. You're only young still.'

He was always saying that. But it wasn't that easy. 'There isn't time. Not with college work to do.'

'Make time. You know I can always babysit.'

'Mm.'

'Nice people?'

'Yeah.' She took a sip of chocolate and thought about it. 'Weird mixture. I mean, we went for a drink after, all us new ones. There was this rich bitch, and a new-agey sort of woman, and an older woman, cosy, you know, nice, and this dancer – you'd call her tarty – oh, and this bossy cow. None of us really wanted her, but she sort of came along anyway. But we got on really well.'

'All women?'

'Yes, well, you wouldn't get men at a belly-dancing class, would you?'

'Perhaps you ought to go to something else. What's it they're all doing now? Salsa? Something where you need a partner.'

Naz sighed. 'I told you, Dad, I don't want a boyfriend. They're nothing but trouble. I'm OK with you and Karis.'

'Just because you had one bad experience–'

One very bad experience. One Dominic was enough to last a lifetime. She wasn't risking going through all that again, and now she had Karis to think of as well. 'I don't want to talk about it.'

'People were meant to be in pairs,' he said, just as she knew he would.

'Then take your own advice,' she retorted.

'Oh, I'm too old to find anyone else now.

39

But you're not.'

'I said, I don't want to talk about it. End of conversation,' Naz insisted.

But when she went to bed, and dreamed she was dancing in a pub in the waistcoat and harem pants, there was a man there. She couldn't see him, but she knew he was there, and he was nice, he wasn't a threat. Which was really weird.

CHAPTER 3

The audience erupted into wild applause. They rose to their feet, clapping, cheering, calling out for more, while she stood there, flushed, breathless, triumphant, a vision of grace and beauty in her flame-coloured costume dripping with beads and flashing with sequins...

'Are you with us, Cathy?'

'What?' Cathy Turner came back to reality. She was standing by the cages at the vet's practice where she worked. She was supposed to be seeing to the special diets of the sick animals.

'Come on, Cathy, you're on a different planet today. I said, would you get Jasmine, please. Her owner's here to collect her.'

'Oh, right, yes. Sorry.'

Ever since the belly-dance class the other

day, she'd not been able to get that music out of her head. She took the pet carrier that was handed to her and looked along the row. Jasmine. Yes. A pretty half-grown female cat, black and white, in to be spayed. She lifted the reluctant creature out of the cage and into the carrier, where it hunched up right at the back.

'All right, puss,' she told it. 'We're not going to do any more nasty things to you. You're going home now.'

Jasmine glared balefully at her. As well she might, poor thing. She'd been deprived of her ability to have kittens. Cathy looked at the label on the cage. Ms N. Randall. She picked up the carrier and went into the waiting room.

'Ms Ran – oh!'

It was the black girl from the dancing class. Or at least, she wasn't very black. Partly, maybe. She had brown skin and black hair, but her features weren't totally African. And she had her daughter with her. Cathy gazed at her. She was a gorgeous coffee-coloured child of five or so, with huge brown eyes and her hair in bunches. Cathy was seized with an overwhelming wave of envy and need.

Naz sounded surprised. 'Cathy! I didn't know you worked here.'

'Oh – yes – I've been here for–'

She hardly knew what she was saying. She gripped the cat carrier with white-knuckled hands, fighting the urge to pick the child up, to hold her to her breast and never let her go.

'Is Jasmine all right?' The child was looking at her pet.

'This is Karis.' There was unmistakable pride in Naz's voice. 'My daughter.'

'Karis. What a pretty name. Unusual.' Cathy's voice came out all croaky. She cleared her throat.

Karis was peering into the carrier. 'She doesn't look happy.'

'She's feeling very sore. But she'll soon be better. She'll be glad to get back to her own home,' Cathy told her.

Her voice still sounded odd. This was awful. She felt hot and cold all over. She must get a grip.

'She's still a bit woozy from the anaesthetic. Just keep her quiet for a while–' she launched into the usual advice for owners, all the while looking at Karis, at her round cheeks, her dear little nose, the way expressions played over her face as she talked to her cat.

'Thanks, we'll do all that, won't we, Karis? Look after poor Jasmine.'

'Yes.' Karis tore her attention away from the cat and looked up at Cathy. 'Mummy said she doesn't want Jasmine to have kittens,' she explained.

'I know. Very sensible,' Cathy said gravely.

It was all right for Naz. She didn't need hoards of animals. She had a real daughter of her own.

'Jasmine's Karis's cat. I thought it'd be good for her to have a pet. As she's an only child.'

Just one would be enough. More would be wonderful, but she didn't mind just one. 'Yes – I was an only child, but my parents wouldn't allow me to have animals. I always longed for a cat or a dog. Most specially a dog. I thought we could go on adventures together, like in Enid Blyton–' she stopped, embarrassed. 'Silly, really.'

'Oh no. I think it's brilliant when children have strong imaginations. I want Karis to be imaginative.'

'I'm sure she is.'

'Cathy, there's a patient to be seen to here–'

'Oh – right.' She smiled apologetically at Naz. 'I'm sorry, it's so busy here.'

'Yeah, I can see that. Thanks for looking after Jasmine. See you Tuesday?'

'Yes, Tuesday. Bye. Bye Karis!'

She watched them out of the waiting room, then turned to help deal with a greyhound trailing blood from a cut pad. She managed to keep her mind on the job until the end of her shift, but as she cycled home she found herself daydreaming again. She sent Naz off to Find Herself in the Far East, leaving Cathy to look after Karis. And when she did not return, Cathy was allowed to keep the little girl for her own... She reached the front door and for a moment she hardly knew where she was. The fantasy had been so vivid. She scrabbled for her key in the chaos of her large crocheted bag.

There was a smell of frying in the air. 'Hello, darling,' her husband Mike called from the kitchen. 'Had a good day?'

'Hello. Yes, OK,' she said automatically. But it wasn't. It had been ruined by seeing Naz and that adorable Karis.

Mike came through to the hall and gave her a big hug. He was a round, untidy looking man with a bushy beard, given to displays of affection. Her teddy bear.

'What's the matter, love? You sound down.'

'Oh – it's nothing,' Cathy sighed.

Sometimes she did not have the energy to talk to him about it. He just would not see things her way. She trudged upstairs to the bathroom, sat on the loo, looked down, and burst into tears.

Her period. Two days early. It was so *unfair*. She sat for ages, sobbing. Nothing seemed worth moving for. She half-heard Mike's footsteps coming up the stairs and stopping outside the bathroom door.

'Cath? What's the matter, love?' She didn't answer. 'Cath – dinner's ready. It's Linda MacCartney sausages–'

'I don't care. Go away.'

'Cath – darling–'

The door started to open. She sprang up and staggered towards it, thudded against it with her shoulder, forced it shut and locked it. 'I said go away!'

'Cath, please–'

Now that she was on her feet she shuffled to the cabinet and found her tampons. When she finally came out, Mike was sitting on the top step of the stairs waiting for her. He came and put his arms around her.

'Oh darling – is it?'

'What do you think?'

A new wave of weeping welled up. She leaned her head on his shoulder and cried and cried, while he rocked her and rubbed her back and made soothing noises.

'Oh darling – there there – I'm so sorry.' And then, 'Maybe next time.'

She pulled away from him, raging. 'But it won't, will it? Next time will be useless, and the next and the next – I don't know why we bother doing it. It's never going to work.'

His gentle face was creased with concern. 'But it might,' he said earnestly. 'It might. There's always hope. It only takes one.'

One. Just one single solitary sperm. That was all that was needed. One sperm strong enough to make it as far as her ovum.

'But it's not going to. We've been trying for seven years. Seven years! And it's never happened. And it's never going to.'

'Cathy, Cathy, darling – you mustn't give

up hope. Never give up hope.'

Hope. Hope was dangerous. Hope let you down. Hope was nothing but stupid fantasies. She broke away and flung back into the bathroom again, locking him out.

Later he gave up trying to reason with her through the door.

Later still he sighed and went downstairs.

Even later still, Cathy stopped crying and washed her swollen, blotchy face with cold water and crept downstairs as well. The Linda MacCartney sausages were in the bin, along with the hand-sliced chips he had made specially for her, because he knew she didn't much like oven chips. Mike was in the dining room, tapping away at the computer. He got up when he heard her, cleared two cats and a pile of magazines off the sofa, sat her down and made her a cup of tea.

'Do you want something to eat? I can get something out of the freezer.'

She shook her head. 'I'm not hungry. But if you want something–'

'I'm not hungry either.'

They sat side by side, limp with misery. 'I don't know what else to say,' Mike began.

A cat leapt onto Cathy's knee. It began kneading her thighs, purring loudly. Cathy stroked it with fierce attention. 'You do,' she said, in a low, hard voice. 'You do know.'

'Oh Cath, please. Not that again. You know what I feel about it.'

'But why? Why? It's so stupid. It would be our baby. It would come out of my womb. I would give birth to it.'

'It'd be your baby. Yours and some other man's. Not mine. It wouldn't be my baby.'

'But it's not as if I was going to sleep with some other man! It's just a simple medical procedure. And they select the donors very carefully. They would find us one who looks like you. And we would bring it up. That's what matters, the loving and the caring, not the – the biology.'

Why couldn't he see that? The frustration was so intense that she felt as if her whole body was about to burst with it.

'It still wouldn't be mine, would it?' Mike said.

She screamed. The sound came from deep in her guts and tore out of her throat. She closed her eyes and opened her mouth and it rang round and round her head. Mike got hold of her shoulders . He shook her.

'Stop it! Stop it! You're being hysterical. Shut up.'

She stopped. Her throat hurt. She was panting.

'I'm sorry, I'm sorry. I know how much you want this–'

'You don't. You don't know how much I want it.'

If he did, if he knew how she longed and longed for a baby, for a small person to love and care for, to watch over and play with and cherish – if he understood that, then he wouldn't hold out on her like this.

'Well maybe I don't,' Mike admitted. 'But there are so many practical difficulties – oh, we've been over all this so many times.'

'Like what?' Practical difficulties were nothing. Anything could be solved, if they could just have a baby.

'Well what would we tell it? I mean, about its father? How could you explain that to a child? And when it was old enough to understand, what a shock – I mean, to find out that your dad isn't really your dad at all.'

'But *you* would be its father. The genetic father would be nothing but a sperm donor. That's all.'

They went round and round it. Like rats in a cage. Getting nowhere.

'I'm sorry,' Mike repeated. 'I'm really sorry, but I can't help the way I feel about it. It revolts me.'

Cathy felt exhausted. Her head was vibrating with pain. She heaved herself onto her feet. Her legs were shaking. 'I'm going to bed.'

Mike sighed. 'OK.'

Holding on to the banisters, she heaved herself up the stairs. She felt like an old woman. She went through the bathroom cabinet, her tights drawer and the heaps on her dressing table before finally tracking down an almost used up packet of paracetamol in her weekend bag. She gulped the pills down with water straight from the tap. They scraped her throat.

She couldn't be bothered to wash. She trudged into the bedroom, peeled off her clothes and dropped them on the floor and collapsed into bed. But she couldn't sleep. One of the cats came in and attempted to curl up in the crook of her knees, but she pushed it off. Nothing as simple as an animal's warmth could comfort her.

Some time later, Mike came up. She heard him plodding around in the bathroom. Then he crept into the bedroom. She lay absolutely still, controlling her breathing, letting him think she was asleep. He got carefully into bed. Cathy stayed dead still. She could feel him trying to study her in the dark. Tentatively, his hand touched her shoulder. Her whole body revolted. She shook him off.

'Cathy,' he whispered, pleading.

She said nothing. She lay with her back to him, stiff. Eventually he sighed and turned over. A while later she heard his breathing steady, and slow. He slept. She lay awake.

She supposed she must have fallen asleep at some point, because she woke with a start to find that Mike was already in the bathroom, shaving.

They went through the morning routines, feeding their collection of animals, making the sandwiches. Mike went into the dining room and came back holding a couple of sheets of paper. He stood in the kitchen doorway, shifting from one foot to the other.

'I – er – I did these for you last night. I looked them up on the net.' He held them out.

Cathy took them. She glanced at them, then looked again, more carefully. Each sheet had four stunning belly-dance costumes on it, heavily beaded and sequinned in beautiful patterns with wafts of semi-transparent fabric for sleeves or skirts or midriff pieces. One set was mostly in pinks, the other in silver.

'It's a shop in Cairo,' Mike explained. 'There's loads of them, all different colours, but I thought, well, you look nice in pink, so I just downloaded these two pages. You can order them by credit card.'

'I thought you didn't like me going belly-dancing.' He'd been dead against it the other day.

She looked at the costumes. She didn't want pink, she wanted flame. Flame and gold.

'Well–' Mike didn't quite meet her eyes. 'I thought, it's nice for you to have a hobby.'

A hobby. A baby substitute. 'Thanks'.

'But I need the car to go to my class,' Judy said.

'Your class?' her husband Alan was momentarily puzzled. 'What–? Oh – you mean your belly-wobbling. You're still doing that, are you?'

'Of course I am. Why would I not?' This was the third week now, and she wouldn't miss it for the world.

'Why on earth did you book your car in to be serviced today, then?'

'I told you, it should have been done by this evening, but they couldn't get a part. A something-or-other joint.'

'I can't think why it's so difficult, it's an Escort, for God's sake, not a Ferrari or something.'

'Well I don't know. That's just what they said.' She hated the insides of cars. When the man at the garage explained things, she just nodded and tried to look knowledge-able. He could tell her anything, really.

Alan sighed, exasperated. 'Honestly, Judy, you let people walk all over you.'

She's the assertive type, your girlfriend, is she? Has she told you to get lost this evening? Is that why you're in such a tetchy mood?

'All right, all right,' Judy turned away and began stacking plates in the dishwasher. The boys had already made themselves scarce. The sound of drum'n'bass came pounding through the ceiling. 'I'll take a cab, then, if it doesn't fit in with your plans.'

He was only going to the golf dub for a

drink. Or so he said.

'No, no–' Alan put on his martyred voice. 'I'll drop you off. What time is it?'

'Eight.'

'And when does it finish?'

'Nine-thirty.'

'Nine-thirty? Bloody hell, Judy, I can't come all the way back for nine-thirty. That's the middle of the evening. I'm not a bloody taxi.'

No, I'm the bloody taxi. I'm the one who usually runs round picking everyone else up at their convenience. 'I'm not asking you to. I expect we'll go for a drink in the Chequers afterwards, and then I'll either get a lift home or take a cab. OK?'

'Yes, yes.'

He lost interest in the argument and went off, leaving her to clear the rest of the dinner things away.

At the last minute things were complicated by Toby and Oliver wanting a lift with all their music gear to a friend's house, which Alan refused to do, causing much swearing and muttering from the boys.

'Bloody kids. Expect to be looked after like babes in arms. You mollycoddle them, you know.'

Maybe she did. They were her unexpected prizes, her surprise bonus extras. They were showered with all the love that Alan didn't seem to want. Judy followed him into the car, carrying her bag. The feel of it gave a new direction to her thoughts. She peeped inside at the folds of slippery fabric. The others would be surprised when they saw her new skirt. She had found an old ballgown in Oxfam, a turquoise satin effort with puff sleeves and a boned bodice. Not at all her sort of thing, of course, but she had cut the skirt off and run some elastic round the waist, or rather the hips, and now it was a dance skirt. She was really rather pleased with it. Thinking about it, she failed to hear most of what Alan was grumbling about.

'Is this it? St Aidan's? Oh bloody hell, what's that idiot doing in the four wheel drive? Why do these women buy those things if they can't handle them properly? Look at–'

He stopped the car right in the entrance to the car park in order to watch the driver of the Range Rover expertly insert it into a very small space at the end. A space that she wouldn't have liked to have tried to get the Escort into. As the light from the church hall fell on the front of the thing, Judy saw that it was Fiona at the wheel and that she had Shauna with her. Yes, Fiona would be good at driving. She was the competent type. Cool and in control.

'Buy them just as status symbols and all they ever do is do the school run in them, when really they'd be far better off with–'

Alan broke off abruptly. Shauna and Fiona

53

were getting out of the car. Two tall women, one blonde, the other redheaded. They made a very striking pair. Judy glanced at Alan's profile. He was staring, his mouth slightly open, an expression of naked greed on his face, though she couldn't tell which one of them he was fixed on. As they walked towards the hall she saw that while Fiona was dressed in jeans and a swing jacket with her hair in a pony tail, Shauna had on a leather biker's jacket over her dancer's leggings and high heels, while her startling mane of hair flowed over her shoulders and down her back.

It isn't fair. It just isn't fair. I never looked like that, even when I was her age. Men never stared after me with uncontrolled lust. Jealousy griped at her, a great black poisonous lump in her guts. 'I'll be going, then,' Judy said, loudly.

'Mm.'

She got out of the car and stood holding the door. 'Bye then. Thanks for the lift.'

'Right.'

She slammed the door. Shauna and Fiona disappeared into the hall. Alan's head snapped round. 'There's no need to slam it like that. You'll ruin the thing.'

She ignored him and walked away, acutely conscious of the difference between her back view and Shauna's.

The hall was buzzing with talk against the

flowing Middle Eastern music. Shauna and Fiona both smiled and said hello as she came in. Judy forced herself to reply. She found herself looking surreptitiously at them as they changed. Shauna had a fantastic body, not a bulge to be seen except where her high round breasts created a perfect cleavage. And Fiona's body was slim and toned too, a size larger, but beautifully proportioned with no sagging bits, and she was possibly ten years older than Shauna and had two children.

Judy felt physically ill. She looked down at her own droopy breasts and bulging stomach. She put her hands on her waist, if you could call it a waist, and gloomily squeezed the handfuls of fat. Horrible, horrible. No wonder Alan went for younger flesh.

'Hello. How's things?'

It was Maggie. Judy pulled her face into a smile. 'Fine, fine.'

'I'm really getting to look forward to Tuesdays now. It's something a bit different, isn't it?'

She wasn't so bad, Maggie. That first time she had thought her a bit of a pain, but at least she wasn't young and beautiful. Probably about the same age as herself.

'Yes, it's fun. Better than aerobics.' She made an effort to keep talking, to appear friendly. 'I've even made myself a skirt. Look.'

She put it on over her green tee-shirt and tied her fringed Indian scarf round her hips. Maggie admired the effect.

'I wish now that I could sew. You don't need to normally, do you? I don't even own a machine.'

Maggie was getting changed. Even she was a lot less bulgy than Judy. She felt horribly inferior. She wanted to go away and hide.

'Hello, Judy.'

It was Cathy. Judy smiled and answered. And then Naz came in. Another smile, another greeting. Naz came over and examined the skirt and asked lots of questions about where she got the fabric and how she adapted the dress. She showed the outfit she was making. She had got as far as a ruby skirt and a wide shaped belt to go round the hips, edged with a trimming of heavy gold drop beads.

'Isn't this lovely?' she enthused, shaking the belt so that the beads quivered. 'There were loads of different ones at the haberdashery stall in the market. I could've spent a fortune.'

Judy found herself drawn into a technical discussion on costume making. The feeling of inadequacy retreated. She was good at something. She could sew.

Cheryl was clapping her hands. 'Come along everyone. I've got a lovely new CD for us to dance to.'

Obediently, Judy joined the class. She warmed up and stretched. She followed the hip drop and the slow figure-of-eight. The movements felt less strange now. The skirt swished and flowed. She copied the simple dance routine and managed to keep in time with the music and Cheryl's steps. There was nothing in her head except the music and her determination to make her lumpy body imitate Cheryl's graceful movements. Cheryl showed them a forward-and-back step she called a kashlemar. In unison, they kashlemarred across the room. Judy found herself smiling. The music accelerated. The class went faster with it, stopping with a triumphant flourish at the end, panting and laughing.

Cathy turned to her, her eyes shining. 'Wasn't that triffic?'

'Wonderful!' Judy gasped, and meant it.

At the end of the session, she realised that she hadn't felt like an old has-been for the whole hour and a half.

'Well done everyone! That was lovely. Next week we'll start putting together a few movements for a dance to do at the Christmas party.'

Christmas. Oh God. The sinking feeling returned.

'What happens at this Christmas party?' Maggie asked.

'Oh, we have a lovely time,' Cheryl said. 'We take over the Arabian Nights restaurant

– you know, the Lebanese one? – and we take all our families along and dress up and take our own music and in between courses we all get up and dance.'

What would Alan make of that? Would he refuse to come? Not if he knew Shauna was going to be there. Perhaps she wouldn't tell him.

'Bye, everyone. See you next week,' Cheryl was saying.

'Who's coming down the boozer?' Shauna called.

'Me!'

'And me!'

'Me too,' Judy heard herself say. More than ever, she didn't want to go back to an empty house.

She found herself next to Cathy and Naz in the pub.

'How's Jasmine recovering?' Cathy asked.

'She's fine. The bald patch has nearly grown over now,' Naz said.

'Who's Jasmine? Not your little girl?' Judy asked.

The other two laughed.

'No, my cat. I took her to be spayed and when I went to get her, I found that Cathy works at the vet's.'

'I work at a doctor's. Part time reception- ist. I bet your patients are less trouble than ours,' Judy said.

'At least yours don't bite.'

'I wouldn't be so sure about that.'

Fiona and Shauna wanted to see Naz's belt again. She explained how she had made it, and what she planned to do with the rest of the outfit.

Cathy shyly produced two A4 sheets of pictures. 'My husband got these over the net.'

They all exclaimed over the exotic costumes.

'There's hours and hours of detailed work in those,' sighed Naz.

'Sweated labour. You shouldn't buy that sort of thing and collaborate in exploiting other women,' Maggie stated.

She was probably right. In fact she was almost certainly right. But why did she feel an overwhelming need to contradict her?

'Bollocks,' said Shauna. 'They're getting paid, aren't they?'

'Poverty level wages...' Maggie was off on a political lecture.

Fiona turned to Naz. 'Do you think you could show the rest of us how to make that? If we're going to dance at this Christmas party, we want to look right. Perhaps we could all get together one evening and pool our ideas.'

'Yeah, OK.' Naz didn't sound that enthusiastic.

'Oh, that's a triffic idea,' Cathy cut in.

'Yeah. I can't sew for nuts, but I might get

my Mum to do it for me,' Shauna said.

Another long-suffering Mum. What would it be like to be Shauna's mother?

Fiona offered to host the evening. 'If that's all right with you, Naz? Can you get a babysitter?'

'Yeah, my dad'll always do it if he's in, or I've got cousins who'll come over. But I haven't got much time. I'm studying most evenings.'

'You choose, then–'

'Now wait a minute,' Maggie broke in. 'The rest of us have got busy lives as well, you know.'

'Don't come, then,' said Shauna. 'Me, I'm going to get an evening off work to do it.'

An exhausting round of negotiations later, the date was fixed for the Thursday of next week. Cathy volunteered to search the net for more pictures, Fiona to go to the county library and Naz to look in her college library. She was doing a part time Media Studies degree.

'You're bringing up a child, running a sewing business and studying for a degree?' Judy said. 'How do you manage to fit it all in?'

They were so energetic, these young mothers now. What was the modern term? Focussed.

'I never seemed to get anything done when I had young children. The time just sort of slipped away.'

Naz shrugged. 'Karis is at school now, so I've got that time, and the evenings.'

But no husband to help her, it seemed. Or hinder her.

They were into their fourth round of drinks – Judy, not having a car to drive home, was on gin and tonics – when a man loomed over their table.

'Hello there. Having a good time?'

Judy swivelled round. It was Alan. The doomy feeling returned, swiftly followed by anger. She had been having a good time, until he appeared. 'What on earth are you doing here?'

'Well, that's a nice way to greet me, I must say, when I've come here specially to give you a lift home.' He kept his voice light and jocular, putting her and her bad temper in the wrong. 'Aren't you going to introduce me, then?'

No. Just go away. Judy swallowed a sigh. 'Everybody, this is my husband, Alan.'

She named the other women. Fiona and Cathy were polite, Maggie and Naz cool, Shauna off-hand. Which was sure to excite his interest. Nothing like the thrill of the chase. Sure enough, he found a chair and sat down in between Shauna and Fiona and started talking to them both. Shauna deliberately turned away from him and began talking across the table to Naz, leaving Alan to Fiona.

'How do you find the Range Rover?' Judy heard him say. 'Marvellous cars, aren't they?'

'I hate it,' Fiona told him.

The evening was ruined. The conversation was split into three. Judy sat sipping at her almost empty glass, feeling like death.

'Don't you think, Judy?'

She jumped at the sound of her own name. It was Maggie.

'That a degree is becoming the basic qualification nowadays?'

She felt a great wave of gratitude. Maggie had seen that she was being excluded, and deliberately brought her in.

'Oh – yes – I think you may be right,' she said, trying to get her head together. 'All my children and their friends either have degrees or are going to go to university. I don't know where that leaves the rest of us, though. On the scrapheap, I suppose.'

Secretarial skills were still thought to be a good enough qualification for girls when she left school. She was thankful when time was called. Alan was quite animated all the way home.

'They're a right mixed bunch, your dancers, aren't they? That Fiona's a cracker, isn't she? They live out at Macey's Green, apparently. Nice village, that. Very choice property. Now would you believe it, they like eating at the Happy Goose and Geraldo's just like we do?'

'Really?' He had never taken her to the Happy Goose.

CHAPTER 4

Thank goodness she had arranged for Naz to make her costume. She really didn't have the time to be doing all that cutting and stitching.

Maggie looked at the huge pile of folders to be marked. Half of them had to be done by tomorrow. The other half weren't due back till Monday, but by the time the weekend arrived there would be another lot to add to them. Not to speak of all the preparation. And then there were the staff appraisals to be set in motion.

She poured herself a glass of Chardonnay and put a chilled low-calorie fisherman's pie for one in the microwave. She wandered into the lounge and sat down. At the end of the day she liked to sit in silence. No radio, no television, no music. Just silence. She lit a cigarette, sipped the wine and surveyed the room.

It was a nice room. A nice house. She had decorated it in whites and neutrals, furnished it sparsely in clean-lined modern pieces and kept clutter to the absolute minimum. It stood on a small well-designed estate on the edge of town and had been brand new when she moved into it last year. A lot of the furniture was new too. There was certainly nothing more than eight years old in the place, as she had brought nothing with her from the home she had shared with Robin, her ex.

A clean start. A line drawn beneath that part of her life.

Normally she found it soothing to contemplate her small kingdom. But since the costume meeting at Fiona's place last week, a chink of dissatisfaction had crept in. She battered it down with logic. Who'd possibly want to live in a great big house like that? And a listed building, too. It was common knowledge that there were terrible restrictions on what you could do to a listed building. And then there were all those antiques and the hand-built arty modern stuff. They might look fine, but they all needed dusting and polishing. And as for some of those pictures on the walls, she thought they were downright ugly. Wouldn't give them houseroom.

Then there was the garden. At the back of Maggie's house there was a patio and some pots of geraniums and a tiny square of lawn. Just enough to sit out on a sunny day, and no bother at all to look after. Exactly what she needed. Whereas Fiona had nearly an acre of wilderness with a boggy pond and a cedar tree to tame. She certainly didn't envy her that job. Though she supposed they would have a landscaping firm in to do it for them.

No, she was quite happy with her own set-up, thank you very much. She closed her mind to the thought of Fiona's handsome, charming, articulate husband.

The microwave pinged. She retrieved her dinner for one and was just about to pour a second glass of wine when the phone rang.

'Mum? It's me.'

'Oh – hello, dear.' It was Ben, her son.

'How are you, Mum?'

'All right. Look, can you call back in ten minutes or so? I've just put my dinner on the table.' He hadn't called her for three weeks. A few minutes more wouldn't do any harm.

'Oh, well – Mum, I just wondered. Is it OK if I come and stay for a bit?'

Her heart sank. That was her silence and privacy gone. 'I suppose so, but–'

'Cheers, Mum. You're a star. Look – er – I suppose you couldn't come and pick me up, could you?'

That was her Saturday gone, and a horrible drive through heavy traffic to Tottenham into the bargain. 'Couldn't you come by train?'

'I have, but I've got all my things.'

It took her a moment to take this in. 'You mean you're here now? At Mellingford?'

'Yeah.'

Whatever had happened? Had he been

65

slung out of his flat? Really, he was so irresponsible. Her fisherman's pie was cooling on the plate. 'Can't you take a cab?'

'Er – well, I didn't have time to get to the cash machine.'

'All right, all right. I'll pay for it.'

'Cheers Mum! I knew I could rely on you.'

That's what mothers were for. Providing money and beds for the night. She ate her dinner automatically. It didn't taste of anything much. Less than fifteen minutes later Ben was at the door. Tall, fair and slightly stooped, he gave Maggie a hug and sniffed the air at the door.

'Smells nice. Is there any left?'

'If I'd known you were coming, I'd've had a meal ready for you.'

They lugged his worldly goods upstairs to the guest room, then Maggie got a lasagne for one out of the freezer while he unpacked. They finished off the bottle of Chardonnay together while he ate and Maggie watched him across the table. His likeness to his father always disturbed her. The way his hair flopped over his forehead, his wide and rather charming smile, his short-sighted blue eyes behind their trendy glasses.

'So what happened about the flat?'

He had been sharing with three others, the latest of various combinations of friends and girlfriends.

'Er – well, it didn't quite work out.'

'How do you mean, it didn't quite work out?'

Ben shrugged. 'Oh well, you know. Disagreements about this and that. Flatshares are like that. Worse than marriages. Easier to get out of, though.'

Which told her precisely nothing. 'You'll have to get up very early here to get the train in to work It's not like travelling in from Tottenham,' she pointed out.

Ben picked up his wineglass and looked very carefully at its contents. 'Yes, well, that's another thing. I'm not actually working in the City at the moment.'

Another job down the drain! 'So where are you working?'

'Er - well – I'm not exactly employed right now. But I'm on the books at several agencies.'

Impatience spurted within her. 'Really, Ben! Isn't it about time you stopped messing about with these temp jobs and started on a proper career? You're twenty-six now. You've been going from one dead-end job to another ever since you left university.'

Why couldn't he be like his sister? Becky was three years younger than Ben and already had a high-powered engineering job and her own flat in Manchester. Becky took after her. She got things done.

'I'll find something. Don't worry. Something always turns up.'

'But that's just it, Ben. Decent jobs don't just turn up. You have to go out and actively look for them. Look at adverts, write a really good CV, present yourself properly. It's a competitive world out there. You're never going to get anywhere just drifting along in this way.'

'Yeah yeah. I'm sure you're right, Mum.'

None of it was going in, that was obvious. He was just agreeing with her to keep the peace. It was so frustrating. 'Yes I am right, Ben, and I wish I could make you see that. You've got a great deal of potential, but at the moment it's all going to waste.'

'Could do better, eh?'

Robin used to do that, too. Mock her gently in order to undermine her. She refused to let Ben put her off. It was for his own good. 'Yes, you could. It's about time you got your act together.'

'I'll see what I can do about it, Mum.'

'You can start tomorrow by looking on the net. There are plenty of job websites. And then you can phone up some agencies. But not temp places, mind. Proper jobs. Careers.'

'Yes, Mum.' He stood up and took his plate and cutlery to the sink. 'I'll wash up, if you like.'

It was like banging her head against a mattress.

Maggie went up to her office to do her marking. Soon the television went on in the living room. She sighed. Goodbye, peaceful house. This was not going to be easy. Still, he was her son, and it was not going to be for long.

The following evening she was booked to go to Naz's flat with her costume fabric to be measured, and discuss what Naz was to make. She dropped Ben off at the High Street, where he was meeting some friends, then drove on to Naz's road, to a tall Edwardian house in a beautifully tended garden. She was slightly taken aback when the door was opened by a man in his fifties with greying fair hair and a pleasant smile.

'Oh,' she said. 'I was looking for Naz Randall.'

'You've got the right place,' he assured her. 'Natalie's been delayed. She said to give you her apologies and ask if you'd mind waiting for a few minutes. I'm her father, by the way. Trevor.'

'Oh,' Maggie said again, quickly readjusting her thoughts. So Naz's mother must have been black, because Trevor was white. She put out her hand. 'How do you do, Trevor? I'm Maggie Stafford.'

'Pleased to meet you.' He had a nice firm handshake.

She followed him into Naz's living room, a light and airy space with stripped boards, white walls and bright rugs and furniture.

'It's very modern, isn't it?' Trevor said,

seeing her take it in. 'She did it all herself, you know – the decorating and the up-holstery, and all this clever paint effect stuff. She's a talented little thing, our Natalie. Take a seat, please. Tea or coffee? Or are you one of these mineral water fanatics?'

Maggie asked for coffee and sat on the low sofa with its bright blue cover and embroidered cushions. She looked about the room as Trevor went off to the kitchen. Children's books were piled on the coffee table, along with a couple of ring binders. A doll's house stood by a chest painted with flowers and birds. Family photos crowded the wall above – Naz holding a tiny baby and gazing at her with the fearful pride of the new mother, the same baby, older now, beaming as she stood holding on to a push-along dog, a standard school portrait, Trevor laughing and displaying a trophy, a big family gathering in a garden, Trevor with his arm round a smiling black woman in a yellow suit. She got up to study them more closely.

'Lovely collection, isn't it?'

Maggie jumped as Trevor came back into the room. She felt faintly embarrassed, as if she had been caught prying.

'My Sadie,' Trevor said, gazing at the picture of him and the yellow-suited woman. 'Wonderful woman. I still miss her.'

'Was it, er – recent?' Maggie asked awkwardly.

'Six years. She just survived to see Karis. She wanted to live long enough for that more than anything, and it was granted to her. She held the baby in her arms.'

He was still looking at the photo, his face open and unguarded.

Maggie swallowed. 'It – er, it must have been a – a wonderful moment.'

'It was. Yes. Very poignant.'

Trevor suddenly came back to the present. 'I'm sorry. I'm being a very bad host. Here,' he handed her a mug of coffee and sat down on the Lloyd Loom chair by the sofa. 'So you're doing this Egyptian dancing thing. Are you enjoying it?'

'I am, yes,' Maggie said, relieved to escape from the emotional tension. She sat down on the blue sofa again. 'I only went the first time on impulse, but it's growing on me. I'm not a needlewoman like Naz is, though, so I've had to ask her to make me a costume.'

'You've come to the right place. She'll make a lovely job of it for you. She's made quite a little business out of sewing, you know. Mind you, I'm glad she's taken up her studies again. She's a clever girl. She should have gone on to college, but we couldn't persuade her. She was set on leaving school at eighteen. Well, you'd agree, I'm sure. You're a teacher, aren't you? It's a pity to let talent go to waste.'

'Oh, absolutely.'

71

'Not an easy job, teaching.' He leaned forward a little, his forehead creasing, his eyes on hers. Kindly, grey-blue eyes. 'I wouldn't like to do it, battling with all those sulky teenagers.'

'It's not all fun and games, no.' She found herself drawn into telling him about life at Watfield Park. She was disappointed when a key rattled in the lock

'Hello, I'm back!' Naz's voice sounded from the hall. Small feet thudded into the room.

'Granddad!' A brown-skinned child with pink ribbons in her hair flung herself into Trevor's arms. He caught her and hugged her.

'Karis, darling! Have you had a good time? How was the party?'

'Wicked! We went to the Jelly Kingdom and I went all the way up the Big Pyramid *and* down the Super Slide *all* the time!'

'I think she should sleep all right tonight,' Naz said, following her daughter into the room. 'Oh – hi, Maggie. Sorry I'm late. I had to pick up Karis from a party, and they were late getting back.'

'That's all right. Your dad's been looking after me.' In fact it was a shame they hadn't been later still.

Karis was led off by her grandfather to have her bath, after a small protest.

'You all seem very close.'

'Yeah. It works,' Naz said briefly. 'Now, where's this fabric of yours and what would you like me to do with it?'

Maggie explained. Naz asked questions, drew sketches, took measurements.

'If I get you some ready-made sequinned motifs to put on the belt and the waistcoat, it will be a lot quicker and cheaper than hand-sewn details,' she suggested.

Maggie agreed. A fitting was arranged for a week's time. Trevor called from outside the living room door.

'She's fine in there. I'll be off, then.'

'OK, thanks a lot, Dad.'

The front door closed. A sinking feeling of disappointment dragged at Maggie's stomach. 'The flats are separate, then? Yours and your father's?'

'Oh yes. We don't live in each other's pockets. We just look out for each other,' Naz said.

She folded up the fabric and placed it on a side table. 'Next week, then?'

'Next week. I'll look forward to seeing what you've done.'

As she got into the car she glanced up at the windows of the top flat. Trevor's flat. Six years. Long enough to have got over the worst of his grief. Long enough to be thinking of looking for someone else. She drove home in a thoughtful mood.

She was transferring the washing from the

machine to the drier when Ben came in, beaming all over his face.

'Hi Mum! Guess what? You don't have to worry about my being a layabout scrounger any more. I've just got myself a job.'

Why was it that she didn't feel a rush of delight? 'Oh yes? That's good. What sort of job is it?'

'In Donatello's – you know, that new wine bar in the High Street.'

Just as she had feared – not exactly a career move. 'Doing what? Bar work?'

'Yeah – that sort of thing. Don't worry, Mum, I'm looking for proper jobs as well. I thought you'd be pleased. I'll be able to pay you rent money now. Anyway, it's a fun job, this. More like getting paid for partying. And there's this incredible girl working there. Wow! Legs up to her armpits. Hot totty–'

'Ben! That's not the way to talk about a woman.'

'Oops, sorry!' Ben grinned disarmingly. 'Naughty old me. But really, if you'd seen her–'

Maggie had a horrible feeling that she had. 'Her name wouldn't be Shauna, would it?' she asked.

Ben stared at her. 'You know her?'

'Yes.' She knew Shauna. She probably ate boys like Ben for breakfast.

CHAPTER 5

'Oh Mummy, you look like a princess!'

Fiona laughed and twirled round in front of her six-year-old daughter, Freya, showing off her new outfit. She had lots of beautiful dresses in her wardrobe, real ball gowns, some of them, with big name labels, but none of them gave her the pleasure that this belly-dance costume did. It had a little silk cropped jacket in aquamarine decorated with sequinned leaf motifs and a long silver beaded fringe that nearly covered her bare midriff, and a matching shaped silk hip-belt over three layers of skirts in greens and blues. One side of her hair was pinned up with a feather and sequin clip and she wore a necklace of silver coins and long coined earrings. She looked at herself in the long mirror and posed, one arm raised. She made a couple of hip drops. The beaded fringes shimmered and swayed, emphasising her movements. Fiona grinned, delighted. She did look like a princess. One from the *Thousand and One Nights*.

'Mummy, can I have a dancing dress like that?' Freya's voice was full of longing.

It was dressing up, Fiona realised. Dressing up and make believe. That was what made it such fun. She looked at her daughter's face. Freya reached out and fluffed up the layers of skirts, feeling the gauzy fabric.

'All right, darling. I'll see what I can make. There were lots of bits left over.'

'Can I have one too?'

It was Richard, her husband, taking in her transformed appearance.

Freya giggled. 'Silly Daddy!'

'Why silly?' Richard scooped Freya up and hugged her. 'If Mummy looks lovely in her dress, why shouldn't I?'

'Because boys don't wear pretty things.'

Richard gave an exaggerated sigh. 'Such stereotypes in one so young. Where have we gone wrong? Don't you think that's not fair, Freya? Girls can wear jeans but boys can't wear princess dresses?'

'Boys would look stupid in princess dresses. Anyway, they don't want to wear them.'

'Perfect logic,' Richard approved.

Why couldn't she get round him so easily? When it came to having a business of her own, Fiona knew precisely why. He had a primitive macho need to be the family's sole provider. He did it brilliantly, of course. They had a beautiful home, wonderful holidays, sent their children to an expensive school. Fiona could indulge her interest in antiques and art and Richard never complained at picking up the tab. But ... but it would be so nice to have a little project that was all her own.

Fiona undulated across the room towards him. 'How do I look?'

'Stunning.'

They had ordered a cab so that they could both have a drink, and picked up Shauna on the way. She bounced into the front seat, a Puffa jacket thrown incongruously over her costume.

'Good this, innit? I been looking forward to it all week. It was a bugger getting Friday night off work, though. I had to promise my mate Mel a Saturday. Hey, guess what? You know that sour bitch Maggie's son works at our place? Ben? He's coming along after work to pick her up. He's been after me for ages. It's a right laugh. He keeps on asking me out and I keep on saying no – well, not always like, no, no. I been stringing him along. Well, you got to, ain't you? At work, it's part of the fun. Anyway, I thought tonight I might say yes, just to see what she says. What d'you think?'

'Well, it's one reason for going out with someone, I suppose,' Fiona said.

'I mean, he's not a freak or anything. He's quite cute in a wussie sort of way.'

'Why do I feel sorry for this guy?' Richard asked.

Shauna threw her head back and laughed. 'Sorry? He's dead lucky, mate.'

They drove down the High Street, past the turning near the church hall, where the shop that Fiona had longed to buy and turn into an upmarket clothes place was, now re-opened selling cards. She was still sure she could have made a huge success of a business, and without sacrificing the children or her marriage. Richard just didn't understand what it meant to her.

When they got to the Arabian Nights restaurant, Shauna threw off the Puffa jacket and revealed a breathtaking costume. A black satin Wonderbra decorated with silver sequinned braid, enormous fake gems and fringing presented her magnificent cleavage to the world, her long supple body had another huge fake gem fixed in her belly button, then very low on her hips she wore a fringed and decorated silver belt over silver and black circular skirts slit up to the thigh.

'What d'you reckon?' she asked.

'I reckon you're right, Shauna, this Ben character is dead lucky,' Richard said.

As Shauna sashayed off to the bar he added, 'Poor bastard hasn't a chance.'

'Do you find her attractive?' The words came out before she could stop them. Stupid. Never show your fears. Richard put an arm round her.

'Darling, the day I fall for something as obvious as that, I deserve to be shot.'

Fiona let out the breath she hadn't realised she was holding. 'Let's get a drink.'

The Arabian Nights was a smallish place with dark blue walls and a tented ceiling, incongruously hung with Christmas lights and decorations. They were early, and it was still a bit chilly, giving out that stiff before-the-party atmosphere. Fiona cast a quick look round. She would have done a much better job on decorating a theme place like this. But before she could start to decide just how they arrived at the bar, where Cheryl was already in place talking to the restaurant owner. Middle Eastern music, a piece that Fiona recognised from the class, came flowing out of the speakers, and introductions were made all round. Maggie was there too, sitting with a gin and tonic, looking rather self-conscious in royal blue and lilac. Shauna gave Fiona a wink

'Hi!' she said brightly to Maggie. 'Hey – I hardly recognised you. Love the costume.'

Maggie took in Shauna's perfect body as it seemed to be escaping from the scanty black and silver. The girl looked exactly the tart that she was. If the top of her skirt was any lower, it would show her pubic hair. But social constraints dictated that she should be polite. 'Thanks. You – er – you look very striking yourself.'

Naz arrived, with Trevor. Maggie sat up straighter and smiled brightly at him. She was rewarded with a brief answering gleam, but his attention was with his daughter. Naz's small dark body was exotic in a tight waistcoat and voluminous harem pants in shimmering copper and green. On her head she wore a little pillbox hat with a long transparent green veil flowing from it, and dozens of thin bangles decorated her arms. Shauna and Fiona both fell on her.

'Hey Nazza, that's really wicked.'

'You really do look the real thing. That's absolutely gorgeous.'

'Doesn't she look a treat?' Trevor said. 'And she made it all herself, you know.'

Naz looked embarrassed. 'Oh Dad! Fiona and Shauna made theirs as well.'

'I didn't. I had to get my mum to do it,' Shauna admitted.

More drinks were bought. Naz was introducing her father to everyone. Maggie decided that the moment to act had arrived. She slid off her bar stool and inserted herself between Naz and Trevor.

'But of course we've met already, haven't we, Trevor? I must say I'm delighted with the costume Naz made me. Now tell me, how are you going to survive an evening amongst all these wild women?'

Trevor smiled, the corners of his eyes crinkling. 'Well, I did wonder, I must admit. But now that I'm here, I think I'm going to have a wonderful time. It's not every day that a man's allowed into the harem, is it?'

Maggie gave a trill of laughter. 'You men and your fantasies! Perhaps we girls should have ordered some bare-chested young men to dance with us.'

'I don't know about young, but I could do bare-chested, if you really want a nasty shock,' Trevor responded.

He was lovely and easy to talk to. Maggie was really enjoying herself.

Other women from the class started to flood in, together with their husbands, boyfriends and various other guests. The temperature shot up, together with the volume of greetings and drinks choosing and mutual admiration of costumes. Behind her, Maggie heard Richard speaking.

'Will you look at that, Fee? That's never the little mousy one, is it? What's-her-name from the vet's?'

There was a moment's stunned silence. Maggie looked up. There was Cathy, dressed in flame and gold. An uplift bra covered in flame satin and encrusted with gold beads and fringing made the most of her cleavage, while her hips were encircled with a matching deep belt, over a skirt that moved like molten gold through a layer of flame coloured organza. Her face was heavily and expertly made up, with her hair piled up on top and decorated with strings of gold beads. The pale body that looked so shapeless in her usual tee-shirts and baggy jumpers turned out to be beautifully proportioned with a tiny waist.

'My God,' Trevor said, 'I've never seen such a transformation in my life.'

Behind this vision stood a short bearded man, looking distinctly uncomfortable.

Shauna swooped on her. 'Cath! Fuck me, what have you done to yourself?'

Cathy flushed. 'Is it too much?'

'No! It's wicked! You look so different – I'm gobsmacked.'

Fiona moved forward as well, with Richard beside her. 'You look wonderful, Cathy.'

'You shall go to the ball, Cinderella – or is it Scheherazade? I think you must have rubbed a magic lamp or something.'

It was still the same Cathy behind the costume and the make-up. She giggled uncertainly. 'I – er, I thought it'd be fun, dressing up. Do you think it's a bit–?'

'No!' Richard and Fiona chorused.

'Yes,' muttered the bearded one.

'I see tension there,' Maggie said to Trevor.

'Ah well, some husbands don't like other men ogling their wives.'

'Ogling! Now there's a word you don't hear much nowadays.'

By the time Judy and Alan arrived the bar area was full to bursting.

'Don't know why they had to choose this

crummy little place,' Alan complained. 'And the food'll be crap. It'll be all couscous and chickpeas and that sort of rubbish.'

'It's Middle Eastern. And the owner loves our dancing.'

'Can't stand chickpeas. They give me wind.'

She nodded and smiled and said hello to women she recognised from the class, all of them decked out in their finery. Some of the costumes were just wonderful. She glanced down at her own. She had opted for a semi-transparent olive green tunic over a dusty pink skirt and leotard, with two layers of coin-edged scarves round her hips and another round her head. She had never worn anything so exotic in her life. Alan, of course, had just snorted and said 'Bloody hell,' when he saw it. She had tried not to let him spoil her pleasure in it.

'Ah, there's our lot,' she said, and began making her way through the crowd.

Alan immediately brightened up. It was obvious why. He accelerated through the packed bodies to where Shauna was perched on a bar stool, bursting out of her sparkly bra, with one leg crossed over the other so that her split skirt fell away to show her slim, smooth thigh right up to her hipbone. If she was wearing knickers they were very brief indeed.

Judy felt sick. Why not just go home now? She stood still, undecided.

'Judy! Lovely to see you! Come and join us.'

It was Fiona, who was tall enough to spot her amongst the crush. Too polite to ignore the invitation, Judy inched her way towards her. She was talking to a short man with a bushy beard and glasses whom she introduced as Mike, Cathy's husband.

'How do you do?' Judy said, all the while trying not to see what Alan was up to.

She concentrated on the man in front of her. Yes, he did look like the sort of man Cathy would have. Sometimes when you met people's husbands or wives, they didn't seem to fit at all. But where was Cathy?

'I love your costume. Those colours look terrific together,' Fiona was saying.

Fiona looked stunning, of course. She was so beautiful anyway, and in sea green and silver she looked like a water nymph.

'Yes, very nice, very ethnic. Far more suitable than some,' Mike said, staring significantly. There was a distinct edge to his voice.

Judy followed his gaze. A girl she didn't recognise was standing with her back to them, talking to Fiona's husband. She was wearing a gorgeous flame and gold two-piece costume, almost as revealing as Shauna's. Then she realised. It was Cathy.

'You can't call that sort of thing authentic. It's a cabaret costume. A Hollywood version of what the East is like,' Mike was complaining.

Dear me, so he didn't like his wife to look sexy, was that it? 'Well, when you're young and shapely you might as well show it off, mightn't you?' Judy said. 'There's time enough to be authentically ethnic when you're middle-aged and baggy like me.'

'Baggy indeed! Don't sell yourself short,' Fiona said. 'Look, you haven't got a drink. Richard! Darling, can you get Judy a drink? What are you having, Judy?'

'Oh, it's all right, Alan will–' She ground to a halt. It was quite obvious what Alan was trying to do, and it wasn't getting a drink for his wife. 'Er, well, thank you very much. Fruit juice please. Tomato. I'm driving.'

'It's a bore, isn't it?' Fiona commiserated. 'We tend to take it in turns, but tonight we got a cab. What about you, Mike?'

'What? Oh, it's my turn. It's Cathy's night out, I suppose.' Grudgingly.

'That's what I like to hear,' Judy said, rather too heartily. What was Alan–?

'Anyway, there's nothing decent here to drink. I'm a real ale man, myself.'

'Really?'

Alan's hand was on that silky thigh.

Fiona was reaching in front of her. 'Scuse me, Judy. Naz! Come and talk to us.'

She touched Naz's arm. Naz, her face like thunder, wriggled through to join them.

'That woman! She's all over my dad like a rash!'

Oh dear, more problems. Not the moment now though to point out to Naz that her father was an adult and a free man and entitled to have a life of his own. Children, even grown up children, could be very selfish.

'Who, Maggie?' Fiona asked.

'Yes, the silly cow. He can't get away from her. You know what she's like when she gets going, talk talk talk, and all the time looking into his face and touching him, like a hand on his arm and his shoulder – so obvious–'

'I shouldn't worry, Naz, your dad looks like he's not the sort of man to fall for the obvious,' Fiona said.

'Oh I know that! But it's just that I wanted to introduce him to all of you lot. I've told him all about you and he wants to meet you, but *she's* monopolising him.'

Judy put a motherly arm round her shoulders. 'It's early yet. There's plenty of time to get him away when we go and sit down.'

Naz didn't look convinced. 'Huh – she's like that thing in *Alien*, stuck on to him.'

Fiona gave a wicked smile. 'Oh I'm sure we're more than a match for Maggie, aren't we, Judy? We'll go and get an arm each and march him off between us, won't we?'

Would we? It was all very well for Fiona to say that, she was beautiful and confident. Fiona and Shauna would easily bring it off, but Fiona and herself?

'Yes, of course–' Judy began, half heart-edly.

A strident voice cut through the hubbub. 'Get your hands OFF, you sad old tosser. I said I'm NOT INTERESTED, OK?'

Judy snapped round. There by the bar was Shauna. Still on her stool, she was glaring at Alan, who was grinning stupidly with both hands raised, as if threatened by a gun.

The roar of chatter died.

'OK. OK. Keep your knickers on. Just being friendly, that's all,' Alan said into the hush.

'Fuck off,' said Shauna, conversationally. She turned to the person on her other side. 'Got a ciggy? Cheers. I owe you one.'

Cheryl chose this moment to bang on the bar with her glass. 'Er – everyone. If you'd like to sit down, the first course is about to be served.'

Frozen with pain and embarrassment, Judy felt arms linking with hers. 'Come on, Jude, we're going to rescue Trevor, remember?'

Fiona was talking to her. Naz was gripping her arm, looking grim. She found herself hustled towards the bar, towards where Alan was still standing looking foolish. Their eyes met, briefly.

'Judy, darling, there you are.' Automatic-ally, she stopped. But her two mentors dragged her on.

'Trevor! I've been dying to meet you, and so has Judy here, haven't you Judy?' Fiona said. 'Now, you are going to come and sit with us, aren't you? Richard, bring Cathy along, and you're with us, aren't you, Mike? That's it. Now, let's see if we can all get a space together.'

There was the usual scramble and chaos involved in seating a large number of people in unplanned places. The tables had been pushed together to make two long units, one each side of the restaurant, leaving a space in the middle for dancing.

'There – in you go,' Fiona insisted, giving Judy a gentle shove.

She found herself stumbling, knees bent, between the table and the banquette built against the wall. She sat down when she came to an empty cover, and found Trevor sitting beside her. Naz sat down next to him, with Fiona on her other side, then Mike drew out the chair opposite her and sat, still looking disapproving, with Cathy obediently by his side and Richard next to her, then Shauna, still smoking her cigarette.

But where was Alan? Part of her wanted to tear him apart for showing her up, for ruining her evening. But the part that had held on all these years still needed to know where he was, to keep a hold on what small part of him was still hers. She felt the base of her wedding finger with her thumb, rubbing the rings embedded between two pads of fat. He was still her husband.

There he was, at the end of her row, sitting down beside Fiona. He avoided her eyes.

Last to arrive was the outmanoeuvred Maggie, who took the only available place, next to Shauna. Judy's sense of humour won through for a moment. Dear me. Maggie and Shauna. Not the best of arrangements.

Waiters appeared, placing little *meze* dishes on the tables, taking wine orders. Richard effortlessly and unobtrusively took charge of the drinks. How nice, to have a man who could do that so well. That was one of the many advantages of being beautiful, having a husband like that.

'Won't you try some of these? They're delicious, quite spicy.'

It was Trevor, dish in hand, ready to serve her.

'Oh–' she stammered. 'Yes – thank you.'

He spooned some onto her plate. Chickpeas. A hysterical bubble of laughter gathered in her stomach, rose up, erupted.

'What is it?'

'Nothing, nothing.' I hope he sits there desperately hanging on to his farts all evening. Her eyes were watering. Something dangerously like a sob was swelling her throat.

'Here,' Trevor pushed something into her hands. It was a hanky, clean and freshly ironed. Thankfully, she buried her face in it.

When she surfaced again, he was holding a bottle of wine in each hand. 'Red or white?'

'Oh – er – neither. I'm driving.'

'One won't hurt you. You've got the rest of the evening for it to wear off and a meal to absorb the effects. Which would you like?'

The pull of a glass of rich red was too much. She really needed it. 'All right then, red.'

Trevor poured. The smell of it wafted straight to her brain. He lifted his own glass. 'Cheers.'

Oh that was better. Judy drew in a long shuddering breath.

'Natalie tells me you work at the doctors' surgery. How do you like it? Do you have to take lots of stick from the patients?'

'Sometimes, yes–'

What was Alan doing now? She couldn't see much of him with three people in between.

'And from the doctors as well, I expect?'

'What? Oh, the doctors. They can be a bit grouchy at times.' She tried to concentrate on what he was saying.

'I'm sure you cope with it all superbly. You strike me as the sort of person who can stay calm and polite under stress.'

Calm? Me? I want to kill my husband. Or take him home and lock him up and throw away the key. I don't know which. I don't know.

'I do?' she managed to croak She took another good swig of wine.

'Oh yes. Not at all like the usual dragon you find behind the receptionist's desk Far too gentle and sympathetic. Far too nice.'

'Oh – thank you.'

She took a nibble of the chickpeas. They were delicious. She began to feel slightly better. The social skills cogs engaged. 'What about you? Naz hasn't said what you do.'

'Me? Nothing earth-shattering, I'm afraid. I'm a shopkeeper. I own Supercook – the kitchenware shop in the High Street.'

'Supercook? Oh, I love going in there. I'm always buying some new bit or piece for the kitchen.'

She was genuinely surprised a while later when the waiters appeared to take away her plate. She had been so absorbed in talking to Trevor she had hardly noticed what she had eaten. Her glass seemed to be empty as well.

Some of the women were getting up. The group that had attended the classes last year performed, a swirl of colour and glitter in the darkened room. They finished with a flourish, to wild applause.

'Now the new girls!' cried Cheryl. 'Come along, don't be shy. You all know this one.'

That was her. No, she couldn't do it. Not in front of all these strangers. Cathy and Shauna and Maggie were on their feet, Shauna already twirling and posing. At the end of the row, Judy saw Alan stand up to let Fiona and Naz slide out. And now Trevor was moving.

'Come on, up you get.' He held a hand out to her. 'Time to dance.'

Judy shook her head. 'Oh no. No. Really.'

'Nonsense. The girls are all waiting for you. They need you. They can't start without you.'

She felt glued to the spot. Her body was heavy. She couldn't move. The others were calling to her, encouraging her. Shauna set up a chant – *Ju-dy, Ju-dy*– She caught sight of Alan, with something close to a sneer on his face. That was it, she would do it. She stood up. The others cheered.

'Yeah, Judy!' 'Good old Jude!'

She found herself in the middle of the floor. Fiona hugged her. 'You're great!' she hissed in her ear.

The six of them formed a group behind Cheryl, who was going to lead them. Judy took her place and raised her arms ready, one up, one out. The music started. Judy moved with the others, keeping an eye on Cheryl, making sure she was doing the right steps. Slowly, a magic seemed to take over. She knew what to do. She didn't need to watch Cheryl. She looked outwards, at the smiling, shining faces of the audience. Her body was moving, swaying, the rows of coins on her scarves jangled and quivered. She got the Egyptian walk right! It felt wonderful, her hips moving double time to the steps she took. She was smiling all over her face. She caught sight of Trevor, clapping in time to the music. He nodded and grinned and raised his hands above his head. A shaft of sheer joy went through her.

It was over, to an outburst of cheering and cries of 'More!'

'More after the next course,' Cheryl promised.

Euphoric, Judy went to her seat. 'You were great,' Trevor told her.

'Oh, it was all over too soon. I could have gone on for ever!'

She caught sight of Alan, who was still standing waiting for Fiona to sit down. For a moment her mood darkened again. No, damn it, he wasn't going to ruin her evening. She was having a lovely time and he – he could just go stuff himself!

Cathy came back to the table flushed and excited. 'There,' she said to Mike, 'you can't complain about that, can you? It wasn't at all provocative.'

'Huh!' Mike grunted, unconvinced.

Beside her, Richard was embracing Fiona. 'Well done, darling, that was wonderful,' she heard him say. 'Fantastic. I always knew you were talented but not like that.'

They spoke a bit more, then Fiona went back to her seat. Richard sat down and turned to Cathy. 'You were great, too. Terrific. Wasn't she terrific, Mike? They've all learnt such a lot in such a short time, haven't they?'

'You could put it like that,' Mike said, heavily disapproving.

'Oh, have a drink and loosen up,' Cathy said.

Grumpy old thing. She'd hoped he would come round as the evening went on, but it didn't seem to be happening. The next course arrived – lamb and couscous for most, vegetables and couscous for her and Mike and the other vegetarians. Opposite her, Judy was in uncontrollable giggles.

'Couscous!' she was stuttering. 'Wonderful!'

She was glad Judy seemed to be enjoying herself. Having a grumpy Mike was nothing to being stuck with that awful Alan.

'What's so funny?'

But Judy could only shake her head helplessly. Naz's nice dad handed her his hanky.

'I haven't had this stuff since we went to Marrakech. In fact, it's much nicer than what we had there. I always suspected we were eating camel,' Richard said.

Oh, to have a husband like Richard! So handsome, so charming, so successful. Not that she was bothered about money, of course. But all the same – and then Richard had such a wonderful way of looking at you as if you were the most interesting person in the world. Even though he had his wife opposite and Shauna sitting on his other side, he had given her his full attention for all of the first course. In fact, she felt quite, well, neglected, now that the conversation was becoming more general.

Richard had such a lovely voice. Cultured. And he was so lively and amusing. He made a story about waiting at the airport sound like a comedy act. Everyone was laughing, even Mike. She looked across at Fiona. She was smiling politely. Like a switch being clicked, Cathy changed from having a great time to feeling hollow and empty inside. It was just pretend, this costume, the make-up she'd had a friend of a friend come and do for her, the attention she'd got from Richard. She wasn't really like this, an eastern seductress, she couldn't carry it off. She was just dull, plain Cathy, married to Mike. It was the Fionas of this world that got the Richards. Being beautiful made everything possible. Beautiful, cool, capable, in control. Everything that she wasn't. The Fionas got the handsome husbands, the lovely houses, the children. And she didn't. She felt horribly depressed.

After what seemed like forever, her half-eaten meal was taken away, and Cheryl was up on her feet again.

'Solo, solo!' people were shouting.

Cheryl laughed and put her hands up and shook her head, but the audience insisted. Cheryl gave in. She danced wonderfully, swirling a pink veil around and above and behind her sinuous body, playing to the audience, holding them in her hand. Cathy gazed, consumed with admiration and envy. She would never be able to do it like that, not if she practised for a million years.

'That'll be you, one day,' a voice said in her ear.

Her head snapped round. Richard was looking at her, his gorgeous brown eyes serious. She felt oddly breathless.

'Oh – I don't think so – I'm not good enough–' she stuttered.

'Of course you are. Anyone can do anything, if they want it enough.'

'C – can they?' she asked.

His head was very close to hers. His shirted arm was touching her bare one. She could feel his warmth, his breath. 'Anything,' he insisted.

'Yes,' she agreed, mesmerised.

'Do you know what I think?' he said. 'I think there's a lot more to you than most people realise. More than you realise, even. It just needs bringing out.'

'Yes,' she repeated. At that moment, caught like a rabbit in his dark gaze, she believed him. Completely.

After the dessert, it was time for anyone and everyone to get up and dance. Maggie joined in with the throng, even though there really wasn't enough room to do anything properly. She might just as well, seeing as the evening had gone pear-shaped. Jostled by laughing, tipsy women and the occasional man brave or drunk enough to get up and join in, she reviewed her progress so far.

It had all started so well. She and Trevor had been getting on like a house on fire until that interfering Fiona had crashed in on her and snatched him away. She'd been left sitting next to that little tart Shauna all evening.

She looked over to where Trevor was sitting with Judy, the pair of them looking at Naz dancing, for all the world like proud parents. It was so *unfair*. Judy had a husband, for Christ's sake. Even if it was that womaniser Alan, who'd been making sheep's eyes at Fiona ever since Shauna had given him the brush-off. She still had a man there. She had no right to go snatching the only free man and monopolising him. She waited until Judy went off to the loo and plonked herself down in Cathy's vacant seat, opposite Trevor. Ignoring Mike and Richard, she smiled across at Trevor.

'Phew, I'm thirsty. Is there any more water left in that bottle? Oh – thanks – that is kind of you. That's better. And how are you enjoying the evening?'

'Very much. How could I not, with such great entertainment?' He waved a hand at the crowd of dancers.

'Has it been what you expected?'

'I'm not sure what I did expect, really.'

He was looking over her shoulder. At his daughter, presumably.

'Naz is a lovely little dancer,' she said. Get them on their weak points.

'Yes, yes she is.'

You're supposed to say that *I'm* good too. 'You must be very proud of her.'

'Yes, yes I am.' Still she couldn't get him to make eye contact. He was searching the crowd.

'Do you often go out together?'

'What? Oh – no, not really. Not evenings out. Trips to the country park of a Sunday with Karis, that sort of thing.'

'Oh yes, Karis. She's a lovely child, isn't she?'

'Mm.' It was like walking through treacle.

'Hi, Mum!'

Maggie started. There was Ben, looming over her. The very last person she wanted to see right at this moment.

'Oh, hello, dear,' she said, without enthusiasm.

'Good do. All the wrinklies giving it all they've got, eh?'

Oh go away, please. 'Why don't you get yourself a drink? The bar's still open.'

'Can't. I'm the chauffeur, remember? That's why I'm here.' Ben's gaze ranged over the heaving, sweating crowd. He was grinning. 'Why aren't you up there, Mum? Thought I was going to see you strutting your stuff.'

'I wouldn't embarrass you, dear.'

'That's all right. There's nobody here I know, except – hey Shauna! Wow – get the outfit. Eye-smacking or what?'

'Hey, Benny-boy. How was it down at the ranch tonight?'

For once, Maggie was glad Shauna was there. She pounced on Ben and dragged him off, leaving her free to talk to Trevor. The crowd began to thin out. Of their table, first Judy and Alan went, then Fiona and Richard had to get back to the babysitter.

'Where's Shauna?' Fiona asked. 'We can't just abandon her.'

Richard laughed. 'Oh, I think she's got better things to do than ride home with us, sweetheart.'

Alarm bells ringing, Maggie looked round. There in the middle of the clearing dance floor were her son and Shauna, locked together.

Once Richard and Fiona had gone, it all fell apart. Cathy and Mike and then Trevor and Naz went. The whole point went out of the evening.

Maggie got up and tapped Ben on the

back 'Come on, we'll get swept out in a minute.'

To her intense annoyance, Shauna got into the car, *her* car, with them, without so much as a by-your-leave. She did sit in the back seat, but in the middle, leaning forward with her elbows resting on the front seats. The whole of the journey she talked non-stop, except when she was shrieking with laughter. Her language was worse than some of Year Ten's playground efforts. But what could you expect, coming from the Watfield estate. The trouble was, Ben appeared to be totally taken in by her.

They arrived at the house. 'There you are then, Mum. Your taxi, right to the door.' He sat with the engine still running, waiting.

'Aren't you–?' Maggie began.

'Just going to run Shauna home.'

'Oh. Right,' she said, in her most disapproving tone, and got out. As she walked up the front path, she heard Shauna's mocking voice.

'Oooo. Who's in a strop then?'

It was gone three, by the green digits of Maggie's bedside clock, before Ben came home again.

CHAPTER 6

Naz drove through the entrance gates of the Dower House. God, it was a beautiful place. She'd been here once before, for the group costume-making session, but that had been in the evening. Now she could see everything better. Even in the post-Christmas gloom of a late afternoon it was very impressive. The gravel driveway swept up to a forecourt in front of the white painted house with its pretty pointed gothic windows. To one side of the house was a huge cedar tree, its lower branches touching the ground.

'Fancy living somewhere like this, eh Karis?'

Nobody else she knew lived anywhere the least bit like this. It had *grounds*, for God's sake. It was like something out of a costume drama. Strapped into her seat in the back, Karis craned her neck to see. They drew up by the pillared front door.

'It's like a palace, Mummy. Does a queen live here? Are there princesses?'

'No, just ordinary people.'

Not that she'd met Fiona's kids. They went to that posh private school, that she did know. They'd better not be snotty with

Karis, or she'd have something to say about it.

The door opened and there was Fiona, casually elegant in jeans and a raspberry pink jumper that just had to be cashmere. Behind her, not quite daring to step forward, was a pretty little girl with big blue eyes and white blonde hair. No mistaking whose daughter she was.

'Come in, come in, I'm so glad you could come,' Fiona said, leaning forward to kiss Naz's cheek. 'This is Freya – and you must be Karis. Freya's really been looking forward to playing with you.'

They stepped into a white panelled hall with a black and white tiled floor, blue and ochre Turkish rugs, two bright modern paintings and a huge arrangement of fresh flowers. Fiona took their coats and led them through to the kitchen. Which was everyone's dream of a country kitchen. Naturally.

'It's much cosier in here, and I can keep an eye on the dinner.'

Dinner? So she didn't have an army of servants, then? 'Right.'

There was a lovely meaty herby smell coming from the red Aga. Fiona gave the children juice and biscuits and sent them off to play.

'I've got a new playhouse for Christmas. Do you like dressing up?' Freya asked.

'Dressing up? Yes!' Karis' eyes lit up. 'You

got a fairy dress? And a princess dress?'

'I've got lots.'

The two of them trotted off. 'Don't forget to show Karis where the toilet is,' Fiona called after them.

'Dressing up's her favourite,' Naz said.

'A bit like us, really, with these dance costumes.' Fiona smiled. 'I love the chance of putting on a bit of glitter. And wearing colours I wouldn't normally be seen dead in. I rather fancy an outfit in hot pink, chrome yellow and oxblood red, with lots of gold.'

Naz tried to imagine cool Fiona in such an eye-searing combination. It was difficult, but Fiona would carry it off. 'Wow! Sounds wicked. But not your normal style.'

'Exactly. That's what it's all about. Look at Cathy at the Christmas party. She turned into a whole new person. Anyway, I'll show you the ideas I had for this spring revue thing.'

Cheryl had asked them to suggest something for the whole group to wear for a charity concert they were due to appear in. Fiona had been appointed chief designer, and Naz the dressmaking adviser. Fiona produced a professional looking art folder and took out some large sheets of paper. Three different ideas were sketched out, and between them they decided on which would be best.

'This is the most practical, too,' Fiona said, tapping the one they had chosen. 'All they have to make is a gold or silver belt and little cropped waistcoat to go with what they've got already. After all, not everyone's got a fortune to spend or the time to make lots of new things.'

Blimey. Who would have thought Fiona would consider things like that? Naz's opinion of her went up. She studied the sketches, thinking of how they would look in front of an audience.

'It needs something on the head. I know we all hate them, and they ruin our hair, but headdresses look really effective on stage.'

'Mm, you're right.' Fiona reached for another sheet of paper and picked up a soft pencil. They both threw off ideas. Naz watched as Fiona drew.

'You know, you're really good at this. Have you had art training?'

'I took an art A-level at evening classes.'

'But you didn't take it any further?'

Fiona's thick blonde hair fell forward as she bent over the pictures, hiding her face. 'I wanted to – but I was at secretarial college during the day, and once I got my speeds up, my parents expected me to get a job. And of course once I went to London, I was too busy doing other things to study in the evenings any more.'

Well. That was a turn-up for the books. Fiona expected to get out there and earn her keep. 'I always thought you must've gone to finishing school or something.'

Fiona laughed. She swung the hair back from her face. 'Hardly! My father's a plumber. I was brought up in one of the tattier suburbs of Wolverhampton. I was lucky in that I at least got to go to secretarial college, and wasn't expected to go straight into a shop or factory. As it was, I was able to get away and go and live in London.'

Double blimey. Who'd have thought it? She had always thought of Fiona as more of a type than a person. The trophy wife. It was as if a cartoon had acquired a third dimension.

'And that's where you met Richard?' Naz guessed.

'Yes. Classic case. Boss marries secretary. But he wasn't well off then. He and Andy, his business partner, had just set up on their own and it was just them and me in the firm. It was all very touch and go for ages. And he was single. I didn't go breaking up any happy homes.'

'You've got a happy home here.'

'Ye-es. Yes, of course. I'm very lucky.'

She said it as if she was convincing herself. Naz gaped at her. Wasn't she happy, then? Was all this just a front? The cartoon finally stepped out and became a flesh and blood person.

Fiona flushed. 'Don't get me wrong. I do appreciate it all. God knows, coming from where I do, I ought to. It's just – well, take all you lot at the dance class. You're studying and running the sewing business and bringing up a child on your own, Maggie's head of science at the comp, Cathy's a veterinary nurse, Judy copes with all those disgruntled patients at the doctor's and Shauna's working towards getting a job as a dancer on a cruise ship. And what do I do? Not a lot.'

Well yes. That was the impression she'd got. 'What do you want to do?'

'I did have my eye on a shop – you know Church Lane, that row of little shops opposite The Chequers? There was one for sale there. I was thinking of either opening a clothes shop – something quite upmarket, you know, designer labels and maybe one or two local makers with talent – or else an antiques place. Or even a gallery. I know a bit about art, after all. Richard and I collect modern pieces.'

There was a wistful note in her voice, like a kid who knew that Father Christmas was not going to bring what she really wanted.

'So what stopped you?' Naz asked.

'Oh – well – someone stepped in and bought it before I could get the finance together.' Fiona frowned at the paper in front of her, embellishing the edges with swirls and flourishes.

'So? There are other places, surely? You don't even have to buy, you could rent

106

somewhere,' Naz pointed out.

'Yes, but – it does have to be the right position. That little shop had just the character I wanted.' Fiona was still doodling on the headgear designs.

'There'll be others. And you don't have to stick at Mellingford. You could look at other towns nearby.'

'True. I'll have to do that.' But it was obvious she wasn't really serious about it.

'Of course, you've got to really want to do it.'

Fiona's head jerked up. 'I do want to do it. It's just – there are complications.'

Naz thought of the complications in her own life, of making the money stretch far enough, of rushing between home and college and the shops and Karis' school, of making sure she was there when Karis needed her, of deciding whether to sit up late to finish an assignment that had to be in the next day or to do a dressmaking job that would pay a bill. She said nothing.

'Well, it's Richard,' Fiona confessed. 'He wants me to be a full time wife and mother. He doesn't see why I want to do anything else–' She gave a small laugh that had nothing to do with humour. 'You must think I'm whining about nothing. I'm sure Shauna did when I told her about it.'

'Shauna?' Naz grinned. Yeah, Shauna would tell it like it was. 'What did she say?'

107

Fiona laughed again, but this time it was genuine. 'She said "Fuck me, what d'you want to do that for? I thought your old man was loaded?"'

Naz folded up. The words sounded so odd coming out of Fiona's mouth. 'Yeah, that's Shauna.'

Fiona got up to make them some more coffee. 'Maybe she's right. Maybe I'm just a rich bitch with too much time on her hands who doesn't know when she's well off.'

Yes. Exactly. And yet Naz found herself feeling just a twinge of sympathy. 'No you're not. But you could do something if you really wanted to.'

There was a clatter outside in the hall, and a spurt of high-pitched giggles. Freya and Karis burst into the kitchen to show off their princess costumes, twirled around and clutched each other, then tip-tupped off again in their sparkly play shoes.

'Don't they look lovely together? Such a contrast. I'm so glad they're getting on well,' Fiona said. 'Karis is a pet, isn't she?'

'She's a monster. I love her to pieces.'

'Do you – are you still in contact with her father?' Fiona asked, not quite meeting her eyes.

Karis' father. Dominic. 'No.'

Fiona looked contrite. 'I'm sorry, I shouldn't have asked. It's none of my business. Forget I said it.'

Dominic. The bastard. Mostly she stamped on his memory so hard that she could almost pretend he never existed. But someimes, a need to talk about him surfaced. It swelled inside her like a growth, nurtured by Fiona's revelations.

'No,' she said slowly. 'It's all right. The fact is, I haven't seen him for over six years. He walked out two weeks after Karis was born.'

'Oh my God. How dreadful for you. Just when you needed him most.' Fiona looked genuinely shocked.

'He wasn't very good at responsibility. Having a baby was bad enough, having a girlfriend whose mother was dying was just too much. He couldn't take it.'

Fiona's hand closed over hers. 'So you had to cope all on your own? How on earth did you manage? I was a complete mess after both of mine when they were born. I don't know what I would have done without Richard and my Mum to hold me together.'

Mess? Yes, she had been a mess. But she hadn't had time to think about it. She'd gone straight from reading Dominic's parting note to sitting by her mother's bedside as she died.

Naz shrugged. 'You'd have managed if you'd had to. That's what you do, isn't it? And I've got my family. All the relatives pitched in. I wasn't all on my own.'

'But you must have been so young at the

time. If Karis is six now, you must have been – what? eighteen?'

'Nineteen.'

'I can't imagine it.' Fiona got up and went over to the huge fridge. 'Time for a drink, I think,' she said, expertly drawing the cork from a bottle of white wine. She poured and pushed a glass towards Naz. 'There.'

'Thanks.'

Naz drank. It was only after the second or third swig that she realised that this wasn't Tesco's special offer plonk. 'This is nice.'

'Don't tell Richard. It's one of his specials. So now you and your father look after each other, do you? There hasn't been anyone since this Dominic bastard?'

'No.' Naz rolled the wine round her mouth. It really was very nice. And Fiona was nice, too. Much softer and more human than she'd thought. She could get to really like her. 'I've been out with a few guys but – well – they're all such kids, aren't they? All they care about is football and going out and getting smashed. And sex, of course. I wouldn't mind if it was just sex. It's all the rest of it I can't be doing with. All the arsing around and showing off. I've got one child, thank you. I don't want to take on another.'

'They're not all like that. A lot of them, yes, but not all.'

She didn't know the half of it. She had her wonderful Richard. Even if he did want her to be a full time wife and mother. It didn't seem like a very high price to pay.

'All the ones I meet are. I'm pigged off with the lot of them.'

'I think you're being too cynical. You shouldn't give up.'

'That's what my dad says. He's always pushing me to go out and meet someone.'

'He's right. You should listen to him.'

Naz grinned. The wine was doing its work. 'We're two of a kind, him and me. Both pig stubborn. I tell him that he ought to find a nice lady of his own. Mum wouldn't have wanted him to be lonely for the rest of his life. But does he listen to me? No.'

'Sounds like you need your heads knocking together.'

'Yeah. Maybe we do. But we're OK really.'

'You wouldn't mind if he found someone new?'

'Well–' Naz thought about it. 'Not if it was the right person, no. But she'd have to be someone very special. I don't want my dad getting hurt.'

'Not Maggie, then?' Fiona had a wicked sparkle in her eyes.

Naz smiled back 'No, not Maggie.'

The door bell rang.

'That'll be Brad the Gardener. I'd better get it before the princesses do,' Fiona said, hurrying out.

She came back into the kitchen with the

111

most gorgeous hunk Naz had seen for a long time. He was over six foot and broad shouldered with it, with an open, friendly face, thick curly brown hair, hazel eyes and a mouth that went up at the corners. He was dressed in worn Levis and an oatmeal jumper.

'This is Brad Storey, he's been replanning our garden,' Fiona explained. 'Brad, this is my friend Naz. She's a dressmaker and designer.'

'Pleased to meet you.'

Naz found her small hand engulfed in his large capable one. 'Me too.'

Fiona brought another glass and filled it up, while Brad spread his plans over the table. Naz leaned forward. He had done the most exquisite design. There was the house and outbuildings, the driveway, the cedar tree, the boundaries. And there were the new gardens he had planned, meticulously drawn and labelled.

'Cheers!' he said, sipping the wine. 'Now, I've tried to make this in keeping with the age of the house, but with all the things you wanted incorporated into it. There's a formal parterre here–'

He detailed features and plantings. Fiona asked questions. Naz looked and listened, enthralled. He really knew his stuff, this guy. Lucky old Fiona, having all this done for her.

'My dad would love to see all this. He's

112

really into gardening,' she said.

'You must bring him over one afternoon, so he can see it before it all happens,' Fiona insisted.

'What sort of a garden has he got?' Brad asked.

'Oh, just an ordinary place. Nothing like this. You know, front and back garden. But it's full of stuff,' Naz said. She knew nothing about it, really, but she did know that this design was incredible.

Brad and Fiona talked some more. Minor alterations were made to the plan. The princesses bounced in again. Naz caught sight of the clock on the kitchen wall.

'Oh my God! I meant to be home ages ago. Karis, go and get your things on. We've got to go.'

'Mu-um—' Karis began.

'You can come another day,' Fiona broke in. 'Freya, go and help Karis find her things.'

After a token show of wheedling, Karis went.

'Lovely kid,' Brad said.

'Thanks,' Naz answered.

He put his pens and pencils in his pocket and stood up. 'I'd better be getting along. When you've shown the plan to your husband, Mrs Meredith, perhaps you'd let me know if you want me to go ahead.'

'I'm sure Richard will love your ideas. I'll phone you as soon as I can.'

Naz stood up and sat down again. God, *how* much wine had they drunk? Two bottles stood empty on the table, and a third was well down. 'Oh God,' she said. 'I don't think I better drive home.'

Fiona's glance went to the bottles. She pulled a wry smile. 'Oh dear. We have got through rather a lot, haven't we? Perhaps we'd better call a cab.'

A cab? All the way back home? It'd cost a fortune. But there was no way she could drive, not with Karis in the back. 'Yes.'

'Whereabouts do you live?' Brad asked. Naz told him. 'That's on my way. I can take you – if you want, that is.'

Naz hesitated. It would save money. And he seemed all right, for a bloke. 'Well – if you don't mind–'

'Sounds like an excellent idea to me,' said Fiona.

Outside in the early winter darkness, a red Mazda truck was parked. In the driver's seat, looking as if it was about to drive off, was a golden labrador. It barked joyously when it saw Brad.

'Oh – I forgot to say. I hope you like dogs. Lady comes everywhere with me.'

Karis brightened up immediately. 'We're going home with a dog? I love dogs!'

'That's good. You'll like Lady, she's very gentle.'

They squashed into the cab, Karis sitting

on the middle seat with Lady's head in her lap.

'She's so lo-ovely,' Karis crooned, stroking the dog's head. 'She's all silky and soft and licky. You're so lucky to have a dog. I've got a cat. She's called Jasmine. She's had an operation to stop her from having kittens.'

Conversation was mostly between Brad and Karis. Brad asked the odd question and made the odd remark, and Karis chattered practically non-stop.

'You're nice,' she decided. 'Not as nice as Lady, but nice.'

'Thank you,' said Brad, gravely.

'Have you got any little girls?'

'No. I live with a couple of mates, in a flat.'

'We live in a flat. We live downstairs and my Granddad lives upstairs.'

'That sounds nice.'

The journey home seemed to take no time at all. 'You can drop us at the end of the road,' Naz said.

'No, no. I'll take you to the door. It's no extra trouble.'

'No really. Just here will do.' You're not seeing where I live, sunshine. However hunky you might be.

'We live at number forty-two,' Karis told him.

'Forty-two, eh? Right you are. You tell me when we've got there, will you?'

They pulled up outside the door. 'Thanks,

I really appreciate that,' Naz said, struggling to get out of the seatbelt. 'Come on, Karis. Don't keep Mr Storey waiting.'

Brad climbed out, went round and opened the door for her. Naz felt stupid. 'Thanks,' she said gruffly.

'Any time,' Brad said. 'Bye, Karis. Give my love to Jasmine.'

It was only later, after she had put Karis to bed, that it occurred to Naz that she might have been set up. 'I'll kill that interfering cow Fiona,' she said out loud.

'Mu-um – when are we going to see Lady again?' Karis called from her room.

'We're not,' Naz told her.

CHAPTER 7

It was odd being out in the morning. Judy felt slightly disorientated as she walked along the High Street. She had agreed to swap shifts with one of the afternoon and evening girls, so here she was, at half past eleven, with nothing much to occupy herself.

At least there was plenty she could do. There's always something to get on with in a house, but she just couldn't settle to anything. So here she was, walking down the High Street.

It had that tatty after-Christmas look. The sales were on, but none of the shops looked inviting. The clothes all seemed to be designed for fourteen-year-olds. She didn't want anything for the house. But then she'd never been one for retail therapy. Comfort eating, that was her weakness, and it showed. She passed a baker's. The smell of fresh bread and sugary cakes wafted out into the street. Judy paused, looking in the window. Danish pastries. Belgian buns. Jam doughnuts. A coffee and a jam doughnut. Yes. Then she caught sight of her reflection. A fat middle-aged woman in need of a haircut. All right, no jam dougnut.

How about a cut and blow-dry, then? A restyle, perhaps? Her daughter Claire had gone on at her at Christmas, saying she should change her look. She hesitated outside her hairdresser's. No. The girl who did her hair was probably busy with another customer. She'd go another day.

It began to rain. A thin, dreary drizzle that made everything look grey. Judy shivered, despite her good wool coat. A display in a shop window caught her eye. A spiral of coloured pot scourers, cleaving like a whirlwind through a sea of bright tea towels. She found herself smiling. Who'd have thought that pot scourers would make such an attractive display? Of course. It was Supercook. Young Naz probably had a hand in the window dressing. Clever girl, Naz. Judy stood staring at the window. She'd always liked Supercook. She often popped in to buy a new bit of kitchenware, or just to look at the pretty serving dishes and chic continental coffee sets. But since the evening of the dancers' Christmas party, she'd been too embarrassed.

Trevor.

He'd been so – kind. Of course, it was only because he'd felt sorry for her. She knew there was no more to it than that. But he'd made her feel like – well – a real woman. One who was worth talking to. It had been a long time since she'd felt like that, basking in an attractive man's attention.

This was silly. She was acting like a teenager. If she wanted to go and look round a shop, she could. She went in. It was warm and bright inside. She wandered round, looking at the piles of coloured tablecloths, the sets of chunky pasta dishes, the racks of shiny tools. She fingered some of them.

Oyster knives. When had she ever felt the need of an oyster knife? Perhaps that was the sort of thing Alan ate when he was with his floozies, oysters. Oysters and champagne. No, she mustn't think of it.

Pastry cutter. She could do with a new one of them. Her old one was getting wobbly. What was she going to cook for this dinner that Alan had insisted on? She hadn't wanted to invite Fiona and her husband round. It wasn't as if she was any closer to Fiona than any of the other girls at the dancing class. But Alan was dead set on it.

'You're always complaining that we never have any of your friends round, and now I'm suggesting it you're making difficulties,' he complained. 'What's the matter with you? You're never happy, are you? You like moaning for the sake of it.'

It was no use trying to explain, so she issued the invitation. Now she had to plan the menu. Go for something really impressive and cheffy, or take it the other way and stick to traditional British, like steak and kidney pie and steamed treacle pud? Might be better. Lots of men loved school dinner food. Not that school dinners were like that these days, of course. Burgers and chips, more like. Well, at least Trevor wasn't in here. That was a relief. She headed for the door.

'Excuse me, madam.'

Judy stopped short. She was in the doorway. She could feel the damp air on her face. A woman of thirty-odd in the Supercook uniform was speaking to her. Her expression was hard, her eyes cold.

'Yes?' A vague unease started up in the pit of her stomach.

'I believe you have some goods that haven't been paid for.'

'*What?*' Judy stared at her. What was going

on? She wasn't really talking to her, was she?

'In your pocket, madam.'

Judy slid both hands into the deep pockets of her coat. Her right hand closed on something hard. She drew it out. The pastry cutter.

'Oh my God—' She felt cold, shaky. This wasn't happening. Not to her. But there it was, real and undeniable, the pastry cutter, dark green plastic and shiny stainless steel, still with its price label on. And it was true, she hadn't paid for it. But how had it got there?

'I – I – didn't know it was there. Really. I must have – oh, this is dreadful, I wasn't thinking, I had every intention— I'll pay for it straight away, of course.'

The woman's face was closed, like a trap. 'It's not quite as straightforward as that, I'm afraid, madam. I'll have to ask you to accompany me to the manager's office.'

People were pushing past them, staring as they went. Judy saw their faces in a blur as the woman's words sunk in. Panic rose in her. Her legs, her hands were trembling.

'You don't think— I wasn't trying to steal it— I just—'

The cutter was taken from her. 'This way, please, madam.'

The woman was holding her by the elbow. Judy found herself being guided back into the shop. Past all the attractive displays, past all the customers, their curious eyes on her. A series of horrors scrolled in her mind. The police station. Alan. The boys. The magistrate's court. The local paper. The shame.

'No!' she wanted to shout. 'No, you've got it all wrong. I didn't steal anything. I'm not a thief.' But her throat seemed to have closed up. No words came out.

Through a door at the back of the shop and into a corridor lit by a harsh striplight. The woman stopped and knocked on a door.

'Come in!'

Oh my God, oh my *God*. Trevor!

A noise forced its way out of her. It felt like a scream but emerged as a strangled moan. The woman opened the door. Judy had a vague impression of a cheerful room, a big desk. Trevor. Trevor was staring at her. She wanted to shrivel into dust and creep under the carpet.

'I found this lady leaving the shop without paying for goods, Mr Randall. She said she was going to pay but she walked straight past the till and was outside the shop–'

'Yes, thank you Carol,' Trevor interrupted smoothly. 'You've been very vigilant. I'll deal with this.'

The woman let go of Judy's arm. She plonked the pastry cutter on the desk, where it lay like an accusation. The door closed behind her.

'I'm not– I mean, you don't think–' Judy

stammered. This must be the most awful moment of her whole life.

'Of course not.' Trevor came round to her side of the desk and pushed forward a chair. 'Sit down.'

Judy collapsed onto the seat. She couldn't look at him. She clutched her handbag on her knee, gripping and ungripping the handle convulsively. Her breath was coming in shallow gasps.

'I don't know how it got there, I really don't. I couldn't believe it when I found it in my pocket. I suppose everyone says that, but I really didn't – I was going to pay.' She looked up, met his eyes. 'I'm not a thief!'

'I know.' Trevor's eyes were warm and kind. 'It was a mistake. I know that. Don't worry.'

'Oh–'

The police station, the court all faded away. It was all right. It was all right. Relief made her limp. Tears welled up and spilled down her face.

'Oh thank you– I'm sorry, this is dreadful.'

'Here.'

A large clean handkerchief was pressed into her hands. Judy wiped and blew and tried to control herself.

'Better? Tea? Do you take sugar?' Trevor was standing by a side table with a steaming kettle in his hand.

'Yes. Please. No sugar,' Judy managed to say.

'There.'

A red and pink mug with comic cows dancing round it was placed on the desk within reach. Judy picked it up and sipped. The hot tea slid down her throat. The comfort of it glowed in her churning stomach.

'What must you think of me?' she said.

Trevor perched on the desk, drinking from a matching mug with pigs capering about on it. 'I think you're a very nice person, and as honest as the day is long.'

'Oh–' She was thankful for the steaming tea. It gave a physical reason for her glowing cheeks.

'I did enjoy that evening at the Arabian Nights,' Trevor said.

It took a moment for her to register that the subject was being changed.

'Yes – er, so did I.' Most of all, I enjoyed your company.

'I went along just to support Natalie – you know – like going to the nativity play.'

Judy managed a watery smile. 'We are a bit like a bunch of kids. Dressing up and prancing about.'

'So what's wrong with that? We all have to spend most of our time being grown-ups. It's nice to take a break from it.'

Oh how true. A break from being dull and boring and middle-aged. 'It is fun, dancing. I'm not very good at it, not like some of the others, but I do enjoy it. And I love wearing something pretty and frivolous.'

'Frivolous is good. I like frivolous. And pretty. Young girls these days seem to wear prison uniform to go out.'

'Combats and DMs,' Judy agreed, thinking of some of the girls that Toby and Oliver brought to the house.

Gentle chat. Judy felt her heart rate steady, her stomach settle, her arms and legs grow still. She felt human again. Almost in control.

Trevor put down his mug. 'Look, I was just going to go and have a bite of lunch. Would you care to join me?'

Judy gaped at him. Had he really said that? Invited her out?

'Of course, if you'd rather not–'

'No–' she found herself saying. 'I mean, yes. Yes, I'd love to. Thank you.'

There. She'd accepted. Good gracious.

'Splendid,' Trevor beamed. He stood up. 'I'll just go and tell them in the shop that I'm off. The staff loo's the next door along, if you want to – you know.'

'Yes. Thank you.'

How thoughtful. She let herself into the toilet and looked into the mirror. My God. What a horrible sight. She scrabbled in her handbag for comb and lipstick and powder and set to work to repair the damage. When she came out Trevor was waiting for her.

'We'll go out the back way, shall we?'

'Oh yes.' Not through the shop again. Not in front of all his assistants.

'The wine bar's quite nice if you fancy that.'

'What, Donatello's?'

She couldn't possibly go there. Shauna worked there, and Maggie's son. They'd be seen. No, wait. What was she thinking? She was only going for lunch with a friend. That was all. 'Yes. That would be nice,' she said.

Donatello's was very modern, very minimalist, all wood flooring and shiny chairs. Trevor found them a table in the corner. No sooner had they sat down than Shauna came sashaying over, looking incredibly sexy in her tight black dress and white apron.

'Well hello! Fancy seeing you here, Judy. Didn't know this was your sort of place. And it's Nazza's dad, innit?'

'That's right. What would you recommend from the menu today, Shauna?' Trevor asked.

Shauna stood with a hand on her hip. 'Well – the squid pasta thingy looks like crap if you ask me, and three customers have told me the smoked salmon's watery, so I shouldn't go for that. But the wild mushroom risotto's OK – oh, and we got oysters in today. I've got to tell everyone that. I think they want to get rid of them quick.'

Trevor looked at Judy. 'What do you reckon? Do you like oysters?'

Judy remembered the knives. That was just before she saw the pastry cutter. 'I – I don't know,' she stammered. 'I've never had them.'

'No? All the more reason to try them. Definitely one of life's pleasures, oysters. And what about a main course? Would you like to try the risotto, or go for something else?'

'No, risotto's fine.' This was all going too fast.

'That's it then, Shauna. A dozen oysters, two risottos and – green salads all right? And have you still got that nice Chilean you had in last week? The Pinot?'

'Yup. Plenty of that.' Shauna scribbled the order on her pad.

'Oh – I don't know about having wine – I've got to go to work at three,' Judy said.

'One glass won't hurt you,'

'Yeah go on, live a little,' Shauna agreed.

Live a little. Yes. Why not?

Oysters were wonderful, she found. Juicy and subtle and succulent. The wine was delicious. She relaxed, glowed, laughed. 'To think I might have gone through life not tasting them,' she said, tipping the last drop of juice into her mouth.

'What a waste,' Trevor agreed.

They talked about their children, and by degrees got on to talking about themselves. The risotto arrived. They finished the wine. They had espressos. The tables thinned out around them. Shauna came over.

'I hate to be a party pooper, but it's half

past two,' she announced.

'What?' Judy looked at her watch, amazed. Yes, it was. She couldn't believe it.

'I've got to go,' she said. 'Shauna, can we have the bill at once, please?'

She wrangled with Trevor over the bill, refusing to let him pay for her. He helped her on with her coat.

'Thank you very much. I've really enjoyed your company,' he said as they stood on the pavement outside the door.

'So have I. It was really lovely.' She couldn't remember when she'd last had such a good time.

'Perhaps we could do it again?'

Alarm bells rang in her head. Once was all right. It was a chance thing. But to meet again, by design, that was different. She hesitated. 'I – don't think–'

'I'll understand, of course, but just a lunch, like this?'

The wine had gone to her head. She was happy. Yes, happy. And he was such a nice man. Live a little. Go on. After all, where was the harm in it? The words came out of her mouth without any apparent effort on her part. 'I'd like that.'

Trevor smiled, a huge warm smile that lit up his face. 'So would I. Thank you.'

She thought about that smile all afternoon.

CHAPTER 8

A whole day, a whole fucking day, and at the end, nothing.

Shauna slumped in the corner of the carriage, amongst the homegoing commuters. A fat businessman was snoring over his *Evening Standard* beside her, his head getting dangerously near to her shoulder. Two silly bitches opposite were prattling on about fitted kitchens. A city type in the aisle was shouting into his mobile. There were paper cups and sandwich cartons swilling round the floor. The air was thick and sour.

She stared at her reflection in the smeary window. She'd really thought she'd got it this time. All that hanging about in that freezing church hall, fighting for space in the smelly toilets, listening frantically as names were called, she'd been through it all before. Only this time she'd made it to the last thirty. She'd have done anything to get this job, anything. Dyed her hair black, worn a G-string, shagged the producer. Not that that would have been any good. He was a fucking gay. All over the male dancers.

What was wrong with her? Why didn't she make it? She was a good dancer, as good as most of those who'd got jobs today. She was a looker. She was tall. The doubt that niggled constantly rose to confront her. Was she too old? All the girls there today had been kids of seventeen or so, and they'd all been in stuff already – ads, panto. They'd been performing since they were at junior school. They had a head start. If only she had been able to carry on with dancing classes when she was little.

Shauna sighed, misting up the window. It wasn't that her mum didn't want her to, but when her dad left there just hadn't been the money spare for that sort of thing. But if she'd been able to keep up the lessons she wouldn't be here now, on this mucky train. She'd be in a West End show, or on telly. She'd know actors and DJs and that. She'd be going out with rich blokes. That was what she wanted, a rich bloke. Someone like Fiona's Richard. Fat chance, the way things were going.

To distract herself, she switched on her iPod and chose one of the numbers from the belly-dance class. Middle Eastern music swelled in her ears, rolled round her brain. She closed her eyes, trying to imagine the dance movements she would do to it. But for once the magic wouldn't work. All she could see was the final line-up of chosen dancers in the dusty church hall, laughing and prancing about, while she and the other rejects put on the their coats and picked up their bags and slunk away into the dark

Shauna got out at Mellingford and trudged towards the station exit with the stream of office workers. Sod it, she was going to get a cab. She couldn't afford it, but who cared? Outside in the damp night people were heading for the car park, the bus queues, the taxi rank

Fuck. The last cab was just pulling away. A whole line of people were waiting, muttering amongst themselves. Shauna went past them and joined the queue for the bus that would take her out to the Watfield estate.

Home looked really welcoming when she finally turned into Constable Drive. Tea. That was what she needed. A big mug of tea and something fattening, like egg and chips. And her feet up in front of the telly. But as she walked up the front path she realised that she wasn't even going to get something as simple as that.

Inside, there was a big time row going on. She could hear young Nicole yelling that she wasn't going to wear poncy peach satin and Mandy yelling that she was the bride, she'd choose. As Shauna opened the door her mum appeared from the living room. After one glance at Shauna's face she turned on Mandy.

'Go and make us a cup of tea, for God's sake, and one for Shauna as well. And don't hog the bathroom. I want to get ready.'

'You going out?' Shauna asked, disappointed. She didn't expect much sympathy from her sisters, but she had thought her mum would sit and chew it over with her.

'Quiz night down the Brickmaker's,' said Denise. She put one foot up on the coffee table and started painting her toenails. 'Anyway, how did it go?'

Shauna took a sip of tea. Somehow it wasn't as soothing as she had imagined. The smell of nail polish made her headache worse. 'I didn't get it.'

'Well I guessed that, what with you with a face on you as long as a wet weekend. Their loss, sweetheart. They dunno what they're missing.'

'I know.' That didn't really make it any better.

'Maybe it's meant. Maybe there's a better job just waiting for you round the corner.'

'Yeah, and per'aps not.'

Denise finished her toenails, took a swig of her tea and stood up.

'Not like you to get down about it. Don't let the bastards get you down, eh?'

'Whatever.' Trouble was, it did get her down.

Her mum went out. Nicole went out. Darren came round and went upstairs with Mandy. Shauna turned the telly on loud. The last thing she wanted was to listen to them shagging. She watched *EastEnders* without really taking in what was happening. The audition went round and round on constant action replay. She took two painkillers, but they didn't work She didn't fancy anything to eat now, either.

The phone rang. 'Fuck off,' she said to it. But in the end she had to pick it up.

'Hi, Shauna?' It was Ben. Calling from work, by the sound of it.

'Yeah, that's me.'

'Oh Shauna – didn't you get it?'

'Nope.' Was it that obvious?

'I'm so sorry. You must be so disappointed. What went wrong? Did they say? They must be blind.'

His real concern flooded down the line and washed over her like a hot comforting bath. It made a such nice change when her sisters couldn't give a toss and even her mum didn't have time to talk about it properly.

'Yeah well, blind or what, I still didn't get it.'

'It sounded such a brilliant opportunity as well. Poor old Shauna, you must be well gutted.'

'You could say that.' Dead on, in fact. Gutted was just about it.

'Look, how about we go somewhere when I've finished here and you can tell me all about it and we'll get really ratted?'

Shauna felt a great swelling of warmth towards him. That was just exactly what she wanted. Suddenly, life didn't seem quite so lousy.

Ben was waiting for her when she arrived outside Donatello's. He had a carrier bag of bottles clasped in one arm. The other he wrapped round her and hugged her to him. 'Glad you could make it, Shauna love.'

'Yeah, well – I didn't have anything else on. Where are we going?'

It was gone closing time, and she didn't fancy going clubbing, not tonight. No way could they go back to her place, not with her sharing a bedroom with her sisters. And he was living with his mum. She didn't fancy having to be nice to that Maggie before going up to his room. Put you right off, it would, having her in hearing distance. And he didn't have a car.

Ben grinned. 'My place. My mother's away on a course. Fancy a takeaway? I've got plenty of booze.'

A takeaway, a load of booze and a nice warm house with nobody interrupting them. Couldn't be better. 'Let's get an Indian.'

Home at last. Maggie came round the corner into her road and looked at her neat little house with pleasure. It had been the right decision to miss the last afternoon of the course. It was nothing but rounding off and summarising, and she could do that perfectly well for herself, thank you. This way, she could have a quiet time to herself to get all her notes sorted out for the staff meeting next week As long as Ben was out, of course. His hours never seemed to be the same two days running.

She pulled into the driveway and frowned. The curtains were still closed. At one o'clock in the afternoon. Ben really was so inconsiderate. The calm she had been so looking forward to evaporated before it had begun.

She heard the music before she even let herself in, the tuneless thump of the stuff they played at nightclubs these days. In the small hall, her arms full of course notes and her overnight bag, the smell hit her. Stale curry. She hung her coat up, anger boiling up inside. Then she heard a female voice.

'You know something? You're a triffic shag.'

Shauna. Shauna was in her house. Maggie was about to march into the living room when Ben's reply froze her. 'You are the most amazing girl I've ever met. I think I'm falling in love with you.'

What? Surely even Ben could not be that stupid? Maggie wrenched open the living room door. Appalled, she took in the scene. Shauna was lounging on the sofa in Ben's towelling robe, which was flopping open to show her long naked body. Ben was sitting beside her in nothing but his underpants. All around them was chaos. Her beautiful orderly room was strewn with beer cans, foil trays, greasy brown paper carriers, mugs, clothes and overflowing ashtrays.

'What *has* been going on here?' she demanded, though it was perfectly obvious what the answer was.

Even Shauna looked uncomfortable, though she managed a weak smile and a 'Hi there, Maggie.'

Ben flushed with guilt and embarrassment. 'Mum! I didn't think you were back till this evening.'

'That's obvious,' Maggie said.

'Sorry about the mess. I was going to clear it all up.'

'You'd better get on with it, then,' Maggie told him. 'I'm going to have a bath, and I expect it to be finished by the time I get down. And then we'll have a little talk about house rules.'

Even a long soak in her expensive bath oil with her favourite station on the radio did not undo the knots inside her. Why was nothing ever straightforward? It was not too much to ask, surely, to have a bit of peace and quiet in your own home.

When she came down Ben and Shauna were both dressed and the house was looking reasonable again. Shauna made off, leaving Ben and Maggie facing each other.

'I was going to do it before you got home,' Ben said.

'It shouldn't have got like that in the first

place. It shows a certain lack of respect, Ben–'

She let off steam for a bit, but she could see that it wasn't getting her anywhere. It was only when she mentioned Shauna's name that he came to life.

'You're such a snob, Mum! Just because Shauna's not been to uni you treat her like she's some creature from the swamp. Life isn't all qualifications, you know.'

'I do know!' Maggie snapped. 'At least Shauna's using what she's got.'

A dangerous light came into Ben's eyes. 'And what exactly do you mean by that?'

'That she's got talent and ambition. She's using her dancing to get away from the Watfield estate and a dead-end job in a bar. Which is more than can be said for you, Ben. You've had a good start in life and a good education, and what do you do with it? Get a dead-end job in a bar! When are you going to buck your ideas up?'

'Oh for God's sake, Mum, lighten up!' Ben turned away and picked up a stray beer can that had rolled under the coffee table.

People were always saying that. At work. Socially. Ben's father used to say it.

'But it's important!' Maggie insisted. 'I don't think you've been to more than two interviews since you came home.'

'I went to one the other day.'

This was news to her. 'Did you? Where?

What happened?'

'They wanted someone with more experience. I'll apply for some more, OK? But now I'm going out. I won't be back for dinner. Right?'

'No it's not all right. Ben!'

But he had picked up his jacket from the floor and was out of the front door. Maggie was left fuming. Why? Why was it always like this? Ben, Ben's father, the boyfriends she'd had since they split, it was nothing but aggro. Maybe it was better not to have anything more to do with men. It was much easier if you just gave up on the lot of them. And yet ... it must work sometimes. It worked for other people. Maybe with someone gentle and kind and amusing ... someone like Trevor.

Maggie made herself a cup of tea and spread her notes from the course out on the table. But it was a long time before she managed to make herself study them.

CHAPTER 9

'I don't know why you're in such a fuss. I thought it was nice of Judy to invite us,' Cathy said.

She thumped the iron down on Mike's

shirt. It didn't matter what he said, they were going and that was that. She'd been looking forward to this dinner at Judy's ever since she'd learnt who else was going to be there.

'I wouldn't mind so much if it wasn't for those other two. Richard and Fiona.' Mike said 'Richard and Fiona' in a silly posh voice. 'I mean, what can you talk about with people like that? I won't know what to say.'

'Fiona's nice, and Richard's ever so easy to talk to.'

Her heart beat faster as she said his name. Could Mike hear it in her voice?

'You certainly seemed to find enough to say to him at that Christmas do,' Mike grumbled.

Richard, Richard, Richard. She was going to see him again.

Cathy switched off the iron and held up the shirt. It would do. She handed it to Mike and galloped upstairs to change.

She'd been into town and bought a new dress in the sales, a red velvet vintage-style number, quite low-cut and curvy. She got it out and laid it on the bed, and one of the cats promptly leapt up and sat on it

'Get *off!*' Cathy squealed, grabbing the creature and dumping it on the floor. She snatched up the dress. In just those few seconds a great patch of hairs had appeared. Then she realised that there were hairs all over the back of it as well. The cats must have been sleeping on the bed all day.

'Oh no!' She brushed frantically at the hairs with her hand. 'Sellotape!' she yelled at Mike. 'Just look at this, and we're late already. Blasted cats.'

She started slapping make-up onto her face. Was that blusher even? The eyeliner was far too thick. Damn. When she'd had it done for the Christmas party it had looked fantastic. She'd bought all the products and they'd lain unused amongst the jumble of beads and brushes and pot pourri and shell baskets on her dressing table ever since. Why hadn't she practised? Why hadn't she started to get ready earlier?

Her hair was a nightmare. The colour she'd put on it for the Christmas party was already fading, and it refused to fall into lustrous locks when she clipped it up, but instead straggled down in untidy lumps.

'Lot of fuss about nothing if you ask me,' Mike said, handing her the sellotape. 'Why didn't you just say we couldn't go?'

'Because it would have been rude.'

Because I want to see Richard again.

'I haven't seen this before, have I?' Mike said, noticing the new dress for the first time. 'You didn't go and buy it specially, surely?'

'Of course not,' Cathy lied. 'It was a bargain, in the sales.'

'I don't like it. Very tarty,' he commented, holding the skirt between his finger and thumb, as if it might bite him.

'For God's sake – what do you want me to wear? A veil?'

Mike had no answer for that.

'What did you have to go and ask them for?' Alan asked.

Defence, that's why. Safety in numbers. 'Why not? Cathy's a nice girl and I think dinners always go better with six. It spreads the conversation more,' Judy said.

'Conversation? With that what's-his-name with the beard? Bloody hell, Judy, he does Morris dancing! What can you talk about with a bloke like that?'

'What you men always talk about. Cars. Pubs.'

Had it really been such a good move, though, inviting Cathy and Mike? At the time it had seemed like a good idea, turning a claustrophobic evening with Fiona and Richard into a proper party. She did find Richard and Fiona a bit daunting – they were so perfect, both of them.

'And she's a bit of a bore too, isn't she?' Alan was saying.

Judy put the final touches to the dining table, tweaking the positions of the glasses. 'Who, Cathy? She's a very sweet girl.'

'That's one way of putting it.'

'Don't be so unkind. Besides, you're the one who wanted me to ask them.'

'I said ask Richard and Fiona, not Morris Man and wassername.'

Why? That was what she wanted to know. Alan surely couldn't think he could chat up someone like Fiona right under her husband's nose? She had toyed with the idea of asking Trevor and Naz as well, but – well – it wouldn't have seemed right. Not that there was anything going on between her and Trevor. Heavens no. They'd just met up for lunch a couple of times. Nothing wrong in that. But all the same, she wouldn't have felt comfortable inviting him into her home as a couple with Alan.

Alan had got bored with the conversation. He wandered off to pour himself a whisky. Judy checked the oven and went upstairs to change. It was going to be a nice evening. Just a nice evening, with friends. So why did she feel so tense?

'Who else is going to be there?' Richard asked.

Fiona looked up from the story she was reading to the children. 'Cathy and Mike.'

'What, Miss Mouse Cathy?'

Freya pulled at her arm. 'Come on, Mummy.'

'From the dance class, yes.' And thank goodness for that. It gave her more of a chance of not having to sit by the ghastly Alan.

'Come *on*, Mummy! Read!'

'"The princess got on her motorbike and roared off towards the mountains,"' she read, obediently.

She didn't want to go to this evening at all. The trouble was, Judy was such a nice person, and she couldn't think of any way of turning down the invitation without sounding rude. What do you say to someone? No, I don't want to come because your husband's a pain?

'Mummy!'

'We're there,' Harry said, pointing to the page.

She realised that her attention had wandered from the book again. It wasn't like the baby books she used to read to them, which she knew off by heart and could repeat with her brain in neutral. This story needed a degree of concentration. She managed to finish the chapter and settled the children for the night. Richard came in and kissed them as well. They stood together in the doorway of Harry's room, admiring their handsome son.

'Aren't we clever, to produce two such wonderful children?' Richard said, as they went into their own room.

'Mm.' What was she going to do about Alan?

'Most of the credit's yours, of course. You're the one who does most of the bringing up.'

'Mm.'

If only she could be as upfront as Shauna. But she could no more tell him to fuck off to his face than she could fly. Then she realised what Richard had said. It was more than just a compliment. There was a sub-text.

'They don't need so much attention now. It's not like when they were really little,' she said.

'Ah, but they still need your influence and support,' Richard said.

'Not all day long.' Naz managed to study and do her dressmaking while bringing up a child, and Karis was a lovely well-adjusted little girl.

'No, but you deserve some time to yourself while they're at school. How else could you cope with me when I get home all grouchy and unreasonable?'

The only thing he was unreasonable about was this business of the shop. But it was too late now. She should have grabbed it while it was available.

It was going to be a disaster. Judy turned down the oven and prayed the pheasants would just sit and keep warm for a while. She had put them in too early, and now Cathy and Mike were late. Alan, meanwhile, was smarming all over Fiona and Richard.

The door bell rang. Thank God. She hurried into the hall.

'I'm so sorry we're late. The car wouldn't start,' Cathy gabbled, as Judy opened the door to them. They both looked stressed and embarrassed.

'Trouble with the spark plugs,' Mike explained. 'I had to–'

'Late? Of course you're not late. Come in, come in. Lovely to see you,' Judy cried, kissing cheeks, taking coats. 'What a pretty dress. Gorgeous colour. Go on in, and Alan will give you a drink.'

'Ah, the lady in red!' Richard said, as they went in. 'Nice to see you again, Cathy.'

'Thank you, yes, nice to see you again – nearly thought we weren't going to make it, but here we are. Isn't this nice – hello Fiona – you know Mike yes of course you do, we've all met before haven't we–' Cathy rabbited.

Mike was going on about the car.

'It's all right,' Fiona said. 'We've only just got here ourselves.'

Alan poured drinks. 'What car have you got?' he asked Mike, as he handed him his beer.

'Metro.'

Alan looked amused. 'You don't get that trouble with your Saab, eh Richard?'

Judy could have killed him.

'Can happen to any car,' Richard said.

'Actually, I would have thought you were more of a push-bike man,' Alan said to Mike. 'Isn't it against your principles or something

144

to go round burning up petrol?'

'Actually, I–' Mike began.

'My first car – God it was a bastard, but I loved it like a baby,' Richard interrupted. 'It was a little Peugeot, and so rusty you could put your finger right through the door.'

That succeeded in distracting Alan. All three men started topping each other's stories about first cars. Fiona caught Cathy's eye and mimed a yawn. But at least the atmosphere had calmed.

'How are you two getting on with your costumes for the spring show?' Judy asked.

'I've bought the material for the top, and I found some lovely trimming in that little shop off the High Street,' Cathy said

While Cathy was stumbling through describing what she had bought, Judy looked at Fiona. She was so beautiful. She was wearing a silver-grey shell top and matching narrow-cut trousers, with a silky beaded cardigan and strappy high-heeled sandals. Her thick blonde hair was shining with health and her nails were all the same length and French manicured. No wonder Alan was fascinated by her. And part of it was Richard as well. Alan had never really been the success he had hoped to be. He had a decent job, but not a top one. He wasn't a high flyer like Richard. He wanted everything Richard had – the cars, the house, the trophy wife. She understood, but it didn't make it any easier to live with. She went into the kitchen to serve the soup.

At least she could set a nice table. She had gone to a lot of bother with the candles and flowers and folded napkins. Everything sparkled in the soft light.

'Oh, that is so pretty,' Cathy exclaimed, as they all went into the dining room. 'Like something from a magazine.'

Alan laughed out loud. Judy wanted to kick him. Why did he have to be so nasty to Cathy? She was now as red as her dress.

Fiona came to the rescue. 'You're right, Cathy. It's really romantic.'

'Ah well, romantic. That's another thing. You like a touch of the romantic, do you? So do I,' Alan said. He drew a chair out. 'Come and sit down, Fiona.'

Judy kept her face neutral, avoiding everyone's eyes. 'Yes, do all sit down,' she said. She could hear that her voice was too bright.

Judy brought in the cauliflower and Stilton soup. Alan poured the wine. Cathy took a swig of hers.

'You're driving,' she told Mike.

'But–'

'We've given up arguing about the driving, it's caused so much aggro. We've ordered a cab. Why don't you share it?' Richard invited.

'Right. Thanks, mate.' Mike sounded as if he didn't know whether he was pleased or not.

The guests all praised the soup. 'She's a good little cook,' Alan said. 'I bet you are too, Fiona.'

Richard picked up the bottle nearest to him and topped up Cathy's glass. 'Have some of this while we're all still sober enough to appreciate it. We picked it up in France last year.' He watched her, as if waiting for some comment.

Cathy took another mouthful. 'Yes. Nice. We went over to Calais a few months ago, didn't we, Mike? We got some terrific bargains at the hypermarket. Some of it was only three euros a bottle.'

Judy could see it coming. Sure enough, Alan gave another of his hoots of laughter. 'I don't think you'd get this for three euros a bottle, eh, Richard? Not a premier cru Meursault.'

Richard ignored him. He was talking to Cathy. 'Never mind what it cost or what's on the label, the thing is with wine, do you enjoy it?'

Cathy tried again. 'It's lovely,' she said.

'Good, that's what it's all about. I can't bear wine snobs.' He and Cathy smiled at each other.

Richard really was very sweet, helping poor little Cathy like that.

'I'm more of a real ale man myself,' Mike said.

Judy could see Alan opening his mouth to

deliver another sarky remark, but Fiona got in first.

'The Green Man did a real ale and food night a couple of weeks ago. It was amazing. I never realised how many different brews there were.'

Talking about beer and food made for easier conversation, though Judy noticed that Cathy was getting through a lot of Richard's expensive wine.

The soup was followed by pheasants in red wine or stuffed aubergines, with a wonderful selection of vegetables. Everyone said how clever Judy was. She began to relax. It was going to be all right.

'It's nice to have something to plan for,' Judy said. 'I hate this time after Christmas. The winter seems to go on for ever.'

'I hate bloody Christmas. Glad to get it over with,' Alan said.

For the first time that evening Cathy agreed with him. 'So do I,' she said, with feeling.

'It's all so bloody hypocritical. I'd like to go away to one of those hotels that ignore it. Spend the whole week without a speck of holly or turkey and end up with a really good party on New Year's Eve,' said Alan.

'Oh, I'd hate that. I know it's terribly commercialised, but I love Christmas,' Fiona said. 'I love the present buying and the cooking and decorating the tree and the house, and I absolutely adore doing the stockings–'

'And pulling crackers and playing silly games–' said Richard.

'And going for long walks and coming back to an open fire and chestnuts and mulled wine–'

Judy looked at Cathy's expression. Naked envy. 'It's not the same now the children are grown up,' she said.

'Of course, you two haven't got children, have you?' Alan said.

Cathy's flushed face went pale. Her mouth tightened. 'No,' she said, a hard little word.

Judy didn't know what she most wanted to do – kick Alan so he hurt as much as Cathy so obviously was, or put her arms round Cathy. Then she saw Richard's arm move slightly. He had not quite concealed the fact that under the table, he was holding Cathy's hand, or thigh, or something. She started talking to Fiona, saying the first thing that came into her head.

'How's your new garden coming along? It sounds wonderful.'

'It's bit of a mudbath at the moment, but it's going to be lovely,' Fiona said. 'Brad's really very talented. And a very nice person as well.'

'I hear Naz has been going out with him.'

'Yes, I was pleased about that. They seem really well suited.'

Richard was talking to Cathy. 'How are all your animals? Have they done anything dreadful lately?'

Cathy managed to pull herself together and started chattering. 'Sprog went for the German Shepherd up the road – he thought it was going to invade our garden. And its owner complained! Sprog's about a third of its size, but he doesn't care, he'll have a go at anything.'

Judy let out the breath she hadn't realised she was holding. Danger over, for the time being. She cleared the plates and brought in three desserts. Everyone made greedy noises. Alan stopped having a go at Cathy and Mike and talked to Fiona instead. Fiona was coolly polite. Cathy looked as if she was finding it hard to focus. They all ate far too much.

When she came in with the coffee, Judy put a CD on the deck. One of the tunes they were using for the spring show flowed into the room.

'For God's sake, Judy, not that ghastly wailing stuff,' Alan protested.

'Don't you like it? I love it. I think it's so evocative,' Fiona said. She began to move her shoulders in time to the strings. Richard beat a drum roll on the table.

'Floor show time! Come on, dancing girls, how about a demo?'

Cathy stood up. Her hair was coming out of its clip. One of her shoulder straps had slipped down her arm. 'Yes! Dancing time!' Her chair fell over.

Mike looked appalled, and put a hand on her arm, but Cathy shrugged him off. She Egyptian-walked sideways into the space at the end of the room and began to undulate to the sensuous winding of the saxophone. Fiona went to join her, Judy followed. Sod what Alan thought, she was going to enjoy herself.

Led by Richard, the men clapped and shouted.

Cathy was putting so much into the dancing that she was actually disappointed when the cab arrived at the door. She kissed Judy and managed to say goodnight civilly to Alan. It was cold and damp outside, cooling her flushed face. She tottered down the front path to where Richard was opening the front door of the cab for Fiona. He had such lovely manners. Mike went round to the outside and got into the back.

'Little one in the middle,' Richard said, holding the rear door for her.

And there she was, sitting in between Mike and Richard, with his body pressed against hers.

'That Alan is a prize arsehole,' he declared.

Hysterical laughter welled up and flooded out. 'Yes, yes, he is–' she gasped.

She couldn't stop giggling. Tears streamed down her face. Her whole body shook. All the way home she was very conscious of

Richard's nearness.

They arrived at their house. Mike had to hold her up to walk inside. 'You made a right idiot of yourself,' he said.

But she didn't care. For Richard had kissed her as they said goodbye and her cheek was still burning.

CHAPTER 10

Judy couldn't quite believe she was doing this.

'Do you like it?' Trevor asked.

'Oh, it's very nice.'

They were in an Italian restaurant in a town about ten miles from Mellingford. It was a pretty little place with trellis and indoor plants dividing up the tables, so that each was in its own little candlelit enclosure. The waiter led them to a corner table. Nice and private, especially as it was Monday, and so far they were the only customers. Ideal for illicit lovers, except that they were nothing of the kind, they were just two friends who liked each other's company. It was the first time they had met like this in the evening, though. It was one step further, towards what, she didn't want to think.

'Don't look so nervous. They'll think I'm

abducting you,' Trevor said.

'Am I? Looking nervous? I didn't mean to be–'

'Relax,' Trevor smiled. 'I just want us to have a nice evening, with a bit more time than when we have to rush off after lunch.'

'We didn't rush off last time.'

'No – we didn't, did we? They had to sweep us out.'

They'd gone to a little country pub, and had been first in and last out. The time just seemed to fly by when she was with Trevor, not like that ghastly evening when she asked Fiona and Cathy and their husbands round. That was over a month ago now, and she'd not been able to bring herself to speak a word to Alan since then beyond agreeing mealtimes and other small domestic matters. She really didn't want to talk to him at all.

'You're very quiet,' Trevor said.

'Am I? I'm sorry.'

Trevor took the hint and did the talking, telling her about Naz's latest project.

'I was glad when Fiona invited her round to her place, because that Brad chap is there finishing off the garden. Now, he is someone I'd like to see her seeing some more of. Just the right sort of young man for her, solid dependable type, but she won't see it, silly girl. But now Fiona has taken on some job planning a party for a ruby wedding. Big flashy do. And she's roped Natalie in to help her. Paying her, of course, but Natalie's got enough to do. If she's running round helping Fiona, it's one more excuse not to go out with Brad.'

'Pity,' Judy agreed. 'But maybe it's just a one-off.'

'I hope so, but I doubt whether Fiona sees it that way.'

Judy sipped a large gin and tonic and studied the menu. She started to relax. This was Trevor Time, where the rules were different. Talking became easy again.

'We had this wonderful man come into the surgery today. He's one hundred and one and he said he thought he was getting a little hard of hearing. A hundred and one! We have people needing hearing aids who are thirty years younger than that. It made me feel quite a spring chicken.'

'You are a spring chicken.'

Judy laughed. 'Oh come on! I'm forty-nine!'

'If you live as long as your man in the surgery, you've still got over half your life ahead of you.'

'Yes, I suppose so – half my life! I could do a lot in that time.'

Judy looked across the top of her menu at Trevor, and felt a surge of fondness to see him using his reading glasses. She had half her life ahead of her still, and she knew this lovely man. She was very lucky.

By the end of the evening, she was fairly drunk.

'When I was seventeen I used to be able to drink half a bottle of vodka and walk home along the tops of all the front garden walls and then walk in and persuade my parents that I was sober,' she giggled. 'Where's that hard head gone?'

'You need more practice. I'll appoint myself your coach,' Trevor volunteered.

'Excellent idea.'

They drove back through the dark country lanes towards Mellingford with Pavarotti singing his heart out from the speakers. Judy leaned her head back and let it all flow over her. And it came to her, out of the velvety night, an astounding fact. She was happy. She reached out and put her hand on Trevor's knee. He placed his over it, and they drove back to Mellingford warmly joined.

Trevor pulled up outside the station, where there were always taxis waiting. She hated this, the subterfuge. It made the whole lovely thing messy and degrading. But if she wanted to carry on seeing Trevor it was necessary.

'I have enjoyed this evening,' she said. If only it didn't have to end.

'So have I. It's been wonderful.' Trevor hesitated.

She knew he wanted to say something. Fear surged through her. 'What?' she said. 'What is it?'

'Well – I was wondering – Natalie's going out on Friday evening and she's asked me to babysit. Would you – would you like to come round and keep me company?'

Judy took a breath. That really was one step further. Was it what she wanted?

She gazed through the windscreen. Outside, it was raining. When she got home, Alan would hardly notice she had been out and the boys only needed her as a provider of food and clean clothes. None of them listened to her when she spoke to them. None of them looked into her eyes, or held her hand. None of them regarded her as a person. She was just The Wife, or Mum, a useful thing to have around.

'All right,' she said. 'Yes. That would be nice.'

'Splendid!' Trevor sounded delighted. In the smeary orange light of the street lamps, his face was young and eager. 'I shall really look forward to it. I'll get some DVDs and we can order a takeaway – or I'll cook something, if you like. I'm quite a good cook.'

'You ought to be. You own a kitchenware shop,' Judy smiled.

'I'll get all my best gadgets out.' He leaned over and kissed her cheek 'Thank you for a wonderful evening. I shall look forward to Friday.'

'So shall I,' said Judy.

As she got out of his car, her legs were as

156

wobbly as a newborn foal's.

It seemed a long time between Monday and Friday. Sewing costumes for the spring show gave her something to do in the evenings, but it didn't stop her mind from going round and round. Several times she nearly reached for the phone and cancelled Friday's date. Was Trevor going to tell Naz? They hadn't discussed that at the time. There was no sign at dancing on Tuesday that she knew anything about it. But then not to tell her was even worse, since it meant that he felt there was something to cover up. Then again, if he did tell her, would he ask her not to mention it to anyone? It was all too complicated, too nasty. It was best to call it all off, and yet – she really did want to go.

The days dragged by until it really was Friday at last, and she woke very early and lay in the dark listening to Alan breathing. All the arguments for and against going to Trevor's seemed very much bigger and more threatening. They chased round her brain until she was lying with her body rigid and her fists clenched with tension. She peered at the clock. Ten past five. Sleep had never felt further away. She rolled silently out of bed and went downstairs to make a cup of tea. Even that didn't have its usual soothing properties. She leaned against the worktop and stared at the oven.

Yes. Time to get busy. She got out the

spray and scrubbed it to within an inch of its life. By the time Alan came blearily down two hours later, she was polishing the windows.

'What the hell are you doing?' he demanded.

'Cleaning.'

'At this time of morning?'

'I couldn't sleep.'

Alan shook his head. 'Bloody menopausal women.'

That was it. She was not giving up an evening with Trevor through loyalty to a man who could make a remark like that. She scrubbed at an imaginary smear.

'By the way – I'm going out this evening.'

Alan was already on his way out of the room. 'What? Oh – so am I.'

Neither of them asked where the other was going.

Getting though the rest of the day was bad enough, but come the evening there was the problem of What to Wear. She worried about it while she showered and shaved bits of herself that hadn't seen a razor in months. Well, it was only good manners to be clean before going out, wasn't it? She would shower before going out with a girlfriend.

Underwear. Yes. Well. Did she expect things to get that far? No. But... No. It was far too frightening. That would mean she really was having An Affair. She couldn't cope with that.

And yet... No.

It was lucky that she didn't have a seduction-type piece of underwear to her name. No basques, not even a pair of French knickers. And she'd given up suspenders years ago. So it was just her newest pair of knickers, her prettiest but decidedly non-sexy bra and the delicious pair of expensive tights her friend at work had given her for Christmas. She looked at herself in the mirror. Oh God. What a horrible sight. There wasn't an item of lingerie in the world that would make that body look less than lumpy. Get dressed quick.

By ten to eight it was panic stations. Everything in her wardrobe was flung on the bed. Nothing looked right. It was either too dressy, too casual, too frumpy or trying too hard. If only there was someone she could ask But she had to wear something. Or call the whole thing off. In the end she went back to her first choice, wide legged trousers, tunic and long waistcoat all in fine charcoal knit. She'd worn them over Christmas and her daughter Claire, who was never one to pull her punches, had been grudgingly approving.

'That's quite nice, Mum. Flattering.'

'You mean it doesn't make me look so fat?'

'That too. But it's quite fashionable. For someone your age.'

Thank you dear. Well, mini skirt and a

crop top were hardly suitable, were they?

Eight o'clock that evening saw her driving slowly down Trevor's road. Where to park? There was room on Trevor's driveway, but – no, best to leave it a few doors up, just in case.

Her stomach churning with nerves, she rang the bell. Almost immediately the door opened. There was Trevor, wearing a blue striped apron, smiling. 'Come in, come in.'

They both hesitated, then leaned forward and kissed cheeks. 'I'm so glad you're here. I was worried you might cry off,' Trevor said.

'I nearly did,' Judy confessed.

Trevor quickly shut the door. 'There! Now you're my prisoner. Come upstairs. Karis is asleep and I've turned on the baby alarm, so we needn't stay down in Natalie's flat.'

He took her coat and ushered her up into a tall, well-proportioned room, comfortably furnished with a burgundy-coloured three piece suite, a big coffee table and a matching rosewood bookcase and dresser. Music – something Lloyd-Webberish – spilled from an expensive looking sound system in one corner, and in the square bay window a dining table was laid for two. A fire burned in the grate.

'Gas, I'm afraid,' Trevor said, seeing her look at it. 'Almost as good as the real thing, and a lot less bother.'

'It's very deceptive.' Judy hesitated. An armchair or the sofa?

'Do sit down,' Trevor said, patting the back of the sofa. 'Would you like a drink? Dinner's nearly ready.'

'Lovely. Thank you. Er – nothing alcoholic for me, please. I'm driving home.'

He didn't argue, fetching her an orange juice and asking about her day. She answered at random. The words didn't seem to come out right. This was ridiculous, she was acting like a fourteen-year-old. Worse, probably. Most fourteen-year-olds seemed to be very self assured young ladies.

'I'll just go and stir a few things,' Trevor said.

He came back carrying two plates of smoked salmon and salad and a bottle of South African white.

'Oh, this looks delicious,' Judy said.

They sat down at the table. Judy took a large slurp of wine. They ate the smoked salmon and talked about food. She began to relax a bit. Trevor produced a spicy chicken dish and refilled her glass. Judy tasted and admired.

'Where's Natalie off to this evening?' she asked. It seemed a safe enough subject.

'She's out with Brad. Gone to the pictures, I think. Full marks to Fiona there, but I'm still not keen on this ruby wedding party thing.'

'Ruby wedding – just fancy.' Forty years. She'd not quite made twenty-five yet with Alan.

'It's our Silver coming up in the summer,' she said.

'Really?' Trevor's voice was – careful. Neutral.

'Mm.'

Twenty-five years ago she'd been madly in love with Alan. Every girl in the office had been madly in love with him. She'd been so surprised when he asked her out. Surprised, flattered, grateful, proud. The other girls had been wildly jealous.

'*You're* going out with Alan Blackwell?' they asked, openly stunned.

She'd been on the chubby side even then. But pretty. Pretty like Claire was now. Not stunning, though, not as good looking as some of the other girls in the office. She never did know why he picked her. She never dared ask

'I just adored him,' she said, remembering out loud. 'I tied myself in knots doing things I thought would please him. Anything, just as long as he kept being my boyfriend.'

'Young love. Painful.'

'Was it painful for you and Sadie?'

'Not between the two of us, no. We had our dramas, of course. Our rows and reconciliations. But we always knew it was true love, right from the start. She was such a lovely girl, so full of life. And so fierce about being good at her job. Nursing had to come first, even before me. Those people needed her, she always said. There was no way she was letting them down, so I would just have to put up with it. And I did, because I loved her, and I came to love her for it. No, it was other people who were our problem. Families. It wasn't so common then, you see, mixed race marriage. Neither side was happy about it, but we just stood our ground. We went out and got married at a register office with a few friends as witnesses.'

'We got married in a register office as well,' Judy said. 'It was a rush job. I was pregnant.'

God, that awful day. It had taken her five weeks to admit to Alan that she was pregnant. They'd had a huge row over it, with him accusing her of doing it deliberately. She'd thought she'd lost him for ever. She walked the streets all one night, weeping. She'd been slightly mad. Definitely. Out of her tree. And then he'd come round, looking hard, indifferent.

'OK then. I suppose we'd better get married,' he'd said. Those words exactly.

She had been delirious with joy. 'It wasn't exactly what I dreamed of. No white dress or bouquet or bridesmaids. I went out and bought myself a new outfit, but it was on the tight side. It would have been more practical to have bought a nice maternity dress, I suppose, but the last thing I wanted was for Alan to see me in a tent for our wedding. But it wasn't just the clothes, it was the whole occasion. I'd always wanted the full thing, you know, church bursting with people, choir, bells, confetti, big reception, the lot. As it was, it was the registrar's office here in Mellingford, which was a dingy little place then, and just our immediate families and a few best friends at the ceremony. I wasn't even sure whether he would turn up. That was the worst part, waiting for him to arrive. I got there before him, you see.

'It was a farce, really. I mean, if it had been a film it would have been really funny. I was in such a state, and my mum was muttering the whole time about how disappointed she was, her only daughter having to get married in this hole-and-corner way and how she'd never get over it, and my dad was silent and grim looking. So there we all were waiting, and Alan's family were getting more and more embarrassed because they'd let him drive off with the best man rather than insist that he came with them, and the registrar kept looking at his watch because there were other weddings booked in after ours and he wasn't going to have his whole system put out because of one groom not turning up and I was on the point of bursting into tears.

'And then just as the registrar was drawing breath to say that he couldn't wait any longer, in came Alan. That was it, I did burst into tears then and I couldn't stop. I sobbed all the way through the ceremony. I couldn't look Alan in the face at all. I had no idea what I was promising. People took photos afterwards and they're so embarrassing! My face is all red with mascara running down my cheeks and Alan looks as if the death sentence has just been pronounced over him. Not exactly the sort of thing you want hanging on the living room wall.'

'Not really, no.' Trevor looked as if he didn't know whether to laugh or sympathise. 'Did it get better afterwards?' He had such kind eyes. And he was so easy to talk to.

Judy looked back down the years. 'It did, yes. I was so proud of my ring and my flat and my married name. I tried really hard to be a good wife. Alan was really rather taken with Claire when she was born. She was a good baby, she didn't cry much and we were a proper little family for a while.'

'But?' Trevor prompted.

'But it all went downhill after Matthew was born. He screamed for three months, and Claire had changed from a pretty baby into a difficult toddler and Alan decided that family life wasn't such fun after all.'

'But you're still together.'

'Yes.' They were still together. Just. Twenty-five years.

'I'm not sure that I can face it,' Judy said.

'Face what?'

'A silver wedding anniversary.'

It had been lurking, the thought of it, ever since the new year. Now it jumped out and confronted her. It was going to be dreadful. It was going to be hypocritical.

'Why not?'

Everybody smiling and congratulating them and giving them cards and flowers and presents. Spending good money on silver gifts.

'I don't think I can keep the pretence up. I can do it from day to day. I'm used to that. But a silver wedding, that's different.'

Everyone talking about twenty-five happy years. It was totally false.

Trevor was concentrating very hard on pushing a small piece of pepper round his plate. 'What are you going to do about it?'

'I don't know.'

Why had she started this subject? She'd wanted this to be a happy evening. Her times with Trevor were for getting away from Alan and ordinary life. She didn't want to spoil it by droning on about her problems.

'That was delicious,' she said, putting her knife and fork straight. 'You're a terrific cook.'

'It was learn or live on frozen pizza,' Trevor said, taking the hint. 'Ready for pudding?'

'Pudding as well! Yes please.'

Trevor brought in chocolate mousse, made

with real cream and chocolate and brandy. He opened a small bottle of dessert wine.

Judy pushed aside the thought of driving home. 'This is far too yummy to just pick at.'

'Good. I do like a woman who appreciates her food.'

Trevor smiled into her eyes and poured the wine. But it wasn't just the alcohol that made her insides turn to jelly. Judy smiled back. There really was something very attractive about him. She raised her glass. 'Cheers.'

'*Santé.*'

'Mmm. Gorgeous.' The wine was like liquid honeysuckle. They finished the lot.

When the last bit of mousse was scraped off the plate, Trevor went out to fetch the coffee. He placed the tray on the coffee table in front of the fire.

'It's more comfortable here,' he said. 'Cognac? Grand Marnier?'

Judy heaved herself up and swayed over to the sofa. Thank God for elasticated waistbands. 'I feel as big as a house,' she said. 'But what the hell? I'll have some Grand Marnier, please.' What did a few calories more matter?

Trevor put *Simply Red* on the sound system. He handed her a glass and sat down beside her. Judy sank back on the sofa cushions. She was warm and full and deliciously woozy. Trevor's face was slightly out of focus.

'I'm so glad you agreed to come here this

evening,' Trevor said.

'I'm enjoying it.'

'So am I. Very much. Do you know, you're the only lady I've ever invited here for a dinner for two.'

Judy felt slightly breathless. 'Am I?'

'There's something very – special about you.'

He reached out and placed a hand on her thigh. It sent a shiver of heat right through her, lighting up–

My God! She hadn't felt like this for ages, not just from a touch.

'Me?' she quavered. 'I'm very ordinary.' I'm fat and boring. Except that she didn't feel fat and boring right this moment. She felt – alive.

'You're nothing of the kind. People have been trying to pair me off for ages, but I've never been interested. Until I met you.'

'Really?'

She was watching his mouth. She wanted very much to kiss it. She leaned forward. Their lips met. His were firm and warm and tasted faintly of cognac. My God, this is me, kissing a man who is not my husband.

Trevor took the glass from her hand and set it down. Then he drew her into his arms.

It was wonderful, wonderful. It was like being young again. Swept along on a tide of lust and sweet music, the person sitting in her head commenting switched off. There were just the two of them, and being wanted and feeling her whole body come alive and fiery and melting until she was crying out with pleasure. She was drifting gently on warm golden waters. Her body was limp and glowing.

Trevor was smoothing back her hair and kissing her face and smiling the same silly satiated smile that was stretched all over her too. 'You see? You are special. That was incredible,' he whispered.

'Amazing,' Judy agreed. Amazing and dazing. She couldn't remember the last time she– Stop it. Just stay in the moment.

'Really? It's been so long, I was afraid that I–'

'You were great,' she said.

The coffee had gone cold. There were bits of clothing on the sofa and the floor. She really couldn't be bothered to put them on, so she settled more comfortably into his arms...

'Hullo, Dad – oh! Sorry.'

The door closed.

Judy shot upright. 'What was that?'

Trevor ran a hand over his dishevelled hair. 'I think it was Natalie,' he said. 'I'm sorry – she's used to – I hadn't told her, you see.'

'It's all right,' Judy said automatically. Was it all right? What had Naz seen?

'I'll have a word with her in the morning,' Trevor was saying.

'My God, what's the time?' She tried to focus on the clock, but the hands were all fuzzy.

'It's gone midnight. I'm sorry, I didn't realise – is this going to get you into trouble?'

'No, no–' Alan probably wasn't back yet. But what about Naz? What had she seen? Enough to guess at what had happened.

'I'll get you a cab.' He went over to the phone. 'What about your car? Will that be noticed?'

Yes, he'd notice that the car wasn't there. 'I'll say–' Her heart was beating uncomfortably. Her nerves were all jangled. Think, she must think. 'I'll say it was a costume meeting, and we all drank too much.'

Yes, that would do. Not that he would be interested in where she had been, just what had happened to the car.

They pulled on their clothes and Trevor fetched her coat. The cab pulled up outside. They crept down the stairs. Trevor drew her into his arms. 'We are going to meet again, aren't we?'

Judy hesitated. She ought to say no. She looked into his eyes. He kissed her, and there was only one answer. 'Yes.'

CHAPTER 11

'You're up early,' Maggie said, as she gulped down her second black coffee of the day.

Ben came into the kitchen, yawning, and pressed the switch on the kettle. 'Shauna's got an audition. I'm going along as moral support.'

Moral support. When had she last had that from any man? 'I thought you worked all day Friday.'

'I've taken the day off.'

'Officially, I hope. You can't just not turn up, you know.'

Ben gave an exaggerated sigh. 'Yes, Mum, I know. It is official.'

Not that she particularly minded if he lost this job. It wasn't exactly a career.

'It's about time you took a leaf out of Shauna's book and looked for something better.'

Another sigh. 'Mum, I like bar work. It's fun. We have a laugh.'

Fun! She was about to point out yet again that there was more to a job than fun, when she noticed the time.

'Christ, it's twenty to eight! I wanted to be in early today.'

She flew about picking up her handbag and briefcase and basket of project folders. 'Bye, dear. See you tonight.'

'Aren't you going to wish Shauna luck?' Ben called, as she went out of the door.

Luck? That little tart didn't need luck, she had sex. Though come to think of it, if Shauna got this job, whatever it was, she'd be out of Ben's way, and then he might see clearly enough to start thinking about his future.

There was no time during the day to worry about what Ben or Shauna were up to. One of her department was away with back trouble and another had just been signed off indefinitely with stress, Year Eleven was now in the run-up to GCSEs, and the whole staff was frantically gearing up for an inspection next term.

'Stress!' Maggie muttered. 'I'll give her stress. Where am I going to find a decent long-term supply? Or any supply at all, for that matter? I'm the one who's under stress, and I don't go whingeing to the doctor about it.' One thing shone like a beacon, guiding her to the end of her day. She had a fitting at Naz's that evening.

Ben and Shauna were flopped out on the sofa when she got in, swigging beer from cans. They both looked deflated. Pity. 'How did it go?' she asked, though it was pretty obvious.

'It was crap,' Shauna said. 'Nothing but a cattle market for fucking Arabs.'

'I felt like a pimp,' Ben said. 'It was humiliating. And there were girls fighting to get into this outfit.'

Despite herself Maggie was curious. 'What was it, exactly?'

'A showgirl troupe to tour the fucking Gulf States. I should of known better,' Shauna said. 'They was nothing but a lineup of tarts. Might just as well of joined an escort agency.'

'You're well out of that. Something better will come along, you'll see,' Ben said, throwing an arm round Shauna and hugging her.

Maggie felt sick.

'Yeah, yeah, you're right. Let's go out and get smashed.'

'Excellent idea.'

They were just so irresponsible. 'Aren't you both working tomorrow?'

Shauna shrugged. 'Yeah, so? All the better reason for going out tonight.'

'Gotta live while you're young, Mum.'

Before you get old and past it like me, I suppose.

Maggie dumped her piles of books and folders and grabbed yet another cup of black coffee before going upstairs to shower and change. She had arranged to go to Naz's at six, judging that she should then be there when Trevor got in from the shop. With a bit of luck he would call in and see

Naz on the way up to his flat.

Driving over to Naz's road, she left the day's strains behind her and let herself think about Trevor. A widower. Ideal. No ex-wife lurking in the background making demands, no bitterness over failed relationships. It was difficult competing with the memory of a dead wife, of course, but it had all happened quite a few years ago now. He must be well over it. And then Naz was a nice girl, if a bit distant, and not likely to spoil things the way teenagers could. Yes, altogether it was very promising. She just needed to give him a little encouragement.

The door was opened by Karis. 'Mummy says if it's Maggie please come in.'

Nice little thing. Well brought up. Not like most of them nowadays. 'Thank you, dear.'

Naz was waiting in the big bright living room with the costume hanging from the picture rail and a box of pins already open. Pity. That meant less time here.

She tried chatting about how the rehearsals were going, but Naz got straight down to business. 'You go and play in your room while I fit Maggie's costume, Karis. Then we'll have tea. If you'd like to get your things off, Maggie.'

'It's such a relief to me that I'm able to call on you to do this, Naz,' she said, as she stripped off her jeans and sweatshirt. 'I really don't know one end of a needle from the other. It would have been a real worry, getting the costumes made for this charity concert thing, if you hadn't been around.'

'I expect you would've managed somehow.'

'Maybe, but they wouldn't have looked half as good.'

She glanced down at her body in sleeveless top and tights. Not bad, not bad at all. Muscles all toned. No flabby stomach. Pretty good, in fact, for forty- well, whatever. It never did to let yourself go, like poor Judy.

Naz handed her a matching gold skirt and cropped waistcoat. 'Put the waistcoat on inside out, then I can fit it.'

She stood with her arms out while Naz fiddled around with pins, making the waistcoat fit snugly round her bust, then got up on a stool for her to get the hem of the skirt straight.

'They're sods to get right, these circular skirts,' Naz said, sitting back on her heels and frowning at the hemline.

Good. The more time, the better. 'It's going to look beautiful,' Maggie enthused.

Which was true. The finished outfit was going to be a royal blue long-sleeved leotard with the royal blue skirt she had had made for the Christmas do over the gold skirt Naz was working on now, plus the gold mini waistcoat and matching belt and a feather-trimmed gold turban.

'Should be effective when we're all on the

stage together,' Naz said, tugging at the skirt, sticking in pins.

A car pulled into the driveway outside. Maggie tensed, listening. The car door slammed, then the door into the shared lobby opened. Karis came flying out of her room and hurtled to the front door of the flat.

'Granddad, Granddad!'

Trevor's voice could be heard. 'How's my best girl today?' and then, louder, 'Hullo, Natalie. Everything OK?'

'Fine, thanks, Dad.'

Maggie took a breath. 'Hello, Trevor. Do come and see what a wonderful job Naz is doing with my costume.'

'Oh – Maggie– Hullo. Sorry, bit of a rush this evening. Things to do,' Trevor said. And to Karis, 'Sorry, poppet. I've got lots of cooking to do. I'll come down and say good-night later, OK?'

Bugger.

Karis tried wheedling, but even she didn't succeed. Trevor's footsteps retreated up the stairs. Karis came in looking sulky. Maggie felt just the same. He might at least have looked into the room. The timing had been just perfect, with her standing up on the stool looking exotic.

'Granddad's busy,' Karis complained.

'He said he'd come and see you later, darling.'

'He's got lots of bags. He's been to Sainsbury's.'

'Does your dad like cooking?'

'Oh well, you know – he likes to try out the things he sells in the shop.'

'My granddad does yummy things. He made chocolate mousse last week. He let me have some.'

Better and better. A man who could cook

'Karis, would you go and fetch my – er – my chalk?'

Karis trotted off.

Naz finished pinning, then made some marks on the back of the waistcoat with the chalk Maggie changed back into her everyday clothes. There didn't seem to be much point in hanging around any longer, but still she was loath to go.

'Are you going out with Brad this evening?' she asked.

How easy it was when you were young. Practically all the men you met were free. When you were in your forties, practically all of them weren't.

'Yes. And I want to get Karis fed and ready for bed before I go.'

It was too heavy a hint to ignore. 'Well, I mustn't hold you up then must I? Thank you so much for all your hard work. Have a good time this evening. Bye bye, Karis. Say goodbye to Granddad for me when you see him.'

She couldn't settle to anything that evening. It was so frustrating. Really, Naz might have been a bit more helpful. She must want to see her father settled and happy again. But there again perhaps she didn't. It was very convenient for her to have him always there to babysit.

She had just got to sleep after lying awake for what seemed like hours when Ben and Shauna arrived back, waking her up again. They stumbled around downstairs giggling for a bit, then had sex very noisily on the living room floor. Maggie put the bedside radio on, but it didn't quite cover the grunts and cries coming from below. She lay rigid with something between jealousy and disgust, mixed with a large dose of sexual frustration. When had she last made love? God, it was months ago, last summer. And even then it hadn't been very exciting. When had she last had really good sex? Oh Christ, it was *three years* ago. Three years! Soon she would hit the menopause, and then it was downhill all the way, even if she did go onto HRT. Was this how it was going to be, all the time until she retired? And then what? Jolly coach trips with other single old ladies? It was unbearable. She had to do something, and soon, before it was too late.

Saturday morning found Maggie walking down the High Street. It was a damp raw day with a nasty wind that blew litter about the street, whipped round the legs and sneaked down the neck Everyone seemed to be with someone. Families sprawled half way across the pavement with their collections of kids and buggies, old couples walked arm in arm, teenagers went about in packs, talking loudly amongst themselves. Only she seemed to be alone.

She bought a couple of things she needed, then hung about Supercook for ages hoping for Trevor to appear. No luck there. Nothing much else in the High Street appealed. Even having a coffee seemed no fun on her own. Best to call it a day. Maybe she would call a friend or two and see if she could fix up something for the evening. She was just marvelling at the ridiculous prices in the florist's when she spotted a familiar figure inside. Fiona.

Fiona wasn't exactly her favourite amongst the dancers, but at least she was someone she knew. She stooped to select a couple of bunches of early daffodils that were shivering in a bucket by the door. A man went past her and into the shop, and as she straightened up she recognised him. Alan. Judy's husband.

Clutching the daffodils, she stepped back. If she peered between the banks of flowers and fancy arrangements, she could just about see them both. Fiona was standing with her back to Maggie, which was a pity. Alan appeared to be doing all the talking.

He was smiling and nodding. At one point he put a hand on Fiona's arm. Fiona spoke to the florist, took some paperwork from her, then turned and went out of the shop, closely followed by Alan.

'Meet whenever you like. It's entirely up to you. Any evening I can arrange, or even during the day. I'm easy. I mean, if you'd prefer daytime, I can always wangle a bit of time off.'

Maggie was so shocked that instead of following and finding out more, she just stood there, staring after them. Had she really heard that right? Was Alan making arrangements to meet?

They'd probably met here by prior arrangement, too. A so-called casual running into one another in the High Street of a Saturday. The bastard! And Fiona. She'd never been that keen on her, but she hadn't suspected that she was such an out-and-out bitch. She had a good-looking and successful husband and all the trappings that went with it, and still she was greedy enough to be having an affair with a friend's husband! She was bored, of course. She had no proper career of her own, unless you counted this party thing she was doing, so she thought she'd have a little adventure with Alan.

'Do you want to buy those flowers, madam?'

'What?' Maggie realised she was being

spoken to. 'Oh – yes – thank you.'

Still staring down the street, she handed the daffodils to the florist.

'That lady who was just in here,' she said. 'Is she a regular customer?'

'Oh yes, she comes in a lot. Buys fresh flowers every week.'

'And the man? Does he come in a lot too?'

'No – I don't think so. Don't know the face.'

All weekend the incident niggled at her. Poor Judy. She knew just how it felt. Better to be on your own than to be stuck in a relationship like that. Not that Judy had to be stuck, of course. Nobody had to be a victim. She ought to just walk out on the bastard.

The question was, what should she say to Judy? She still hadn't made her mind up when Tuesday evening came around. All she knew was she had to find an opportunity to help her.

It was only three weeks till the Charity Concert. The dances still looked very ragged. Some people hadn't yet memorised the choreography and the technique varied from graceful and controlled to embarrassingly bad. Cheryl was such a useless teacher. A good dancer, yes. But she was a terrible organiser and appalling at getting over what she was trying to explain. Maggie knew her own performance was all right. When she took something up, she did it properly, so she had taken a tape of the music home and practised the sequences of steps until she knew them. Poor Judy hadn't got it at all. She kept moving the wrong way and was half a step behind the entire time. Fiona was irritatingly good and of course so was that tart Shauna. Cathy and Naz were getting there.

'Do try to practise at home,' Cheryl begged them. 'It's dress rehearsal in two weeks. It has to be right by then.'

'Oh dear,' Judy muttered to Maggie, who happened to be beside her at the time. 'I think that was aimed at me. I do find it very difficult to remember what comes next all the time. Perhaps I shouldn't be in it at all. I feel I'm letting the side down.'

It was an opportunity on a plate. Maggie jumped at it. 'Why don't you come round to my place one evening and we'll go over it until we both know it inside out?'

Judy looked doubtful. 'Oh, I don't think–'

'Yes, you must,' Maggie insisted. 'It will be fun, and we'll both feel more confident when we've had an extra practice. Now, no arguments. When can you come? Tomorrow? Thursday?'

Judy gave in.

When she arrived at Maggie's the next evening, she looked different. 'You've had your hair restyled,' Maggie said, taking her coat.

Judy flushed and touched a lock over her

ear. 'Yes. I thought it was about time. Do you like it?'

It was a shorter, younger cut, and it had been carefully highlighted. 'I do. It's really nice. Suits you much better,' Maggie approved.

Poor woman. It was so obviously a pathetic attempt to make herself younger and prettier for Alan. But what chance did she have against someone as stunning as Fiona?

'Drink before we start?' she offered. 'I've a bottle of Australian Chardonnay in the fridge.'

'Oh – no, thanks. I've got to drive home,' Judy said, with a little smile, quickly smothered, as if it were a joke.

'Perhaps afterwards,' Maggie conceded.

She pushed back the sofas and put on the tape. The two of them went over and over the bits Judy had difficulty in remembering until they both had the choreography foot perfect.

'Thank you,' Judy gasped. 'That's been really helpful. I feel much better about it now.'

That had to be a good thing. But how much should she be told about her husband? Learning a couple of dances was hardly in the same league as keeping a marriage together.

'Fancy that glass of wine now?' Maggie suggested.

'Well – just one. Thank you.'

Judy collapsed on the sofa. 'Dear me. I am out of condition. You're hardly out of breath at all.'

'I go to the gym at least once a week. Twice sometimes,' Maggie said, looking complacently at her firm body. 'Why don't you come along? They're very good where I go. They start you off very gently and don't make you do anything that's beyond your ability, then you gradually work harder as you get fitter.'

'I've never fancied going to a gym. All those young girls in lycra, you know, but – yes – perhaps I will. It's about time I paid some attention to myself.'

Well. That was a step in the right direction. As long as she's doing it for herself and not just for Alan. 'We all owe it to ourselves to stay fit,' Maggie said.

She handed Judy a glass of wine and sat down on the other end of the sofa. 'My downfall's the smoking,' she confided, lighting up. 'I know I shouldn't, but I just can't give them up. Them and men. They're both bad for me.'

Judy smiled. 'We all deserve the odd little sin.'

'Let me guess. You're a chocoholic.'

Judy gave her a wary look. 'Er – yes. Yes, you're right.'

'Well, it does you less harm than men.

They're none of them any good when it comes down to it, are they? They all let you down in the end. I mean, I thought I had a reasonable marriage. We got on all right, we liked a lot of the same things, we shared a group of friends, we had a nice social life, we had two super children. I thought we were the ideal family. But I was wrong. A new member of staff arrived at his department, a little tart fifteen years his junior, straight out of university.'

God, the humiliation of it! It made her physically sick with anger and jealousy even now.

Judy was nodding sympathetically. 'It is very hard,' she was saying. 'How did you cope?'

Cope! She had wanted to kill the bitch. She found herself telling the whole sorry tale. She refilled her glass and lit another cigarette. 'And of course once someone had the guts to tell me, that was it. I went ballistic. I threw all his things out of the house and had the locks changed.'

The wild frenzy of chucking his precious things from the upstairs windows. His albums, his books, his stupid carnivorous plants, all in a heap in the rain. The sheer freedom, of letting go, of not fighting to keep control of herself, of wreaking revenge. Wonderful.

'Yes, it's best not to know. If you turn a

blind eye it can all right itself again, but once it's all out in the open there's only one way to go,' Judy said.

Maggie stared at her. 'How can you think that? You'd rather live a lie?'

'I think it's often for the best.'

'But how can it be for the best? Sharing your man with someone else? Oh no. You're wrong, definitely. I'm free of him now. Free to choose someone else, someone better.'

Judy raised her eyebrows. 'I thought you said they were none of them any good?'

'Well – some of them are better than others. Some are almost civilised.'

The need to confide was too strong to resist. She'd not told anyone up till now. Certainly not her colleagues. Not even her close friends. They knew too much about her past. 'In fact, there is someone I've got my eye on.'

'Oh – really?'

'A widower. So much better, don't you think? You can't avoid the luggage second time around, but at least if the wife's dead there's no ex hanging about the place. Or worse still, a current wife. There's plenty of them that will tell you they're divorced when they're nothing of the sort. But this time I know it's absolutely above board.'

'A – widower?'

'Yes. Well, you've met him, so you know he's nice. Trevor. Naz's father.'

Judy choked over her wine. 'Oh – dear – 'scuse me – went down the wrong way.'

Maggie patted her on the back and got her a glass of water and a couple of sheets of kitchen towel. Judy recovered, though she still looked a bit red in the face.

'I'm so sorry – so silly–'

'It's all right. Happens so easily,' Maggie assured her.

Really, she was terribly lacking in self-esteem.

'Yes, I really do think that Trevor is one of the good guys. As far as men go, that is. Do you know, he's an excellent cook, for a start. I always think that's a good sign, don't you? And there's the way he cares for little Karis–'

It was pleasant, being able to talk about him like this. And it might well be a lesson for Judy, too. If she saw that there was an alternative to sticking with that cheating bastard of a husband, she might make a move to assert herself, to take control of her life. Because she must know, in her heart. She was turning a blind eye, like she said. Well, blind eyes never did anyone any favours. She seemed to be taking it all in, sitting there nodding.

'And has he – er – shown any – er – interest?'

'It's early days yet,' Maggie said. 'Mustn't rush these things. I mean, it's all right for the young girls now to do all the chasing, but that generation of men like to make the running themselves, don't they? A bit un-PC, I know, encouraging the cave man instinct in them, but you have to make some concessions, don't you?'

'Yes, I – I suppose so.' Judy stood up. She was still looking a bit flushed. 'I really think I must be going. Thank you for your help, Maggie, I really appreciate it.'

Maggie found her coat and saw her to the door. 'Now, what about starting at the gym? Which evening is best for you? Or we could go at the weekend, if you prefer?'

'Oh – well – I'll think about it.'

'No, no, that's not good enough. You said you were going to go.'

'I'll think about it,' Judy repeated. 'See you Tuesday. And thanks again.'

And she was gone before Maggie could pin her down to a date.

CHAPTER 12

Monday began badly for Cathy. She started her period. So that was the end of hoping-against-hope for a baby yet again. Which brought on a row with Mike about fostering, which in turn made her late for work. Usually her job soothed her, but after the crushing disappointment of not getting pregnant even seeing to the needs of sick animals didn't help. The owners were bad tempered. One of the vets snapped at her for not listening properly. Two dogs and a guinea pig bit her. It was her turn for evening surgery, so it was nearly eight o'clock before she left and by then she was close to tears. To top it all, when she went outside to fetch her bike to cycle home it was tipping down with rain.

'Bloody weather!' she said out loud.

Bloody life. It just wasn't fair. Other women had babies, why not her? Some women had everything, women like Fiona. Fiona had two beautiful children and a gorgeous husband. Richard. He'd been so kind to her at that awful dinner party. The way he looked at her, like she was the only person in the room...

She stood holding the handlebars as a steady stream of cars growled past her from the station, tyres hissing on the wet road. Richard drove up here from the station each day. He'd told her that when he came into the surgery on Saturday with those two adorable children and their rabbit.

'Poor old Boris the Bunny here should have been brought in earlier, but Fiona seems too busy with this party thing of hers to do anything else,' he'd told her.

Stupid Fiona, neglecting her husband and her children's pet just for someone's silly party. Cathy made a sympathetic noise.

'But it was lucky you were on duty today,' he went on, smiling that white smile of his. 'Now I can picture you here when I drive past to the station.'

It had made Cathy's legs go all funny.

She pushed off up the hill, wobbling as she went. A car hooted at her, making her wobble more, and then another one splashed water over her. Then a car had pulled over and stopped in front of her.

'Bugger!' she squealed, hauling the bike back onto the pavement. There wasn't room to ride round it, not in this traffic.

The passenger door of the car swung open in her path, lighting the interior.

'Richard!'

'Cathy – I thought it was you. Would you like a lift?'

Oh those gorgeous dark eyes. That lovely voice.

'I – I–' she stuttered.

'Come on, you're going to get soaking in this lot. Put your bike back at the vet's and hop in.'

In a daze she obeyed. Inside the car it was warm and dry. The seats were real leather and comfy as armchairs. Something soothing was playing on the sound system.

'Lucky I came by just then. Had a good day? Any tricky cases?'

Cathy managed to tell him about an emergency they'd had in.

'I should think you make an excellent nurse.'

She glowed. 'Well – I try.'

'You seem to me to be such a caring person. Do you get very involved with your patients?'

She sighed. 'I do, rather. I've a whole litter of abandoned kittens at home at the moment.'

'Earth mother, eh?'

If only. 'Sort of.'

'Do you grow your own vegetables as well? I see you as a sort of *Good Life* figure.'

'Do you?'

'I've always rather fancied Felicity Kendal.'

Oh God. Her insides turned to jelly. 'Oh–' she squeaked. 'Have you?'

She was very conscious of his body only inches away from her. Her hand itched to touch his thigh. Nearly home. And she wanted this journey to go on for ever, enclosed in this secret space in the wet evening, just the two of them.

Richard pulled up outside her house. 'Thank you so much, it was so kind of you,' she said, trying to extend the moment.

'My pleasure. Any time.'

'I'm on late turn Mondays and Thursdays,' she heard herself say.

'Really?' He was looking at her in that intense way, so that she felt she might drown. 'I'll remember that.'

She wanted to reach out, to fall into him, to be burnt up.

He leaned forward and kissed her lightly on the cheek. *'Au revoir,* little Cathy.'

She had no idea how she managed to walk to her front door.

Maggie pulled up outside the convenience store. Having to stop for yet more milk dissipated the good feeling from the workout she'd just had at the gym. What did Ben do with it all? Life was just one long treadmill. And now it was raining.

Inside the shop some louts from her school were pushing and guffawing by the shelves of canned beer. Having to sort them out did nothing to improve her mood. She watched them as they slunk off, paid for her milk and headed for the door. If only she could be sure of going back to a tidy house. Fat chance, when Ben had been home all morning. The thought of the chaos he'd probably left was distinctly off-putting.

Back in her car an idea came to her. She could go round to Naz's and pick up the costume. She rang Naz's number, and to her delight got Trevor. She kept him talking for quite a time before she finally had to own up to why she had called.

'She's out at the parents' meeting at Karis' school at the moment,' Trevor told her. 'I know she's finished your costume, though.

She's bringing it to the class tomorrow.'

'Ah – well – I'm not sure whether I'm going to be able to make it tomorrow,' Maggie lied. 'But I did want to have the costume ready for the dress rehearsal next week. So if I could just pop round now?'

He wasn't really able to say no.

The world suddenly seemed a more hopeful place. With a bit of luck, she would have a good long talk to him without Naz being there. She knew how long parents' meetings went on.

To her disappointment Trevor had her costume all ready for her when she arrived, but she stepped into the hall anyway and admired it as it hung from the picture rail. 'She's made a lovely job of it, hasn't she? She's a talented girl, your Naz, you must be very proud of her.'

Trevor couldn't very well contradict her. They talked a bit about Naz, and then she asked him about Supercook. Maggie was enjoying herself. And then a key turned in the lock outside and Naz burst in.

'That woman! She doesn't know what she's talking about! Do you know what–? Oh – Maggie. What are you doing here?'

Naz was obviously fuming. Her small body was stiff with anger. Maggie smiled and indicated the costume. 'I just came to pick this up. It's beautiful, Naz. But what's the matter? Was there a problem at Karis' school?'

'Problem! There's no problem with Karis, I can tell you that,' Naz raged. She had just enough control left to speak in an undertone, so that Karis would not hear her. 'She's a very bright little girl. It's her teacher that's the problem. She thinks Karis is behind in her maths work. Great list of things she says Karis can't do, when I know she can. She does it for homework. And she's such a hypocrite, she says all that and then she gives me this sickly smile and says, "I do hope you don't think I've got some sort of a down on Karis, Miss Randall. She's a dear little girl, always cheerful, and excellent social skills. She's very popular with her classmates." I could have killed her!'

Maggie had to hold back a grin of delight as she saw the big golden opportunity opening out before her. Instead she arranged her face in an expression of concern.

Trevor had a soothing arm round his daughter's shoulders. 'It's all right, pet. We know she's doing just fine.'

Naz brushed a hand over her eyes. 'It's these bloody teachers,' she growled, glaring at Maggie. 'They don't understand.'

The poor girl did have a lot on her plate, bringing up a child on her own.

'I'm wondering, Naz,' Maggie said carefully, 'do you think Karis would benefit from some one-to-one coaching? Even the brightest child can sometimes get swamped in a large class. Some individual attention, perhaps an hour a week, might make all the difference. Just give her that bit of extra confidence she needs?'

You could almost see the words sinking into Naz's brain. The truculence drained from her eyes as she turned the idea over. 'Well,' she said 'I suppose–'

'It does sound like a good way forward,' Trevor said.

'But it would cost–'

Trevor started to say that cost didn't matter, when Maggie jumped in.

'I'd be delighted to help.' She was about to say she would do it for free, when she realised that that was being a too pushy. Naz was very prickly about her independence. Her eye lighted on the dance costume. 'How about I swap my skill for yours? You made my costume, I'll coach Karis.'

'Well – I–'

In the end, Naz couldn't think of a reason not to agree. They arranged for lessons to start on Wednesday. Maggie left walking on air.

Naz got Karis' tea while trying to read a book for an assignment she had to get in by Monday. She didn't get very far, not with Karis loudly practising the song she was learning for the school Easter concert and demanding total attention and lashings of admiration.

There was so much to do. All this stuff with the party wasn't helping. It was eating into her studying time far too much. She should never have agreed to go along with it. It was just that it seemed like easy money. She hated having to borrow from her father. Not that he ever made a fuss about it, but that wasn't the point. She wanted to be independent.

The phone rang. As if summoned by thought, it was Fiona.

'Hello Naz. How are you ? Good. Listen, did you manage to get those quotes from the printers?'

Printers, printers – oh yes. 'Yes. Wilson's was the best.'

'Oh splendid. Can you finalise that, and then that's one more thing out of the way. I'm going to sit down this evening and make a list of last-minute things to do. Once the children are in bed I'll have a clear run through, since Richard's got a late meeting. He probably won't be home till gone eleven.'

'Really? Well, I have to go, Fiona.' Some of us do have things to get on with.

'It's funny, isn't it? Before this party commission came up, I used to get really cross when he was late. I tried not to let him see it, because he does work very hard and he'd rather be home than at the office, but I couldn't help resenting it. But now I'm almost pleased, because it gives me a free evening to do what I want.'

'Yes, lovely. See you, then, Fiona.'

A free evening. Now that was a nice thought. Naz looked at the notes and pile of unread books on her desk Perhaps she shouldn't go out this evening. Perhaps she ought to get some work done, but that would mean being in when Judy was upstairs with her dad. A night out it was, then.

By the time Brad came round, Karis was playing up. 'I don't want to go to bed. I'm not tired. I want to come out with you and Brad.'

'Well you can't. You're too young.'

Trevor appeared, picked her up and threw her over his shoulder. 'Bedtime now,' he insisted.

Karis yelled and beat his back with her fists.

Trevor ignored her. 'Off you go, you two. She'll be all right,' he said.

Karis screamed. 'I won't go to bed! I won't! I want to go out with you!'

Naz hesitated.

'Come on, your dad's right. She'll be fine once we've gone,' Brad said.

Incensed, Naz rounded on him. 'How do you know? That's just what you want to believe.'

'She's playing to an audience now. My nieces and nephews are just the same. They create when their mum and dad are going out, and it's all a show. Once we've gone she'll calm down.'

He was right. Which was infuriating. 'You're so bloody reasonable,' Naz complained.

It was that Maggie's fault. Karis was overtired from the coaching session yesterday. The doorbell rang and they all went quiet, even Karis. Naz started towards the door.

'No, I'll go,' Trevor said. 'It might be–'

Judy. 'It's all right,' Naz said, and hurried to open it.

It was Judy, looking very bright and attractive with her new hairstyle and her more modern make-up. When she realised who was standing there, she looked acutely embarrassed.

'Oh – Naz. I thought you were – only I tried the upstairs bell and nobody came and I heard voices–'

'That's all right. Come in, he's in here. Karis is being difficult,' Naz said, stepping back to let her into the narrow hallway.

'Look, er, Naz – it's not what you think–' Judy stammered.

Naz looked at her. Her dad's girlfriend. Married girlfriend.

'Isn't it?' she said, and led the way into the living room.

Only Brad was there. Karis' high voice and Trevor's low one could be heard next door in Karis' bedroom. Negotiations seemed to be going on. Naz took a breath. She waved a hand at Brad. 'This is Brad,' she said.

'Brad – Judy.'

'Oh, you're the young man who did Fiona's garden. It looks wonderful.'

And there they were, chatting away like old friends. In the end, Naz practically had to drag him away.

'So that's the secret girlfriend, is it? Nice lady,' Brad commented, as he started the truck

Naz folded her arms across her chest and stared straight ahead down the dark street. 'She is the secret girlfriend, yes.'

'You weren't very polite to her.'

He was right, which made it worse. 'So?'

'So she's your dad's choice, he seems to be happy and you shouldn't spoil it for him.'

'She's married. When I saw them together I was shocked. I didn't think Judy was that sort of person. She seems so nice and kind and loyal and–'

And like my mum, except that my mum wouldn't have had an affair with another man.

'If your dad doesn't mind, why should you?'

Bugger it. He was so *reasonable*. They were still arguing about it when they got to Donatello's.

The bar was jumping. It was Friday night and everyone was out to have a good time. Brad's friends had bagged a table in one corner and had already got a couple of rounds in. Naz downed a Red Bull and vodka. She still felt wound up and cross and betrayed.

Shauna came sashaying over with the tapas they had ordered. 'Hiya, Nazza! How's this gorgeous man of yours?'

She wrapped herself round Brad while everyone on the table whistled and shouted. Shauna gave them a stage wink 'Wait till Nazza's in the lavvie, then it's you and me for a full-on snog.'

Naz's fingers curled. 'I'll have to have a go at your Ben, then,' she said, trying to keep the edge out of her voice and not really succeeding.

Shauna flapped a hand at her. 'You're welcome to him, darling.'

Brad's friends included her in the talk, making sure she didn't feel left out. They were nice people, a good laugh, friendly. Brad was caring, sexy, fun, solid. She should be enjoying herself. It was a great evening. Everyone was having a brilliant time. So why did she feel so knotted up, so confused, so – trapped?

By tennish she couldn't stand it any longer. She wanted to go home but she couldn't, because Judy was upstairs with her dad. She went into the loo.

'Hey Nazza–' Shauna was right behind her. 'You got the hump with me?'

Naz shrugged. She just wanted to lock

herself in a cubicle and be alone.

Shauna put an arm round her. 'I didn't mean nothing, mate. It was just a laugh. Look, here I am with you just to prove I'm not having a try at him.'

Naz exploded. 'I don't fucking care, right? You can do what you like with him but leave me alone.'

Shauna rubbed her shoulder. 'OK OK, I get it. Just cool it, eh? What's the matter? Tell old Shauna. I'm your mate, Nazzie. Is everything all right with you and Brad?'

'Yes! How many times–?'

'He is gorgeous, Naz. I mean, I'd have him if he wasn't yours, and if I wasn't going off dancing. 'Cos he's, like, not a quick shag and gone, is he? He's the settle down and roses round the door sort. You can see that. But not boring. Not an anorak. I mean, he's dead sexy. You're just putting on the act, are you? About not caring? To get him gasping? I mean like, you must fancy him rotten really–'

Yes. 'No!'

'Oh come on–'

'I do fancy him. Yes. But – not the rest. Not the roses round the door.' Naz had her arms folded tightly round herself. 'I don't want to be in anyone's power ever again,' she said slowly. 'Once you love them, they can hurt you. I went all through that with Dominic. I went through it and I came out the other side and I'm never going back. A quick shag's OK, but nothing more. Not the roses round the door. Because it doesn't work, does it? They all let you down in the end. They're all bastards.'

'Not all of them. Look at – look at–'

Shauna hesitated. Someone was thumping the tampon dispenser and swearing. The hand dryer was roaring. 'Look at Cathy and Mike. Now Mike's not a bastard.'

'But would you want to be married to him?' Naz demanded.

'No.'

They were both silent, thinking of being married to Mike. Shauna snorted, then erupted into laughter. 'Fucking Mary, what a nightmare!'

Suddenly, Naz found that instead of weeping she was howling with hysterical laughter. She held onto Shauna, tears streaming down her face.

'All right now?' Shauna gasped. Naz nodded. She wasn't all right, but she was a lot better than she had been.

The group welcomed her back as if she'd been to the North Pole. The evening surged on, noisy and cheerful. The bar staff swept them out at closing time.

Outside, it was cold and windy. The High Street echoed with the shouts of other groups that had just been turned out of the pubs. Some of the others were arguing over whether to go for an Indian or a Chinese.

Brad slung an arm round Naz's shoulders and pulled her close to him. 'Coming back to mine?' he asked.

Naz tried to wriggle free. 'No – not tonight.'

'Oh Naz.' For once, Brad sounded annoyed. 'Look, if it's your dad – you're not his keeper, you know. You're not responsible for him. You're acting like you're the parent and he's the child.'

'I'm not!'

'You are. You're like one of those fathers who thinks no one's good enough for their little princess.'

'I'm *not!*'

'You are. You're being totally unreasonable. He's not going to thank you for acting like this.'

He wrapped his arms round her, nuzzled against her head, kissed her neck 'Come on, come back to mine.'

His body was big and strong and warm. She felt a surge of desire. She did want him. More than that, she wanted to lose herself, to stop worrying about college, work, Karis, her dad. She wanted to be swept down into that whirlpool of pleasure... Brad was running his hands over her. Even through her thick jacket it was exciting. He was talking in her ear.

'Look at it this way, it's a good thing if your dad's got someone of his own. That means there's more room for you and me, a future–'

'No!' Naz struggled out of his arms. 'There's no you and me, right? Get that clear. No future. Nothing.'

She started to march up the street. She had to get away, before it was too late, before he got under her skin and into her life. Before he became necessary to her.

Brad strode after her and caught her arm. 'What the fuck's got into you this evening?'

It was the first time she'd ever heard him swear. 'Nothing,' she said. 'Just leave me alone.'

She wrenched out of his grasp and walked on. Like a beacon in the dark, there was a taxi rank just yards away. 'Naz, don't do this. I love you.'

She whirled round. 'No you don't. You don't know the meaning of the word! None of you does!'

She pulled open the door of the nearest cab and fell inside. Then she cried all the way home.

CHAPTER 13

Maggie arrived at the school where the charity concert was being staged. A harassed looking woman with a clipboard directed her to the classroom assigned to their group. She ran a professional eye over the displays in the corridors as she went along. Not as good as Watfield Park, and this was a better catchment area than the Watfield estate. Chattering voices and snatches of music wafted out of the rooms. The corridors were full of excited performers – little girls half dressed as fairies and elves, spotty boys got up like something out of *Riverdance*, blue robed members of a gospel choir, fat geishas from a production of *The Mikado*, lurid shirted steel band players ... she began to feel the first fluttering of nerves.

She found the right room and was welcomed in by Cheryl.

'There you are, Maggie! Wonderful! Only half a dozen more to come now. Isn't this exciting? There's some space over there for you to change. There's loads of time, so don't panic. We're not on till quarter to ten.'

'Ten! I thought we were half-eight.'

'It's been changed. We're second from last now.'

Fiona was standing nearby. 'One off top of the bill,' she said. 'I suppose that's an honour. But I'd really rather get it over with. And besides, Richard was going to take the children home after they'd seen me, if they were tired. Now they'll have to stay up till the end.'

Maggie fought against envy. Fiona's family were here to support her, as were everyone

205

else's. It must be so nice to have someone out there rooting for you. Ben was coming along, but to see Shauna. She was quite sure that he wouldn't have considered it otherwise. She found a space in between Cathy and Judy and hung up her costume.

'Oh dear, I do wish I hadn't said I would do this,' Judy said.

She looked pale with nerves, her cheeks loose and flabby.

'You'll be fine,' Maggie told her, though she doubted it. At least Cheryl had had the sense to put her at the back, where she didn't show too much. She was nice, Judy, but she was a rubbish dancer.

Cathy let out a wail. 'Oh no! I forgot to do my nails! You've all got lovely red nails and mine are horrible!'

'It's all right, I've got some polish with me and you've plenty of time to do it,' Fiona said.

Cathy looked acutely embarrassed. 'Oh, no, really, it'll be all right.'

Fiona ignored her and searched in her expensive-looking vanity case. She came out with a choice of three nail colours. 'Here you are,' she said. 'Take whichever you like.'

Cathy actually backed away, as if the things might bite. 'No, really.'

What was the matter with the silly girl?

'For Christ's sake, which do you like best? Here, this one's nice. I'll do it for you,'

Shauna said.

She marched Cathy over to a desk and sat her down. Cathy's hands were shaking. 'I feel sick,' she moaned.

Fiona was saying something about the party she was organising, but Maggie couldn't concentrate on it. It was all so trivial. Instead, she found herself watching Cheryl as she plugged in a portable CD player. That was a turn-up – Cheryl being efficient enough to bring the means for them to have a last run-through. Cheryl rummaged in her bag. She brought out two CDs and kept looking. Her face was going redder and redder. Then she turned the bag upside down and tipped the contents on the floor. Maggie could guess exactly what was wrong.

'You haven't left some of our music behind?'

She hadn't meant to say it so loudly, but she was so disgusted that her words cut through the hubbub. A horrified silence fell.

'We haven't got our bleeding music?' Shauna cried.

'I thought I had it, it was in my deck at home. I must have picked up the wrong one. I don't know how–' Cheryl sounded close to tears.

'Why on earth didn't you check before you left home?' Maggie demanded. It was basic common sense, after all.

Fiona, cool as ever, had her mobile in her

hand. 'Is there anyone at home who can bring it over for us?' she asked.

Cheryl shook her head. 'My mum's looking after the girls, but she can't drive.'

Fiona glanced at her watch. 'If you phone her and tell her exactly where it is, I'll ask Richard to stop by and pick it up.'

In a few minutes, it was all arranged. 'There, crisis over,' Fiona said, snapping the mobile shut.

'Richard really is a star. Not all men would run about after things for you like that,' Judy said.

Maggie could hear the longing in her voice. She knew just what Judy meant. It must be nice to have someone totally devoted to you.

'I know,' Fiona was saying. 'I should appreciate him more.'

Maggie chanced to look between the bobbing heads of the group round Cheryl to where Cathy was still sitting at a desk with her nails half done. She appeared to be staring at Fiona with an odd expression on her face, most unpleasant. And then their eyes met and Cathy gave a weak smile. Nerves. They were all suffering.

She went over to Naz. 'What a to-do. Are you all right?' she asked.

Naz shook her head. Under her dark colouring she was pale, giving her skin a strange greyish tinge.

'What's the matter?'

'Nothing.'

'We're all nervous. It's natural. And this business with the music didn't help. Cheryl really is a hopeless organiser.'

Naz took a long breath. 'It's not that,' she said.

'What is it, then?' She liked Naz. She wasn't a whinger. She got on with things and was working hard to better herself and look after Karis.

Naz pressed her lips together, but it didn't stop them from trembling. 'It's Brad,' she confessed, her voice coming out as a squeak.

A bubble of excitement formed in Maggie's stomach. Naz was going to confide in her. A very good sign.

'You've had a row?' she asked gently. Naz nodded. 'A bad one?'

'Yes. I – it was the Friday before last,' Naz hesitated, then her expression closed. 'But you don't want to hear my problems.'

Maggie sat down on the table by her. 'It always helps to talk.'

Tears were swimming in Naz's eyes now. The temptation to tell was too much. 'It was all my fault. I ran off and got a cab home by myself on Friday. Then he didn't phone me all weekend and I wasn't going to phone him and when he did on Tuesday I – I – really blew it. I said all the wrong things. You know, how you do, sometimes?'

Oh yes. However much you rehearse things

in your head beforehand, it never comes out the right way at the fatal moment.

Around them, women were putting on make-up, spraying their hair, admiring each other's over-the-top fake jewellery.

'Yes,' she said. 'I do know. But things can still be sorted out, Naz. I'm sure it's not too late.'

Naz took a big sobbing breath. 'That's why it's best to make a break now. If it hurts like this now, what will it be like later?'

'What do you mean, later?'

'When we've been together for longer. When Karis has had time to get to like him–'

'I thought she liked him already?'

'She does, that's just it, that makes it all far worse. This time there's her to get hurt as well as me. I can't do it.'

'Is he going to be here this evening?' Maggie asked.

'Yes – no – I don't know. He *was* going to be, but now I don't know–'

'My guess is he will be. And that he'll be waiting for you afterwards. Make it up with him then, Naz. All you'll have to do is run up to him and it'll all be all right.'

At her age that was all it needed. It was later that things got beyond a simple gesture.

Naz shook her head. 'It isn't as easy as that.'

'It could be, if you let it.'

'I don't know–'

Maggie put a hand on hers. 'Just do it.'

There was a stir at the door. It was Richard, with the CD. Maggie watched Cheryl as she was all over Fiona and Richard. Stupid woman. Cheryl was clapping her hands.

'Er – girls, please, now that we've got the music – thanks to Fiona, and Richard, of course–' Claps and cheers.

'Perhaps we could just have a quick run through, just to refresh our memories.'

The intimate moment with Naz was broken. Naz got up and joined the other dancers in the middle of the room. Reluctantly, Maggie followed.

'If we say that way's the audience – no – perhaps that way would be better.'

They all got into their starting positions. Cheryl slotted in a CD and the opening bars of the first number shivered round the classroom. There was a sharp knock at the door. It was one of the organisers.

'Two minutes to the start. Can you be quiet now, please? Any noise from here can be heard in the hall.'

Everyone groaned. Cheryl was panicking. 'Oh dear, oh dear. Now we won't have time. We really needed a run through–'

'We can do it in the interval,' Maggie pointed out wearily. For heaven's sake, couldn't she work that out for herself? 'The audience will all be talking then and won't hear us,' she added, just in case Cheryl couldn't work that out, either.

'Oh – yes, yes of course. That's what we'll do.'

The classroom door was shut on them. The group tried to be quiet. There were hissed conversations and bursts of giggles. Really, they were like a class of twelve-year-olds. Maggie concentrated on putting on her make-up.

From the hall the buzz of the audience went quiet. Then there was a burst of applause. Tension in the room rose palpably. This was it. It had begun. Someone could be heard speaking from the stage, but the words couldn't be made out. There was another burst of applause, and then music. A children's choir. Their sweet young voices echoed down the corridors.

Maggie was seized with a sharp nostalgia for her own offspring's childhood. How much easier everything was then. They'd been a proper family – father, mother, son and daughter. They'd gone on family holidays and spent Christmas playing silly games. She'd been able to refer to 'my husband'. Where had it all gone wrong? Robin, that's who had ruined it. It was all his fault, chasing after that tart. He'd broken up their happy family.

One act followed another. Some sounded dire, others pleasant. All were heartily applauded. Cheryl got them all warming up, then when the interval came round she actually managed to put the CDs the right way up in the deck and see them through the three dances. Everyone made mistakes, and they only just finished rehearsing before the second half started.

An edgy hush fell on the group. The gospel choir sang. A folk group played. Shauna was going round checking everyone's make-up. There was a tap on the classroom door. The organiser who had come round before put her head round.

'Two minutes! Come and line up to get onstage.'

Everyone leapt up, picking up veils, adjusting head-dresses There was a lot of muted gasping and squealing. They got into the right order.

'Have you got the music?' Maggie hissed at Cheryl.

Cheryl went bright red and leapt at her portable player, stabbing at the eject button. She handed the CDs to the organiser. It was a good thing somebody was on the ball.

They padded along the corridor in their bare feet, the coins on their hip-scarves jingling to their steps. The act that was on now, a piano duo, got louder and louder as they got nearer to the stage doors. They were handed over to the guardians of the doors while the organiser went off to give their music to the sound man.

'Don't forget – smile!' Cheryl muttered to

each dancer.

'Six hip arches left, turn to the count of eight, pause, two, three *then* triples forward,' Judy muttered.

Oh dear, supposing she got it wrong? Supposing she turned the wrong way, or went forward when everyone else had paused? She felt ill. She wanted to go to the loo.

Behind her, Cathy gave an encouraging squeeze to her shoulder. 'You'll be fine, Jude,' she breathed.

If only.

The piano duo finished with a flourish. There was thunderous applause. Trevor was in there somewhere, waiting to see her, as well as Naz, of course. He was willing her to do well. That made her feel a bit better.

Alan was there as well. She'd been surprised when he'd said he would come, since he'd always been so disparaging about her dancing. Then a split second later she realised why. He wanted to see Fiona. It no longer hurt. Alan could do what he liked, it didn't bother her.

The pianists came out of the stage door, flushed with success.

The dancers who had been with Cheryl last year went silently in to line up on the steps to the stage and into the wings. The rest of them crowded into the small space each side of the stage. It was dark and dusty and hot. Judy broke out in a sweat.

'And now, ladies and gentlemen, a touch of the exotic. All the way from the Middle East – the middle of east Mellingford, that is – we have the Queens of the Nile Egyptian Dancers!'

A ripple of anticipation, then more applause from the audience. The first notes of the music flowed out into the hall, a sensuous solo flute that wound up and down, sometimes slow, sometimes fast. One by one the more experienced dancers went on to the stage and struck a pose. As the notes of the flute died away the last one was in place. Then the music changed, became a quick, flirty little tune with flute and drums and strings. The group began to move, swaying and hip-dropping and Egyptian-walking.

From where Judy was packed in, she could just see a slice of the stage between two side curtains. She was on a level with the dancers' feet, but even from there it looked good. The costumes glowed in the intense stage lighting, the dancing was lively and accurate.

Oh God, let me be all right. Don't let me be the one to let the others down.

All too soon the number ended. The dancers were unwrapping their long coloured veils from around their hips. The rest of the women were going onto the stage to join them.

This was it. Judy concentrated on not tripping over her skirt as she climbed the steep steps. Onto the stage. Into her position. Pose – one arm up, the other out, so that the veil drapes elegantly. Bend the elbow slightly. Don't look stiff. Smile. Thank goodness she was at the back. Three ranks of dancers in front of her hid her from too much public scrutiny. All the same, she felt horribly exposed.

The lights were very bright and surprisingly hot. The hall beyond was very dark. But though she couldn't see the audience she could hear them shuffling and muttering, sense their intense gaze. The audience was a monster wanting to be amused.

The next number started, a slow serene tune that soothed and calmed. The dancers stayed practically on one spot, swirling and sweeping and turning their veils like a cloud of bright butterflies. Judy kept her eyes firmly on Cheryl at the centre front, following each movement.

It was all right, it was all right. She was keeping up. Right, swoop and up, left swoop and up, undulate, undulate ... and the final turn and – pose! It was finished. They were clapping! She had got through her first dance without any mistakes! Now the finale.

The veils were tucked into the hip-scarves, the dancers formed two lines. The drum beat began, quick insistent tapping of fingers and slapping of palms. The dancers skipped into action, circling, advancing, retreating, quick steps and slow. Pipes joined in with the drums, adding the melody, earthy, folky music, in complete contrast to the last one. The audience took up the beat of the tune, clapping in time. The dancers' hips dipped and shimmered.

They formed a semi-circle round the sides and back of the stage. Shauna came forward as the music changed pace and rhythm to do a solo spot. Judy gazed at her, entranced. She was good. She performed. The rest of them just danced, but Shauna performed. She gave her all to the monster in the darkened hall, she sparked with life and energy, she was sensuous and graceful. Her spot ended with a sensational shimmy that got the audience whistling and whooping. How wonderful, to be able to do that!

Two lines of dancers circled round Shauna, one clockwise, the other anticlockwise. The music accelerated to a climax. They whirled into a tight bunch and stopped, Shauna with her arms up in the middle, the inner circle kneeling up on one knee with their arms out, the outer circle sitting down on both knees with their arms reaching forward.

The audience erupted.

They had done it! Judy couldn't believe it. They were bowing. She'd managed to get through both. It was wonderful. There were two curtain calls, and then they escaped. Euphoric, elated, they scampered back to their changing room, hardly able to contain their excitement. After all that waiting, it was finished so soon.

Naz wanted to do it all over again. For those brief minutes on stage, she had forgotten everything except the dance.

Cheryl closed the door behind them. 'Shh, shh, well done, you were fantastic, all of you, wonderful–'

They were all laughing and squealing and hugging each other. Cheryl was passing round chocolates. They were all congratulating Shauna for her dancing and Cheryl for her choreography and Fiona and herself for the costumes and everyone else for just sticking the course and being there. They were a team. They were a hit. They had made it.

And then the classroom door burst open and people came flooding in, husbands, parents, children, boyfriends.

Naz found herself breathing fast. Her heart was thumping. Had Brad come? Her dad came in, carrying Karis, who wriggled down and ran straight to her. Naz swept her up and hugged her close, taking comfort from her hot little body until Karis begged to be put down again. That dreadful Alan walked straight past Judy and went to speak to Fiona.

'All over her like a rash,' someone said in her ear. It was Shauna.

'Yeah,' she said absently, still staring at the door.

More people, strangers, relations of the other dancers. Her dad was enthusing on about how good they had all been. Richard came in carrying a crate of champagne bottles and a box of glasses. There were shrieks and cheers as the corks began to pop. Someone pressed a glass into her hand.

'To the Queens of the Nile! Long may they reign!' Richard toasted.

'The Queens of the Nile!' everyone repeated.

Richard and Fiona were standing together, arms round each other, children at their side, the perfect couple. Mike came in and congratulated Cathy. Everyone was in pairs, it seemed. Naz felt excluded.

Cheryl was banging on a table and yelling for quiet. 'Everyone. Girls, listen–'

Gradually, some of the hysteria subsided.

'Speech!' somebody called. Gales of laughter.

'No, no, no speeches. I'm no good at them. I just wanted to tell you all some news. We've just been invited to perform at the Mellingford Midsummer Festival!'

Cheers, yells, clapping. That was it. He wasn't here. Karis was tugging at her arm. Naz turned away from all the cheerful faces and ran into Cathy. To her amazement, she saw that Cathy looked as unhappy as she felt.

'What's up?' she asked automatically.

'Nothing,' Cathy said.

Naz shrugged. Cathy had a sweet, faithful husband, even if he was a bit weird. What did she have to worry about?

'It's all right for you,' she said. 'I should never have gone out with him in the first place. I knew it was a mistake.'

People were jostling round them, laughing, spilling champagne. Karis wandered off to join her grandfather.

'What?' Cathy said. She was looking over Naz's shoulder.

'I let myself be pushed into it. Dad, and Fiona. They think they know best, but they're not me, are they? They don't see–'

'Your Brad's here,' Cathy said.

'*What?*' Naz spun round. There he was, looking uncharacteristically uncertain, scanning the room, looking for her.

'Brad–' she whispered. She clutched at Cathy's arm. 'He's here. He came. He did watch the show.'

Joy shot through her. She hadn't blown it. He still cared. She pushed through the crowd. From the doorway, a beaming Brad was shouldering his way towards her. They met in the middle, flinging themselves into each other's arms.

CHAPTER 14

How did other people cope? It was so exhausting – the lies, the adolescent mood swings, the having to get on with everyday life. You needed a handbook. *The Menopausal Woman's Guide to that First Affair.* Perhaps she should write it herself. Judy smiled to herself as she stood over the sink peeling potatoes. That's what most people would think, if they knew. Poor old Judy's gone off her nut, she's having a last fling. Except that she wasn't having a fling. It was more serious than that. Much more serious.

Her hands stilled as she thought of the evening of the Charity Concert. There she had been, in that hot classroom full of excited women. She'd been excited herself, triumphant at having managed to get right through her two dances without disgracing herself. And then Trevor had appeared with Karis in his arms and she'd wanted so much to rush up to him, to have him put his arms round her and tell her she was wonderful, like Fiona and Richard, like Shauna and Ben. But she couldn't. She had to stand there, ignoring Alan who was ignoring her, and pretend that she and Trevor were nothing more than passing acquaintances, while Karis ran up to her mother and Trevor smiled and congratulated his daughter.

Then, to make things worse, Maggie had come up to her and started on about going to the gym again, and in her distracted state she'd agreed, just to get away. And just when she thought she couldn't stand it any longer, there he was, Trevor, at her elbow.

'You were terrific,' he murmured in her ear, and out loud, 'Hello, Judy, nice to see you again. It all went very well, didn't it?'

They chatted about this and that, trying not even to look at each other too much, and all the while she wanted to claim him, to hold onto his arm, to be part of him. She could see Maggie making her way back to her in a very determined fashion.

'Of course, I'm not surprised you're a good dancer,' Trevor said softly. 'It's a well-known fact that people who are good at dancing are good in bed.'

'Well-known by whom?' she asked, glowing with delight.

'By me. I'm an expert.' His hand rested on her bottom, sending shafts of pleasure through her.

Maggie was at his side, her face all bright and expectant. 'And what are you an expert on, Trevor? I'm sure you know about all sorts of things.'

'I know a good act when I see it. You lot

were splendid,' he said.

His hand closed round her buttock. Judy suppressed a squeal. Maggie looked at her curiously.

'Pardon me. Indigestion,' she gasped, pressing a hand to her mouth.

Maggie evidently decided not to be distracted from her aim. She stood there gazing into Trevor's face, plying him with questions and remarks.

'I think the whole thing was very much enhanced by Naz's costumes, don't you? You must be so proud of her.'

'We all like to think our kids are wonderful, I suppose. Do you think your twins are wonderful, Judy?'

'Well I–'

'I'm not sure that I agree. I'm not too happy about my Ben at the moment. He could be doing a lot better for himself in lots of ways. But little Naz is such a talented girl. How's she getting on with her degree?'

'Not well enough, she's got too much else on. What do you know about this party business with her and Fiona, Judy?'

'They seem to be–'

'It's so important that she doesn't neglect her course work,' Maggie interrupted. 'You know that if she needs any help I'd be only too willing to advise her?'

'Thank you, but–'

Alan appeared, with a face like thunder.

'Come on, we're going,' he said.

'But I'm only half changed!' Judy protested.

Alan glanced at her. She was still wearing her skirt and leotard. 'Put a coat on over it,' he said.

Over his shoulder, Judy saw that Richard and Fiona were leaving. Richard was carrying a very sleepy looking Freya. They were taking the children home to bed.

Trevor's hand closed surreptitiously round her wrist.

'Aren't some of you girls going for a drink after?' he said.

To her credit, Maggie rose to the occasion magnificently. 'Yes, we are. I can give you a lift home if you like, Judy.'

'I – er–'

Go drinking with Maggie in tow or go home now with Alan? Difficult choice. But being with Trevor a bit longer in any circumstances won.

'Thanks, yes, if it's no trouble,' she said.

But then Brad turned up and he and Naz staged a great reconciliation, and Trevor had to volunteer to take Karis home. Judy was stuck with going out with Maggie, Cathy and Mike. It was not a success.

'When's dinner, Mum?'

Judy started. Toby and Oliver were at the kitchen door. She looked down at the sink. She'd finished the spuds and hadn't even noticed. 'Oh, er, twenty minutes. I think,' she said.

'Mu-um! You said it'd be at half-six. It's that now. We're going out, remember.'

'Are you?'

Groans. 'We *told* you, Mum. This morning.'

Had they? She couldn't recall. 'Well, you'll just have to wait.'

More groans. 'You're getting really dozy, Mum. You never got those photos I asked you to collect the other day.'

'And you let us run out of crisps.'

'Did I? Well, it won't hurt you.'

'Mum! We can't live without crisps.'

She always kept the crisp supply up because she was addicted to them herself. Or used to be. That must have been why she had forgotten to buy them. Somehow, she didn't need snacks these days. She put her hands to her hips. Definitely getting slimmer. These were size fourteen trousers.

The boys were still going on about her household failures. She waved them away.

'Dinner'll be when it's ready. Go and lay the table for me if you're in such a hurry.'

The phone rang. She picked up the one in the kitchen before either of the boys could reach the one in the hall.

'Hello, it's me.'

Excitement thrilled through her. 'Hello you.'

'Can you talk?'

'Not for long—'

Oliver's head appeared round the kitchen door. 'Is that—?'

'It's for me,' she mouthed at him.

He made a disappointed face and left. 'So, what did you want?' she asked.

'Does it have to be anything special? I just like to hear your voice. But as it happens, it'd be even better to see you, and Naz is going out this evening to finalise the arrangements for this wretched party of Fiona's, so do you think you could come round?'

Oh God, she was supposed to be going to the gym with Maggie – but then that would make a good cover story. She only had to phone Maggie and cancel before Alan got in. 'Yes. Yes, I can manage that.'

'Wonderful! I'll look forward to seeing you. When can you be here?'

Oliver looked in again. 'Hurry up, Mum. I'm expecting a call.'

'Use your mobile.' And go away.

'I'm out of credit.'

'Use your brother's.'

'He's using it.'

Go away! 'About half-sevenish,' she told Trevor.

'Can't wait. Have you got someone there?'

'Yes.'

'I'd like to take all your clothes off.'

Judy swallowed a delighted giggle. 'Me too,' she said, conscious of Oliver still glaring at her.

'And then cover you with honey–'

'That'd be nice.'

'Mum! I *need* the phone.'

'Buzz off, Ollie.'

'And then lick it all off slowly–'

'Yes, thank you. We'll do that, then.'

'How much longer are you going to be?' He sounded just like his father. She almost expected him to start making money counting gestures and tap his watch.

Trevor's voice rolled into her ear. 'Then make passionate love to you on a tiger skin.'

'Yes, right.'

'We're on, then, are we?'

'Absolutely.'

'I'll hold you to that.'

'I hope you will.'

'Mum! My life depends on this.'

'See you, then,' she said briskly, and put the phone down. 'All yours, Ollie.'

'About bloody time!'

He flung out of the kitchen. Judy held her sides and doubled up with silent delicious laughter. Toby came in, mobile clamped to his ear. He gave her a suspicious look

'You all right, Mum?'

'Yes, spot of indigestion.' She seemed to be getting quite a lot of it lately.

Alan turned up just as she was getting dinner on the table. He spent the first part of the meal grumbling about the state of the trains, while the boys made faces and guessed what he was about to say.

'Worst run line in the country is it, Dad?'

'Not fit for human beings to travel on?'

'Like being in some banana republic?'

Alan slammed his knife down. 'For Christ's sake! I have to travel on that poxy line every day of the week just so I can keep you and your mother in food and drink with a roof over your heads! I can do without your stupid remarks.'

Oliver and Toby looked at each other. Oooo! They mouthed, in mock terror.

Alan gave up on them. 'Can you video that film for me this evening?' he asked Judy.

'Er – no, sorry. I'm going out.'

'Out? What do you mean, out? You don't go out on Wednesdays.'

Judy took a breath. I'm going for an evening of passionate sex with my lover. 'I'm going to the gym with Maggie.'

It came out remarkably coolly. Oliver and Toby fell about.

'You! Going to the gym!'

'What are you going to? The Nifty Fifties?'

'Workout for Pensioners?'

'Aqua Stretch for the Bodily Challenged?'

Judy reached over and flicked them both round the head with her table napkin.

Alan was scowling. 'One of you two will have to do it,' he said. 'Mind you don't forget. And don't record over my Formula

One like you did last time.'

The boys shovelled down the last of their meal and stood up. 'Sorry Dad, we gotta split.'

'What do you mean? You're going out as well?'

'You got it.'

They picked up their plates to put in the dishwasher, and left.

'Bloody hell!' Alan slammed his knife down again. 'Now how am I going to get the film taped?'

'Set the timer,' Judy told him.

'It's not working.'

Then stay in and watch it, if it's so important. 'You'll have to get it fixed,' she said, and picked up her own plate and the serving dishes.

'Where are you going? I haven't finished yet.'

'I told you. Out.'

Judy put the serving dishes down again and followed the boys into the kitchen. She couldn't wait any longer to get out of the house. All the way to Trevor's place she sang along with the radio. She was out! She had escaped. She was going to see her lover.

She, Judy Blackwell, sensible middle-aged woman, respectable wife and mother, doctor's receptionist, had a lover. Judy Blackwell, belly-dancer, had a lover. That was it. It was all because of her new identity. She had turned a corner the day she started that class.

Trevor was downstairs in Naz's flat. 'Come in, darling, I'm just putting her to bed.' He folded her in his arms and hugged her close. 'Mmm. Lovely to see you again. I'm so glad you could come.'

'Me too.' It was wonderful to be held by him again.

Karis came bounding up, dressed in her pink Barbie pyjamas. 'Hello! I've got a new fairy story book. My mummy bought it for me.'

'You're a lucky girl, aren't you? I like fairy stories. Which is your favourite?'

They debated the merits of *The Sleeping Beauty* over *Rapunzel* for some time, until Trevor insisted that Karis got into bed. She tugged at Judy's hand.

'Can you read me my story?'

Who could resist those gorgeous brown eyes? 'I'd love to,' Judy said, and meant it.

They settled on *Little Red Riding Hood*. The years rolled back as she read the tale, changing her voice for the different characters and putting all the drama she could into the words. Karis snuggled against her and chanted the 'Oh grandmother,' lines along with her. Judy was enjoying herself. She'd forgotten what a pleasure it could be to be with a small child. The sweet smell of them fresh out of the bath. The innocent warmth of their little bodies.

Karis sighed with content as the story ended and settled down under her duvet.

'I haven't got a grandmother,' she said.

Oh yes, she'd forgotten this as well, the ploys to keep you hanging on for as long as possible. 'I know. But you've got a lovely granddad,' she said.

'My mummy's mummy died when I was just a baby and I haven't got a daddy or a daddy's mummy.'

Judy stoked the frizzy dark hair that splayed out on the pillow. What did you say to that? 'I haven't got a grandma or a granddad either,' she said. Or a grandchild, for that matter. Yet.

Karis had her lower lip caught between her teeth. She was thinking. 'You could be my grandma.'

Judy caught her breath. 'Oh. Karis – what a lovely idea.'

But what would Naz say to that? And Trevor?

'The trouble is,' she said slowly, 'I can't be your proper grandma, because I'm not your mummy's mummy. But I can be a pretend one.' Not a stepgrandma. Stepparents had a bad press in fairy stories.

Karis's face fell. 'But I want a grandma,' she insisted.

'Tell you what, I'll be a special auntie instead,' Judy suggested.

'I've got aunties. And cousins.'

'Great-aunt, then. How about a great-aunt?'

'Great-aunt...' Karis tried it for size. 'Great-aunt Judy. Yes. You can be that.'

That decided, she curled up on her side and closed her eyes. 'Night-night.'

'Night-night, Karis. Sleep tight.' She padded out of the room and turned the light off.

Trevor was hovering in the hall outside. He gave her a smile of approval and they went to sit in Naz's lounge until they were sure Karis had gone to sleep.

'Was that all right? About being a great-aunt, I mean?' she asked anxiously.

He put an arm round her. 'I think it's a terrific idea.'

'But what will Naz say?'

'Naz will have to get used to it.'

'She doesn't approve of us, you know.'

'I do know. But she'll get used to that too.'

Judy wasn't so sure. But when Karis was asleep and they went upstairs, she had other things to occupy her thoughts.

The days when she didn't see Trevor were troughs through which she had to drag herself. She woke on Thursday morning convinced that she ought to end the whole thing. What was she doing? She had a nice home, a family, even a marriage of sorts. She'd hung on to that marriage through thick and thin – mostly thin – and she'd kept it going for nearly twenty-five years. Why risk all that now just for the sake of a bit of romance?

She tried not to think ahead. If she did, it frightened her. For she knew it couldn't go on forever like it was now. Something had to change. Either what she and Trevor had would end, which would break her heart, or she would leave Alan, leave her home and the twins, and that would hurt the boys horribly. She couldn't stand either prospect, so she tried to blank them out. Just look as far as the next meeting with Trevor. Or plan the next phone call. It had to be enough, for now.

She was doing the afternoon and evening session that day at the surgery. It was a particularly difficult one. Everyone seemed to be bad tempered – the doctors, the patients, the other receptionist, even the nurse, who was usually a haven of calm and patience.

Judy took five minutes to go to the loo. Tomorrow. Tomorrow was Friday, lovely lovely Friday, and she would see Trevor again. Just hold on, just get through the rest of the day, and by this time tomorrow it would be nearly time to get ready.

When she got back to her post Naz was waiting to check in. She wasn't looking happy. Judy pasted a big smile on to her face.

'Hello, Naz. We don't often see you here, do we? You're such a healthy person. We could do with more like you.'

'Yes, sure. Doctor Ahmed. Six-thirty.'

'That's fine.' Judy checked her in. There was nobody waiting behind Naz.

'You're lucky. Doctor Ahmed's running practically on time today. You should be back in time to put Karis to bed.'

'Good.'

Naz glanced at the other receptionist. She was answering the phone. Naz leaned forward. 'You are *not* Karis's great-aunt,' she hissed.

Judy felt cornered. She knew something like this was going to happen. 'I – I know that, Naz. But when Karis said she wanted a grandma, I didn't want to reject her. That wouldn't have been right, now would it?'

'You're not any sort of relation to her.'

'I know. But like I said, I didn't want to–'

The other receptionist was looking curiously at them. Naz shot a furious glance at her and the woman looked away.

'Just remember that,' she said to Judy, and went to sit down at the far corner of the waiting room.

Judy found she was shaking. She had handled that all wrong. If she could just explain to Naz. But now was neither the time nor the place.

By the end the session she had never been so glad to leave work

Toby and Oliver were sprawled over both the sofas watching a film and spooning cereals into their mouths. Plates and mugs littered the floor. They both grunted vaguely at her when she said hello. She didn't have the energy to make them clear up, or even to ask whether they ought to be revising for the fast approaching A-levels. Tea, that was what she needed, or even a drink. Yes. A coffee and brandy. That would save her life. She backtracked to the living room door.

'Oh Mum–' Toby suddenly came to life, though his eyes never left the TV screen. 'Someone phoned. Er – Maggie?'

'Oh – did she?' She didn't want to know. The last thing she wanted to do was to speak to Maggie. She was so exhausting.

'Yeah, she said would you ring about going to the gym? As you didn't make it yesterday.'

'Ah – right, thanks, dear. I'll do that.'

She was just about to go out of the door when Oliver surfaced. 'I thought that was where you were going yesterday? The gym?'

Oh my God. Excuse. Think of an excuse. 'Oh, yes, I was going to but there was a change of plan at the last minute–' Her mind seemed to have gone totally dead.

'Chickened out, did you?' Both boys snorted with laughter.

'Something like that, yes,' she agreed, and backed out of the room.

Oh my *God*. That was close. Supposing Alan had been in? The boys didn't really care where she went, but Alan might not have left it at that. He might have questioned her further. Her legs felt quite weak. She staggered into the dining room, poured herself a large brandy and flopped down at the table. She took a large gulp, choked, and shot it all over the polished surface. Coughing and gasping, she looked at the mess. She wasn't cut out for this sort of thing. She hated lying, and she was bad at it. She hated causing friction, and she was obviously doing that in Trevor's family. She couldn't go on like this.

But she couldn't bear for it to end.

CHAPTER 15

Maggie swung into the driveway and braked hard. The pile of folders on the back seat slid to the floor. 'Hell.'

It had been another horrible day. The pressure was really building up to the inspection. The Head had been on to her about all sorts of ridiculous details that needed to be sorted out beforehand. What did these people think she was? A teacher or a civil servant? Because that was what she was turning into – someone who did nothing but fill in forms and chase irrelevant pieces of information. It wasn't what she had gone into teaching for.

She got out of the car to pick up the folders. Loud music was coming from the house. 'Hell*fire!*' she growled. That Shauna was here again. Ben never made that much noise when he was by himself. They'd probably been upstairs having sex all day. Shagging. That's what those little tarts in Year Nine called it.

'I shagged Damian last night.'

'Oh, I shagged him at the party last Saturday. Him and Sean.'

And then they wondered why they got pregnant.

A thought struck her, bringing her out in a cold sweat: supposing Shauna got pregnant? She would be a grandmother. It was horrible, horrible. She felt quite sick. She stormed into the house, slamming the front door behind her. They were in the kitchen making toast.

'Hi Mum! Cup of coffee?'

'Hiya, Maggie.'

They both of them looked soft and glowing and satisfied. It was obvious what they'd been up to.

'Hello,' she said, giving them a hard look 'Yes, I would like a coffee.'

Maggie sat down on the sofa and lit a cigarette. Behind her in the kitchen there were smothered giggles. She took a long drag down into her lungs and waited for the calming effect. That was better. The room was a shambles. There were newspapers and trainers and dirty mugs and crisp packets all over the place. How could they manage to make such a mess in just one day? They'd better clear it all up. She couldn't sit in this.

Ben ambled in with two mugs. He handed one to her. 'There you go, Mum. Sorry about the mess. We'll have a go at it in a mo.'

Shauna followed with another mug and a plate of toast and Marmite. 'Want a bit?' she asked, waving the plate at Maggie.

'No thanks.' She'd put on enough weight lately, thank you, without snacking between meals.

The pair of them sat down together on the other sofa. Shauna tossed her hair back from her face and stretched out her long legs. Even in combats and a black crop top, she looked stunning. Young, supremely fit, beautiful. Everything that Maggie wasn't.

Ben leaned forward. 'Hey Mum, triffic news, Shauna's heard of a dancing job. And what's more, she's got to be a dead cert to get it.'

On a cruise ship? That would be good news. 'That's good, Shauna. Where is it?' Maggie asked.

'Only in a restaurant, you know, that Turkish place over in Arnleigh, the Marmaris Palace.'

Pity. 'Oh, so you're using the belly-dancing,' she said.

'Yeah, should be good. The pay's got to be better than the bar and it'll get me out of the house for another evening and that is a result. All I hear about there now is Mandy's bleeding wedding. God, I'll be glad when this wedding's over. We'll all get a break from hearing her going on about it. You'd think that now she's living with her Darren we wouldn't get to see her so much, but no, she's round our house every day still. It's driving me mental.'

Seeing Shauna in her house like this was enough to drive you mental. Her language! And the way Ben looked at her, as if he could hardly believe his luck at having her there. 'Still no luck with your cruise ship plan, then?' she asked Shauna.

'Got another audition in six weeks' time.'

'Really? That's good.' Maggie smiled at her son. 'Maybe a year abroad is what you need, Ben, rather than start a proper career at this point.'

'Well yeah–' Ben looked surprised. 'That was just what I was thinking of, Mum. Only I didn't think you'd approve. When Shauna gets her break, I can apply for something on the same ship. Bar work or something.'

Maggie nearly groaned out loud. Hadn't he any ambition beyond having sex with Shauna?

'I was thinking of something more worthwhile, actually. Something that would look good on your CV. Teaching in Africa, that sort of thing. You've got a degree. They'd be

239

delighted to take you. They even welcome people my age.'

But Ben just shook his head. 'Can't see me doing that, Mum. You going out tonight?'

She tried a bit harder to convince Ben that he'd like to volunteer for something useful, but all he was interested in was getting her out of the house that evening. It was tempting to say that she was staying in, but if she didn't keep up going to the gym, she would start getting saggy, and that would never do.

'I'm supposed to be going to the gym with Judy,' she said, watching the hope dawn on their faces. 'But whether she'll come with me, I don't know. She did agree to, but so far she's only made it once. There's always some sort of excuse at the last minute.'

Disappointment drooped their shoulders. Whose house was it, anyway? If she wanted to stay in, then she would. They'd have to find somewhere else to paw each other.

'P'raps she doesn't like sweating away on the machines,' Ben said.

'She needs to.'

Judy couldn't be that much older than her, but nobody would know it. She'd let her body go completely. Maggie looked down complacently at her own toned stomach.

'Oh, I don't know,' Shauna said. 'I think Judy's really got her act together. Haven't you noticed? When you think what she looked like when we met her. She's had her hair done different and she's lost weight, and she's wearing, like, more younger clothes. It's like she's really changed.'

Had she? Maggie hadn't really noticed, to tell the truth. Other people had commented on Judy's hairstyle or clothes, but Maggie had always regarded her as someone to be pitied. But now she thought about it, Judy did look different from the woman who had first come to the dance class.

'Yes,' she said slowly. 'Well, it's nice to see that she's making an effort. It shows that her self-image is improving. I just hope it's not just to try to hold on to that ghastly husband of hers.'

Shauna grinned. 'P'raps she's got a boyfriend,' she said.

Maggie laughed out loud. The very idea of someone as conventional as Judy having a boyfriend! She'd probably never slept with anyone but that rat Alan. 'I don't think so.'

'Why not? I used to work with this woman what was older than Judy and fatter and all, and she'd had this boyfriend for years. They even knew each other, the boyfriend and the husband, but the husband never knew what was going on and the boyfriend kept holding on hoping she'd leave the husband and go and live with him, but she never did, because the husband was boring but he looked after her proper.'

A husband and a boyfriend. How did

some women manage it?

'I don't think that's true in Judy's case,' she maintained. 'Why does there have to be a man involved? She's probably taking more interest in her appearance simply because she feels better about herself. Maybe when her boys leave home she's going to surprise us all and leave that husband of hers and become an independent woman.'

'Yeah, well, I still think she's got a bit on the side, and good luck to her. She deserves it. If I was married to that Alan, I'd of cut his balls off years ago.'

Beside her, Ben winced.

One thing you could say for Shauna, she'd put Alan off in no uncertain manner when he'd made a pass at her. Which was more than you could say for Fiona. Fiona had everything. Rich husband, lovely house. She swanned around all day long having beauty treatments and pretending to run a business and on top of all that she had to play around with Judy's husband. It was disgusting.

'I do take your point, Shauna. He is dreadful, but it does take two to have an affair, you know. The women are to blame as well. They shouldn't go out with a married man to start with.'

'You're dead right,' Shauna said, to her surprise. 'Me, I don't hold with it. I seen the trouble it makes. Friend of mine, her friend went off with her husband. She was like, betrayed twice, wasn't she? Fucking tragic, it was.'

'Some women have no sense of sisterhood. They'll do anything just for some amusement. I was really shocked the other day–'

The secret she'd been harbouring had been smouldering inside her, getting more difficult to hold each time she saw Fiona. Now the need to tell somebody welled up in her, unstoppable. She leaned forward. 'I saw Alan go into a florist's shop and come out again with Fiona. And then the two of them went off down the street together. Fiona! I would have thought that she would have known better.'

She waited for gasps, anger, a torrent of Shauna's foul language. She was disappointed. Shauna laughed. 'Oh come off it, Maggie! Fiona? With *Alan?* Pull the other one.'

She might have known better than to expect a proper reaction from such an ignorant little tart. 'I saw them together, with my own eyes,' Maggie insisted. 'He came out of the shop with her and he was talking away nineteen to the dozen trying to arrange a meeting.'

At this point Ben spoke up. 'You were near enough to hear what they were saying and yet they didn't see you?'

Lurking guilt made her angry. 'You make it sound as if I was spying on them! As it so happens I was just passing, and they were so engrossed with each other that I don't think they would have seen me if I'd jumped out and shouted at them.'

'He might just have happened to have been passing as well,' Ben said.

'Maybe, but why did he go in and speak to her? Why did they come out together?' It was perfectly obvious why.

'He might of gone in to see her, but it doesn't mean to say that she wanted to see him. You know what he's like – say one word to him and he's all over you like a rash. Can't get rid of him,' Shauna said.

'You got rid of him,' Maggie pointed out.

'Yeah, but I got a mouth on me, ain't I? Fiona's too much of a lady.'

'A lady! Making assignations with your friend's husband is hardly ladylike behaviour.'

'Yeah, but she wasn't making assig-whatsits, was she? He might of been asking, but I bet you she wasn't having any.'

'Yeah, you're reading far too much into it, Mum. After all, this Alan bloke might just as easily have seen you first, and then Fiona would've seen you talking to him,' Ben said.

'Are you two the Fiona Is Innocent movement or something? Don't you think there's anything even remotely suspicious in the situation?'

'No, not really,' Shauna said.

Maggie lit another cigarette. It was useless. She couldn't get any reaction out of them. They just sat there, the two of them, refusing to believe what was patently obvious.

The phone rang. 'Maggie?' Judy's voice floated down the line. 'I'm so sorry, but I'm afraid I'm going to have to cry off again.'

'Again? What is it this time?' That sounded rude, but she didn't care.

'Oh – well – a friend of mine's just phoned up and she's in a bit of a tiz, and I really think I ought to go round and talk to her. Calm her down a bit, you know.'

Was she lying? Maggie forced a jokey expression into her voice. 'I'm beginning to think that you don't want to go out with me, Judy.'

Flustered laughter from Judy. 'Oh, no, of course not – it's just the way it seems to work out. Next week definitely, all right?'

'I'll hold you to it,' Maggie said. And meant it.

She looked at Ben and Shauna, lounging against each other on the sofa. 'Well, that's my evening out scrapped,' she said.

It took a while for them to take the hint. They hung around for an hour or so, then went to get a takeaway from the kebab place on the other side of the estate while Maggie made her evening meal. But eventually they set off for a drink in town.

Peace at last. Except that her mind wasn't

still. Fiona and Alan. Judy and somebody –
but no, that couldn't be true. Not Judy. Ben
and Shauna all over each other. Naz with
her Brad, despite the fact that she had a
child in tow. Why was it so easy for everyone
else to find someone? It was the same with
single friends of her own age. They all
seemed to have some man to go out with.
They sat and compared restaurants and
bargain breaks when they had a girls' night
out, and she had to just sit there listening to
them and feeling totally left out.

She looked at the pile of folders she had to
mark. No, she couldn't face it. She would go
to the gym on her own, and maybe after a
good workout she would feel better. She
went upstairs to fetch her sports bag.

'He's well fanciable, your Ben, ain't he?' one
of Shauna's cousins said.

A heaving crowd of women were repairing
their makeup in the ladies lavs of the church
hall on the Watfield estate. Outside, the tables
were being tidied away and the DJ was setting up. Mandy's Big Day had finally arrived.

'Yeah, he's all right,' Shauna said, her
mouth hanging open as she retouched her
mascara.

All round them women were dressed in
their best gear. Shauna was condemned to
off-the-shoulder puff sleeves, a badly fitting
bodice and a gathered, frilly skirt in an

especially nasty shade of green.

'You been going out with him for long?'

'What? Oh, Ben. No – well, yes, I s'pose. Six months.' Shit, that was a long time. The longest she'd been out with anyone.

Shauna stuffed her make-up into her bag and backed out of the scrum in front of the three tiny mirrors. Six months! And she'd only gone out with him in the first place to piss that Maggie off. She shoved her way past sweating aunts and cousins and family friends, all of them talking away at the tops of their voices, slagging off the other side's family, the food, everyone else's outfits. It was a relief to get out into the hall again.

Ben homed in on her like a heat-seeking missile. He wrapped his arms round her and snogged her.

'Mmm. I've been gagging to do that all day! Stuck down on that table with all your relatives while you were doing your bit supporting the bride. Mandy and Darren look happy, don't they?'

Shauna looked across the room to where the bride and groom were still sitting at the top table, drinking cheap Spanish bubbly and gazing at each other. Enough to make you puke. 'It won't last.'

Ben hugged her closer. 'Cynic, you don't mean it really.' And snogged her again.

The afternoon staggered into evening. The DJ played lots of crap numbers for the wrinklies to dance to, three of the male cousins tried to get off with Nicole, two fourteen-year-olds were found shagging behind the staging, the drink ran out and two of the men had to go down the offie to get some more, some relative of Darren's picked an argument with one of Shauna's cousins and a whole bunch of men bundled into the fight. All pretty normal, really.

The floor of the church hall was slippery with spilt beer. People were passed out under the tables. The DJ was on to the slow numbers.

'Lady in red–' bawled drunken voices all over the hall.

Shauna and Ben were smooching in the half dark. She was beginning to feel really ill. She'd been drinking since before lunchtime and now it was getting on for eleven at night.

'Christ, I hate weddings,' Shauna said.

'No you don't, not really.'

'I do. They're crap.'

The DJ turned the volume up.

Ben was kissing her neck and shoulders. His breath was hot and his lips soft. Shauna wished they could get away, but they were stuck here right to the end. Ben was speaking in her ear.

'You know I love you, darling?'

'Mmm–'

'I never loved anyone like you. You're amazing.'

'Great soft git.'

'No. I mean it, Shauna. I do. Shauna, are you listening?'

'Yeah, I'm listening.'

'I want us to get married.'

Shauna laughed. 'Yeah, and the rest.'

'I mean it. I love you and I want you to marry me. Will you? Please?'

Fuck. He was serious. She stood still in the middle of all the swaying couples. Her head was thumping and she felt sick. His anxious face was blurring before her eyes.

'Sorry–' she said. 'Gotta go to the lav–' She made a dash for the toilets, leaving him gazing after her.

CHAPTER 16

'Tea, Karis, come and get it.'

'Not hungry.'

Naz growled with impatience. Karis had been grouchy ever since she'd picked her up. 'What d'you mean, not hungry? It's fruity chicken and rice, your favourite.'

'Don't want it.'

Naz flung down her oven gloves. You go to all the trouble of making a proper meal, not frozen pizza or burger and chips, and this is what happens. She strode into the living room. Karis was slumped on the sofa, looking listless. Instantly Naz felt guilty. What was wrong with her? She should have noticed earlier.

'What's the matter, sweet pea?' She put a hand on Karis' forehead. She did feel hot. Did she have a temperature?

'Don't feel well.'

'Poor thing. You just lie there, and I'll get the thermometer.'

Ninety-nine point six. Not a big rise, but a temperature all the same. Should she give Karis a children's aspirin? She didn't want to run to pills the moment something was wrong, but Karis was looking so poorly. This was when she needed her mum. Now, when she had to be the responsible grownup and make these big decisions was when she felt most in need of someone to turn to.

The phone rang. It was Fiona. Karis started coughing. She coughed till tears streamed from her eyes.

'Oh, Naz, I'm having a major crisis. I need your help. They rang this morning asking for a horse and carriage to take the parents to the party. Apparently they wanted one for their wedding and couldn't get one and the mother's been disappointed over it for forty years so they want one for the ruby wedding. Now, why they didn't know this when we first discussed it I don't know—'

Naz managed to break in. 'Fiona, I can't

talk right now. Karis isn't well.'

'Oh – oh dear, what's the matter?' Fiona didn't really sound that interested, but Naz detailed all her symptoms all the same.

'Mm, yes, yes – sounds like one of these things that does the rounds. Have you tried Calpol? It always works for mine.'

'I suppose that might–' Naz began.

'Try it. But look, Naz, I've been on the phone all day trying to find this wretched horse and carriage. I've done all the stables, all the wedding hire places, all the people I know who've got horses or have friends with horses – nothing! They're all booked up months beforehand. Naz, I'm really rather desperate. I just feel that if we fail to deliver on this, our reputation is zapped before we even begin. We really do have to find one.'

That old familiar problem of being torn in two directions. She had promised to help Fiona with this party thing, and Fiona was going halves with the fee, which was more than generous because Fiona had done over half the work. But right this moment Naz didn't want to know. Karis was sniffing and looking miserable. Naz sat by her on the sofa and stroked the damp hair off her face. If Fiona would just shut up.

'I think Dad knows someone who's got one. She seems to be getting worse–'

'Can you ask him? Now? So that I can ring them straight away? It really is important.'

'I wonder if I ought to take her straight to the doctor?'

'Naz! Will you please ask your father? Now?'

'What? Oh. Well. Yes, I suppose. I'll ring you back.'

Anything to get her off the phone. Naz fussed about giving Karis orange juice, getting aspirin down her, putting a wrung-out face flannel on her forehead. Then she tried to get her father. He wasn't at the shop and his mobile was off. She left messages, cursing silently. He was with that Judy. He had to be. He never normally turned his mobile off. She rang Fiona to give her the bad news.

'God, no! Look, ring me as soon as you speak to him, will you? I've got nothing ready for dinner and Richard said he'd be early this evening. He'll go ballistic.'

Thank you so much for asking after Karis. Selfish cow.

An hour or so later Karis was getting more and more fretful, complaining of a headache and hot eyes. Naz took her temperature again. *Ohmigod!* One hundred point three! And then she noticed the rash.

That really did it. What if it was meningitis? Children died of that. Perhaps she ought to get Karis to the hospital straight away–

A key rattled in the front door. Naz leapt up and flew into the hall. 'Dad! Oh Dad, I think we ought to take Karis to hospital.

She's got a temperature and a rash and–'

She stopped short, for there with her father was Judy, who smiled at her rather uncertainly. 'I've been trying to phone you,' she told her father. 'Your mobile was off.'

'Oh, was it?'

From the living room Karis called her granddad. Trevor hurried in, followed by Naz. Karis, with a new audience to play to, made the most of her ailments. While her dad was sympathising with his grandchild, Naz could feel Judy hovering somewhere in the background.

'Well, she certainly does look poorly, but I don't know about the hospital,' her dad said.

'But she's got a rash – what if it's meningitis?' Naz insisted. She felt as if her head would burst with the worry. She must not get this wrong.

Her dad looked beyond her to where Judy was standing. 'What do you think, love?'

Naz turned to Judy. One part of her didn't want That Woman anywhere near her child, whilst another part was desperate for any authoritative voice.

'It's so worrying when they're ill, isn't it?' Judy said. 'A temperature does knock them back so quickly. But meningitis–' she stepped forward. 'May I?'

Naz nodded. Judy knelt down by the sofa so that she was on a level with Karis.

'Does your neck hurt, pet?'

Karis moved her head. 'No,' she admitted, sounding somewhat put out.

'Well, that's a good sign. Could I have a glass, do you think?'

Trevor handed her one, and Judy pressed over the spots on Karis's arm. 'There,' she said, smiling. 'See that? The rash has faded. It wouldn't have done if it was meningitis. So I think we can rule that out.'

A huge weight lifted off Naz's heart. 'Thank God for that! But what is it, do you think? I mean, this rash?'

'I'm not a doctor,' Judy said. 'But we have had a lot of children come through the surgery with the same sort of thing this week, which is just a nasty virus-y thing.' She went through what the doctor recommended. 'But you can call the surgery if you like, or I could. I expect I could get you squeezed in this evening.'

That dreadful feeling of being alone and responsible had dispelled. There was help all around. Naz felt quite limp with relief.

'Oh, I don't know. Perhaps we'll do what you suggest and see–'

'You were doing it right anyway, keeping her cool, giving her drinks and something to reduce her temperature,' Judy told her.

It was all right. She was a good mother. She did know what was best for her child. 'I'll get her some more water. And – what about you? Would you like some tea, Judy?'

Judy smiled at her. 'That'd be lovely, Naz.'

It was only much later that she remembered Fiona and her horse and carriage crisis. With Karis now calmer and cooler and tucked up in bed, she felt able to put her mind to more frivolous things. She didn't like to disturb her dad and Judy upstairs. Well, they deserved a bit of privacy, after all, and if it was something really important, like Karis suddenly getting really ill again, she knew they'd be down the moment she asked them. But after a bit of trawling through her memory she came up with the name of her dad's horse-owning friends and gave them a ring. Ten minutes later she rang Fiona.

'Naz! Oh, wait a moment–' Fiona sounded slightly distracted. 'OK. Just came into the kitchen. Richard hates it if I take business calls in the evenings. And seeing as he came home with a fabulous bunch of flowers for me today, I must do my bit to keep the peace. So – any luck?'

'Sorted,' Naz told her.

'Really? Oh Naz, you're a star! I can't tell you how relieved I am. You've really managed to find one?'

'I have. A beautiful open carriage, with hoods in case it rains and a matched pair of grey horses. They'll dress them all up with ruby ribbons for us and be round at the happy couple's place in good time to ferry them to the party.'

Fiona congratulated her again. 'Oh, I nearly forgot. How's Karis?'

'Much better,' Naz told her. 'I was in a right state. I was beginning to think she had meningitis, but then – er – a friend of dad's did this test thing, with the glass on the rash, you know? And it wasn't. And now she's sleeping.'

'I'm so glad. Now I must go and do my Stepford Wives bit. Million thanks again, Naz. Bye.'

Shit! Nearly gave Judy away there. Mustn't do that.

It was easy, lying to Mike. He trusted her totally and never thought to question her. Which of course made Cathy feel even more guilty as she set out to meet Richard. Seven-fifteen found her turning into the pub car park, early for the first time in her entire life. One glance was enough to tell her that Richard was not there. After the third attempt, she managed to back into a space facing the entrance. She felt exposed, sitting in the car. She huddled down in the seat, peeking in the rear view mirror to do her make-up. Every time a car came in she felt sure that its occupants were wondering what she was doing there waiting on her own.

Seven-thirty came and went.

Seven-forty-five. Perhaps he had been held up. If she had a mobile, like rest of the world, he could have let her know. Seven-fifty-five. How much longer should she wait? She remembered Shauna, holding forth in the Chequers.

'I never wait for no one longer than half an hour. If they can't be arsed to be there on time they're not worth it.'

Eight o'clock. She was getting cold. She had a headache from the tension. She ought to go home, but then what would she tell Mike? She had said that she was staying round at Naz's all evening. Besides, she couldn't leave, not yet, not while there was still a chance that he might turn up. If she left now and he did arrive, he might never phone her again.

At three minutes past eight a familiar-shaped car came tearing in through the entrance and braked heavily right in front of her. At last! Shaky with relief, she got out of the car. Richard leapt out, strode over to her and swept her into his arms.

'Cathy, sweetheart, I'm so sorry. I thought you might have given up on me.'

Never. Safe in the warmth of his embrace, she had just enough confidence to lie. 'I was just about to.'

'I'm so glad you didn't. Bloody trains. There was a breakdown, so they said, and we were stuck in the middle of bloody nowhere for half an hour. Look, I'm going to get you a mobile. It's ridiculous, not having one.

Even my gran's got one. Come on, let's go and eat. I'm starving. Only had time for a quick sandwich at lunchtime.'

Cathy hadn't expected a meal. The last two times, they'd just driven to a dark layby and had glorious and very energetic sex in the back of the car. So now she nibbled a limp cheese salad, which was all the place could offer in the way of vegetarian fare, while Richard ate his way through scampi and chips.

'Now I know why I never usually come here,' he said. 'Still, it serves as fuel, I suppose.'

Richard was full of a new project he was engaged in at work Cathy listened, entranced, as he explained all the different stages of planning and launching an advertising campaign.

'It's so refreshing to talk to someone who's really interested,' Richard said, pushing aside his empty plate. 'Fiona's so engrossed with this stupid party thing that she can't be bothered with what I'm doing at all. It's even encroached into our time now. Yesterday evening she did nothing but make phone calls about a bloody horse and carriage.'

'Oh dear. That's a shame.' Cathy could hardly stop the triumphant grin from spreading over her face. This was where she had the edge over Fiona. She leaned forward, fixing her eyes on his narrow, clever face. 'So where have you got to with this one?'

'We've just identified our target groups–'

He could have been telling her about drain clearance or tax returns and she would still have found it fascinating. Just hearing his voice and seeing his lips move and watching the changes of expression on his face was enchanting. He used his hands a lot when he talked, like an Italian. Long-fingered hands with wiry black hair growing on the backs. Soon they would be touching her.

She gave up on the salad. She wasn't hungry. All she wanted was him. She grinned to herself, thinking of her little secret – she wasn't wearing any knickers. It made her feel wild and free. Different rules applied to women who didn't wear knickers. Richard's foot met hers under the table. Red hot lust ran straight up her leg to her groin. He smiled into her eyes.

'Coffee?'

'No thanks,' she managed to croak

'Good, neither do I.'

She sank into the enveloping luxury of his car. Funny how she'd always despised people who drove executive cars. 'Immoral waste of money,' she'd always said. 'All a car needs is four wheels, an engine and some seats.' But she had to admit that this really was rather nice.

They pulled off the road onto a track leading into a wood. 'Like being a teenager again, isn't it? Finding somewhere the parents won't see us,' she said.

Richard switched off the engine. 'You certainly make me feel young again. But maybe next time I'll fix us somewhere a bit more comfortable.'

Oh, what heaven. 'That'd be lovely.'

They got into the back of the car. A short, swirling time later, Richard got out a packet of condoms. Through the haze of desire, desperate hope dawned. Different rules applied to women who didn't wear knickers. Cathy put a hand over his. 'You don't have to use one of those,' she said.

Richard tore the top off the packet. 'I think it's best if I do.'

'I'm on the pill,' she lied.

'All the same, it's safest all round. Then neither of us has to worry.'

His hand explored where she should have been primly covered with knickers. 'You won't know it's there, I promise you.'

She was no longer in a state to argue.

The only way to get through it, Fiona decided, was to put Richard and the children right out of her mind, forget they even existed, and think of nothing but the job in hand. She and Naz arrived at the party venue at the crack of dawn. Flowers were delivered and were banked round the rooms, the pictures were put up, the sound system was tested, the tables laid, the balloons blown up... Items on Fiona's clipboard were steadily crossed off.

The hostess and her family arrived and were lukewarm about everything. Fiona smiled and smiled and felt like screaming.

'Snotty bitch,' Naz muttered. 'Hope her breast implants explode.'

Fiona had a sharp mental picture of the woman's pneumatic chest bursting all over the reception room. She broke into howls of hysterical laughter. 'Oh Naz,' she gasped, hanging onto her friend and sobbing into her neck. 'I'm so glad you're here.'

Naz was gazing at her in amazement. 'I've never seen you lose your cool before,' she said.

'I'm really on the edge. Richard and I had the most dreadful row over this the night before last, and then he was terribly late home last night – later than he's ever been before – and he just went to bed and pretended to be asleep. I thought – but then this morning he was so sweet – I don't know what to think. And now if this is a flop–'

'It won't be.'

Fiona just hoped she was right.

And then everything started happening. Guests piled in, the happy couple arrived in their carriage and grey horses and made their entrance, champagne was disappearing like prohibition was starting at midnight. Fiona and Naz checked details, kept everything flowing. The happy buzz of a successful occasion began to build.

'Listen,' Fiona said, as they met at the kitchen entrance.

They listened. People were talking, people were laughing. It was going to be all right. By two in the morning she knew it was all right. It was more than all right, it was a huge hit. Dozens of people had said so. The anniversary couple were about to make their way up to the honeymoon suite, when a dark woman in a gold dress that looked as if it had been sprayed on caught hold of Fiona's arm.

'Ah – you're the one who's organised this, aren't you? Good. Now are you available on the ninth of June?'

Richard's voice muttered warnings in the back of her head. 'It's only a one-off, isn't it?' he had said, and she had sort of agreed with him.

'Um–'

'Only my bloody stepdaughter has just told me that she's getting married then. Booked the register office, for Christ's sake! The register office – nobody uses them any more! Now what am I going to do? It's only three months away, everything will be booked up and I've got to make it the biggest event in the county, and annihilate her bitch of a mother for good. And I don't mean your average do with a marquee and a naff band and a disco. I mean fantasy, I mean *A Midsummer Night's Dream*, I mean–'

'Hot air balloons?' Fiona suggested. 'Elephants?' Now where did that pop out from?

'Yes! Exactly. I knew you would understand. Now can you do it?'

For a moment she hesitated. Richard would go ballistic. And yet – and yet this was just too good to miss. 'It won't be cheap,' she said.

'Darling, don't worry about the expense. That's the least of my problems. Just tell me if you can do it.'

Fiona took a breath. Her hands were shaking, but her voice was remarkably steady. 'Oh yes,' she said. 'I think that's possible.'

CHAPTER 17

Naz was so angry she could hardly see straight. She stormed past nervous parents seated on small chairs outside classrooms and out into the playground. The teacher's words chased round and round in her head, knotting and tangling themselves up. *Slow start – lack of concentration–* They were all alike, these teachers. Thought they knew the lot. That Maggie was just the same.

She managed to get inside the cab of

Brad's truck and turn the ignition. Somehow she drove home, muttering to herself and screaming at any drivers who dared to cross her path, and dumped the truck with two wheels on the pavement. She switched off the ignition and laid her head on her arms on the steering wheel. Calm. Calm. Take deep breaths. Karis might wake up if she went in yelling. She didn't want Karis upset. She had enough problems as it was, with That Woman as her teacher.

When she thought she had the surging emotions held down, she walked up to the door. Her legs felt like string. Brad was stretched out on the sofa, reading the sports page. He smiled lazily and held out a hand to her as she came in.

'Hello, love. How did it go? All–?' He broke off and stood up as he took in her expression. 'Hey, what is it?'

'After all the hard work Karis has done with Maggie!'

Brad took her in his arms, rubbed her back, rocked her. 'I thought Maggie said she was making good progress?'

'She did. She is. I've seen the work she's done, Brad. All those things That Woman said she couldn't do last time, she can do them now. I mean, Maggie is a good teacher. A pain in the arse, but a good teacher–'

From Karis' room, there was a sleepy call. 'Mu-um.'

Naz froze. Don't let her know. She pitched her voice low and soothing. 'Go back to sleep, love.'

Brad padded into the kitchen, came back with two cans of Bud, opened them and handed one to her. 'Here,' he said. 'Sit down, drink this and tell me the rest. Didn't she think Karis has got any better? What about her maths? I thought she was getting really good the other day. She actually wanted me to test her on mental adding and subtracting when we were driving along. She was enjoying it.'

Naz gulped some beer. Her chest felt so tight it was difficult to swallow. 'I know. That's what I mean about Maggie being good. It's worth putting up with her coming round here and hanging about trying to see Dad. But That Woman – she's never satisfied. She admits Karis has improved but just says she's got more to do. Don't you see? She's been pigeonholed. Mixed race child of single parent family, on free school meals, therefore she's not going to achieve anything. She's been written off! At six years old!'

'Look,' Brad said, 'it's nearly the end of the school year, right? Next term she'll have a new teacher.'

'But she'll still be compared with all the other kids. All these wonders who can read Shakespeare and understand quantum physics or whatever.'

'Perhaps she's just a bit of a slow starter. Some kids are. Everyone thought my brother was thick, but when he got to the Juniors, he suddenly put a spurt on and now he's the brains of the family. Got a degree and everything,' Brad said.

'Yes. Yes, that could be it. A slow starter. She just needs a bit more help from Maggie and she'll be fine.'

She took another swig of beer, and nodded. The tight feeling was ebbing. It was all right. They could win. 'We'll show her, Karis and me. No one writes her off as disadvantaged.'

'Of course, we could do something about that,' Brad said.

Something in his tone of voice made her look sharply at him. He had lost some of his cool. His cheeks were pink. 'About what?'

'About the single parent thing. If you married me, we could be a family.'

For several seconds she gaped at him. It was all happening too fast. She felt a surge of resentment. He was getting her while she was down, backing her into an emotional corner.

'What?' she said, to gain time.

'You heard me.'

For a few moments she was tempted. It seemed like the easy answer – get married, be a perfect family. Except that it didn't work like that. Slowly, she shook her head.

'No.' She wasn't risking everything she'd worked for since Karis was born. It had all been too hard won.

The first thing Maggie did when she got to the dance class on Tuesday was to find Naz. 'How did the consultative meeting go? I've been trying to phone you to ask.'

Naz looked stony faced. 'She was really negative. Said Karis still didn't concentrate – oh, I can't talk about it. It just makes me so mad!'

Maggie was hit by contradictory emotions. The professional in her wanted Karis to have improved because of her help, the woman wanted the excuse to carry on going to the flat.

'Concentration comes with age and she has got better, I've noticed it just after the few sessions I've done with her.' She questioned Naz closely, finding out exactly what had been said.

'Yes, yes. Well that's actually quite positive, you know. I think Karis's teacher has an unfortunate way of putting things. In fact, I think it sounds as if she's quite pleased with her. What we need to do now is to build on what we've done, and not let Karis forget everything she's learnt during the summer holidays. By next term she'll have a head start.'

'Oh–' Naz had that stubborn look to her.

'I really can't ask you to keep coming. I mean, I can't afford–'

'Nonsense,' Maggie said. 'All that sewing pays for the lessons. We agreed that. And besides, it's a pleasure to teach a bright willing little thing like Karis after all the sulky teenagers I have to deal with all day.'

She wasn't going to be put off now. Trevor had been getting quite chatty and friendly when they met. 'You mustn't worry,' she said, putting a hand on Naz's arm. 'Karis is fine. You must think about your own exams. If I can help you there at all–?'

'No, thank you,' Naz said. 'I think Cheryl's about to start.'

The class followed its familiar pattern – warm up, some points of technique to work on, then into practising their set piece dances. They were working towards the summer festival now, the big do in Mellingford Park. As well as the dances they had performed at the charity concert, they were adding on two new numbers and Fiona and Shauna were doing a duo. Maggie felt the stresses of the day disappear as she concentrated on getting the steps right.

'Smile!' Cheryl called. 'Smile everyone! Naz! Look as if you're enjoying yourselves, and the audience will enjoy it with you.'

'Seven, eight and *right* turn,' Maggie muttered at Judy, who was just ahead of her. Judy flashed her a slightly desperate smile as she turned – the correct way, for once. What was she going to do about Judy? She ought to know what was going on, not shut her eyes to it.

'One more time,' Cheryl called. 'Remember – two slow figures-of-eight and one ve-ery slow one. Very controlled, with a slight bounce to it – see.'

She demonstrated. They all copied. They did the dance one last time.

'Lovely!' cried Cheryl. 'That's going to be ready well in time for the festival.'

They cooled down and changed and walked out into the warm summer evening. Hanging baskets were bright with flowers. Kids were cruising round on their bikes and skateboards.

'It's so nice. We ought to sit outside,' Judy said.

'Oh yes, excellent idea. There's a nice little courtyard garden behind The Chequers,' Maggie said.

Shauna and Fiona were both bursting with news, Shauna making them all howl with laughter over happenings at her belly-dancing night at the Marmaris Palace, Fiona relating the latest outrageous requirements of the wedding she was planning.

'You're well out of that,' Maggie said quietly to Naz. 'It sounds crazy.'

'Yeah, I've far too much on as it is,' Naz agreed.

It just seemed like they were going to get into a nice confidential conversation, when Shauna interrupted. 'How's it going with that gorgeous Brad? You ain't said nothing about him for ages.'

Naz went bright red. 'He wants us to get married. But that's not–'

The rest of the sentence was drowned in gasps and cries of delight from round the table. Judy reached across and hugged her on one side, Cathy on the other.

'That's wonderful news, Naz. I'm so pleased for you–'

'He's lovely, you lucky thing–'

'Fuck me, that's a turn-up–'

'I always knew you were meant for each other–'

Naz held her head in her hands and yelled. 'Stop!'

They were all so surprised that for a moment there was quiet.

Naz took a breath. 'I turned him down.'

More gasps and cries, this time of amazement.

'Naz, how could you?'

'You idiot!'

'But he's lovely.'

'Why, for heaven's sake?'

Maggie jumped in to back Naz. 'I'm appalled,' she told them all. 'This is the twenty-first century, and still you all seem to think that getting married is the be-all and end-all of life. I think Naz is very wise to think twice, or think several times before committing herself.'

'Right,' said Naz.

'I don't care which century we're in, marriage is still the best way to live. People were meant to be in pairs,' Judy maintained.

'Oh for pity's sake,' Maggie scoffed. 'You can sit there and say that when your marriage–' She broke off abruptly. Whatever had made her say that? But the words were out now, and there was no way of calling them back.

'My marriage is what?' Judy asked quietly.

There was a stillness round the table. Faces were horrified, amused, fearful.

'Well,' Maggie said, trying to put it as tactfully as possible. 'You're not exactly Derby and Joan, are you?'

'Who the fuck–?' asked Shauna.

'But at least we are still married, which is more than can be said for some people.' It was the nearest thing to a bitchy remark that Maggie had ever heard her say.

'Yeah, Judy – let's hear it!' Shauna applauded.

Maggie rounded on her. 'I thought you were against marriage? You've said enough against your sister's wedding.'

'It works for some people. Look at Fiona and Richard, and Cathy and Mike. They're happy,' Shauna argued.

Maggie caught sight of Cathy, who was sitting across the table from her. Her face was wooden.

'Yes, I happen to think that marriage is a very good thing,' Fiona was saying. 'Maybe I'm old-fashioned, but I think most people are happier when they're married. Why do you think there are so many dating agencies and singles clubs around? Because people aren't happy on their own. They're desperate to find partners–'

'You believe in being faithful within marriage, do you?' Maggie asked. Try as she might, she couldn't keep the edge from her voice.

Judy was holding on to the table. Her knuckles were white.

'Yes, I do, actually,' Fiona said. 'I don't think it can work without trust on both sides.'

Maggie could hardly believe her ears. How could she be such a hypocrite?

'You amaze me, you really do. You say things like that when–'

'Naz ain't the only one round here what's got a proposal,' Shauna said loudly.

'Really, Shauna? You mean you've had an offer? How very exciting,' Judy responded, also loudly.

'Wh – who is it, Shauna?' Cathy asked, with an odd squeak.

As Shauna's words sank in, Maggie felt herself going cold. Surely not? Ben couldn't have been that stupid, could he? She stared at Shauna, who leaned back in her seat and grinned.

'Yeah, it was at our Mandy's wedding. You know what they say about one wedding bringing on another? And I never even caught the fucking bouquet. Blinding, innit?'

'Ben proposed to you? Congratulations, Shauna. How very romantic,' Fiona exclaimed.

'That's brilliant, Shaws,' Naz said.

'He *didn't?*' Maggie exploded.

Shauna was smiling in her face. 'Oh yes he did, Maggie. Your precious son wants to marry little old me.'

'And what – what–?' Try as she might, Maggie couldn't get the words out. They were strangled in her throat.

'What did I say?' Shauna prompted.

'Yes, what did you say? We all want to know,' Judy said.

Shauna half swallowed her smile. She looked slowly round the table. 'Ah well, that's for me to know and you to wonder.' And no one could get any more out of her.

Maggie left the pub early. Naz, Trevor, Judy and her problems, Fiona and Alan – they were all chased out of her head by the appalling prospect of having Shauna as a daughter-in-law. Where would they live? In her house? And then she realised that of the pair of them, it was Shauna who had her head screwed on. Ben was just besotted. He would do whatever Shauna asked. She would have to rely on Shauna not thinking Ben was good enough for her.

Oh God. Oh help. Why did I agree to do this?

Judy's legs felt as if they were about to drop off. Her lungs were screaming. Sweat stood out on her forehead and gathered in all the many creases between the rolls of fat on her body. Beside her on the exercise bikes Maggie was spinning away at twice the speed and hardly looking warm.

'Don't give up now, you're nearly there!' she trilled, just like the sports mistress at Judy's old school.

Miss Valentine. Now there was a misnomer if ever there was one. The boot-faced old cow could never have received a valentine in her life. Might have sent a few though. To young girls.

'You're doing really well,' Maggie encouraged.

I want to strangle her. I really do.

At last the torture came to an end. Oh the sheer bliss of a shower! Judy stood for ages as the hot water cascaded onto her head and shoulders and over her shaking, aching body. It wasn't such a bad old body. She soaped it dreamily. She had nice breasts. Trevor liked them. And she'd lost some weight in the last few months, got her waist back, was working her way to a size twelve. Trevor loved her just the way she was. He didn't like stick insects, he said. He liked real women. Trevor Trevor Trevor. Just two days and she would see him again. Just two days and they would–

'Judy! Are you nearly ready? I'll go and order us some fruit juices from the bar.'

I don't want a fruit juice, I want a G and T. A large one.

'All right.' Wimp. But what else could you do with Maggie? The woman was unstoppable.

Judy dried herself, put on her tracksuit and joined Maggie in the bar.

'There now, don't you feel better for a good workout?' she said, pushing a large glass of water and a small tomato juice towards her. 'Have the water first, you need to replace what you've lost.'

'No, I don't. Feel better, I mean,' Judy dared to say, and gulped down the water.

'You will when you've been coming a few times. Your muscles will begin to firm up and your fitness levels will rise,' Maggie assured her.

Judy doubted it. Besides, she didn't plan on coming even a few times more, if she could possibly avoid it. 'I liked Naz and Fiona's ideas about the costumes for the festival, didn't you?' she said, to change the subject.

'Yes, they seemed very effective. Design

275

isn't really my thing,' Maggie said, as if design wasn't worth discussing in that case. She lowered her voice a little and leaned towards Judy. 'I must say, I thought Naz was a silly girl not to even consider marrying that Brad.'

Judy was stunned. 'I thought you said that Naz should think several times, and that marriage wasn't the be-all and end-all of life?'

She had said a lot of other things that evening as well, things that Judy did not want to go into again.

'In principle, no, it isn't, but in Naz's case I think it might be a good thing. Living in the same house as her father like that isn't good for either of them.'

'Oh I don't know,' Judy said. 'It seems to suit them both very well.'

'But it makes them far too interdependent. Trevor will never be able to form a new relationship with Naz and Karis to consider.'

I shouldn't be so sure about that.

'And besides, this Brad seems very suitable, from what I have heard.'

'Yes, he is a nice young man,' Judy agreed, without thinking.

Maggie's expression sharpened. 'Oh, you've met him, have you?'

God, what do I say now? 'Yes, I – met him at the performance, remember, and then – I ran into them in the High Street. He was very pleasant, and obviously crazy about Naz.

Couldn't keep his eyes off her. And from what Fiona says he's very good at his job. He's done wonderful things with her garden.'

It appeared to do the trick. 'Yes, and Karis seems to like him, too. She often mentions him when I'm working with her.'

Ah yes, the coaching sessions. That was sure to lead to Trevor, and Maggie was the last person Judy wanted hear from about him.

'Did you ask Ben about proposing to Shauna?' she asked.

Maggie suddenly looked a lot older and bleaker. Judy felt a bitch.

'Yes,' Maggie said. 'I did. It's all too true. He did ask her to marry him. The good news is that she refused. The bad news is that he hasn't given up. He's besotted with the – the girl.'

Poor Maggie. She might be a pain in the neck, but you had to feel sorry for her at times. 'Perhaps she'll get this cruise ship job she's hankering after,' she offered.

'She's not a good enough dancer for that. If she was she'd have made it already. No, I've just got to hope that she'll find someone else. I did try to interest Ben in going abroad himself. Some sort of voluntary service. He's just wasting his life at the moment. He doesn't seem to know what he wants to do as a career, so I thought if he went out to Africa or South America or somewhere and did something worthwhile he might get his head together and actually make some plans–'

Judy found herself switching off. It was so much nicer thinking about Trevor. The next thing she knew Maggie was leaning forward again and putting a hand on her arm. There was a look of earnest concern in her face.

'Judy, there's something I've been keeping from you for some time. I wasn't sure whether it was right to tell you, but now I've made my mind up. You have a right to know. Then you can take what action you feel is best.'

People had said things like this to her before.

'I don't want to know,' she said, automatically.

'It's best that you do,' Maggie insisted. 'Believe me, I understand. I've been there. When you know your enemy, you can fight.'

Except that she had never been a fighter. More of a dogged hanger-on. She shook her head, but even as she did so, she realised that the feeling of dread was missing.

'It's Alan, isn't it?' she said.

Her voice came out quite matter-of-fact. She might have been discussing some irritating problem with the washing machine.

'Yes,' Maggie said gently. 'Judy, there's no easy way of putting this. I saw him with – with someone. They were planning a meeting.'

'I don't think so,' she said.

'Judy, you cannot hide your head in the sand like this. It was him.'

'Then you must have mistaken what was going on. There haven't been any signs.'

'Signs?'

'Oh you know, the usual – working late, new clothes, unexplained phone calls, guilt presents.'

And even if there had been – she almost gasped as it hit her like a brick. Even if there had been, it hardly mattered, because I no longer care. It would still hurt. No one likes to be rejected, to be found wanting. He was still her husband, was supposed to be hers and hers alone. She couldn't hear that he was hankering after somebody else and not suffer. But it wouldn't be the gut-wrenching pain, the obsessive jealousy that used to seize her, not that poisoned cauldron that once boiled and seethed beneath her calm exterior. Not that she could explain that to Maggie.

'I know what to look out for. I'm used to it,' she said, lamely. 'You learn to cope with these things.'

'But you don't have to just *cope* with it,' Maggie told her. 'This is the twenty-first century, for pity's sake. Women aren't doormats, they aren't chattels. You wouldn't catch me putting up with your situation. When I found out what my ex was up to, I threw him out.'

Really? I thought you said that *he* left *you.*
'And are you happy?'

Maggie flushed. 'I'm better off without
that bastard, I can tell you. I'm independent.
I'm my own person. Look, Judy, you've got
to face up to him. Give him an ultimatum.'

'And if it is what you say, risk losing
everything? My marriage, my home?'

'You won't, I promise you.'

Judy's long fuse was burning away. 'How
can you say that?' she demanded. 'What
makes you such an expert?'

Maggie just couldn't let a challenge like
that go. 'Because the other woman's got far
too much to lose, that's why. She's just
amusing herself.'

It took a second or two for that to sink in.
Judy stared at her. 'You know her, then?
Who is she?'

Maggie started blustering. 'Oh, nobody
you'd know–'

'You're lying. I can tell. Who is she? You
can't go telling me to face up to things and
then only give me half the story.'

'Really Judy, it's best. I shouldn't have said
this much–'

'I want to know.'

'Very well, but on your head be it. It's –
Fiona.'

'*Fiona?*'

No, that couldn't be right. Alan fancied

Fiona, yes. He'd made her invite Fiona and Richard to that dreadful dinner. *Could* there be something going on between them? There it was now, the ringing in the ears, the breathlessness, the tangled barbed wire knot of pain.

'But – I thought she was my friend,' she wailed.

Maggie's mouth was hard. 'Friend? That woman doesn't know the meaning of sister-hood. She's just a spoilt rich bitch with not enough to do. She's bored, and your Alan is convenient.'

Wait a minute. Let's just get this straight. 'You saw them?'

Maggie told the tale of the florist's. Judy tried to sort it all out in her head. 'You say he met her in there, and they came out together. Setting up a meeting.'

'Yes. They must have arranged to meet in the shop, obviously.'

Was it obvious? They arranged to meet in the shop so that they could arrange to meet somewhere else? Or had she got it muddled up somewhere? She wasn't sure what to think now. 'I'm going home.'

Maggie patted her hand. 'Call me if you want to talk,' she invited.

No thank you. 'Right.'

The more she thought about it over the next two days, the more bogged down she became. Sometimes she was convinced that Maggie was right, more often that she had got it all totally wrong. Sometimes she was hurt, angry and betrayed, then she realised with a jolt that she was doing just the same thing to Alan. Sometimes she cared, desperately, sometimes she was almost glad because then it justified her doing whatever she liked. And then, early on Friday morning, the most amazing, most obvious revelation burst upon her. She had choices!

When this had happened in the past, she always felt there was nothing she could do but to hold on in there and wait for Alan's infatuation to pass. Which it always did. For here they were, still married, after nearly twenty-five years. But now – now she had Trevor. Which was both wonderful and far more difficult. She couldn't wait to see him again.

Friday evenings had fallen into something of a routine. Karis would be ready in her pyjamas for Brad to say goodnight before he and Naz went out, Judy would read her a story and then Trevor would finally settle her down. This Friday, Judy read on autopilot, her mind on other things.

'So what *are* they?' Karis demanded, pulling at her arm.

'What?' She hadn't heard the original question.

'Commles.'

'Commles?' There was nothing in the story with a name remotely like that.

'My teacher said we had to find them. In the sentences.'

Light dawned. 'Oh, *commas*. These little marks, like full stops with a tail.' She pointed to one. 'Can you see any?'

They hunted for commas. Judy explained as best she could what they were for. She finished reading the story. Trevor came and rescued her. Then at last they were able to go upstairs and flop down on the sofa.

The rest of the evening's routine usually went drink, eat and make love. She still wasn't sure whether she wanted to tell Trevor about Maggie's suspicions. She sipped her G and T, ate Trevor's latest dishes (chilli chicken and croutons on a bed of baby spinach followed by raspberry parfait) and tried to come to a decision.

'You're very quiet tonight,' Trevor said.

'Am I?'

'Yes. Sort of distracted.'

'Oh – sorry. I've got a lot on my mind.' Tell him. No. It will look as if you're hinting. Pushing.

'I've been doing a lot of thinking lately as well.'

A surge of irrational panic made her gasp. He wasn't thinking of ending it, was he? 'H-have you?'

Trevor reached across the table and took

her hand. 'I want to you answer me something honestly.'

'Right.' She was good at honest. It was lying she found hard. Except lately, of course. To Alan.

'Just how much of a marriage have you got left?'

She had to laugh. 'Oh God, how can I answer that?'

He was looking steadily back at her. 'Try.'

'But it's so complicated. I don't know. I really don't.'

'Do you still love him?'

'No.' No, she didn't. That much had been proved the other day, when Maggie spoke to her. She'd been far more upset that it should be Fiona than that Alan might be cheating on her.

Trevor gave a tight smile. 'Good. That's one big step. Does he still love you?'

Did he? Did he ever? He always said he did, when an affair was over. But words were cheap, after all. She always grabbed them greedily, held them in her heart, taken them out and looked at them when things were bad. *He loves me. He does really. He just needs the excitement of other women.*

'He loves – no – needs the security of me and our home and our children and – and the status it gives him.' Yes. That was what Alan needed. That was what had always brought him back

'And you? Do you need all that? Is it enough?'

'That's what I've often asked myself. Often,' she admitted. Slowly.

'And what answer did you come up with?'

'It had to be enough – until recently.'

'Recently?'

'Until I met you.'

'Yes!' Trevor said. 'That's it exactly. That's how it was for me. After Sadie died, I thought I could never find another woman as wonderful as her. And when I got over the worst of it, I decided I'd just have to aim for a sort of contentment. I had Natalie and Karis, and I had the business and the garden and my friends. It was enough. I told myself it was enough. Until I met you.'

Judy could see where this was heading. She didn't know whether she was more fearful or overjoyed. Her heart was thudding in her ears, bursting out of her chest. 'But unfortunately I happened to be married.'

'He doesn't deserve you, darling,' Trevor insisted. 'I haven't brought this up before because I don't like to be a homebreaker, but the more I hear about your Alan, the clearer it is that he simply doesn't appreciate what he's got. Why carry on wasting your life with him when we could be happy?'

This was it. Decision time. Judy looked into his anxious face, his kind eyes. He was right, they could be very happy. But – they weren't teenagers. There were others to consider. 'So – what are you saying, exactly?' she asked, playing for time.

'I want you to move in here with me.'

It sounded so easy, put like that. And it was what she wanted, more than anything else in the world. If it was just herself...

'I can't make a decision like that, not all at once.'

'Think about it,' Trevor urged. 'Think about it, and then say yes.'

CHAPTER 18

Richard would never do something so hackneyed, surely?

Fiona stood in middle of the dressing room, his jacket in one hand, a circle of paper in the other. She stared at it, as if she might change it if she looked hard enough. But it stayed the same. It was a paper coaster, white with a green edge, with Oasis Motel and a palm tree printed on it in green. There had to be an explanation.

All she had to do was to ask Richard, and he would laugh and tell her – what? That it was a joke, played on him by the guys at work? An advertising campaign? A – at this point her imagination ran out.

She knew the Oasis, vaguely. It was on the A road about ten miles the other side of Mellingford. It wasn't the sort of place she and Richard went to, or indeed that any of their friends went to. It did serve food, but it certainly didn't have the type of restaurant they frequented. Richard was very knowledgeable about food and wine. He appreciated top class places. And the Oasis wasn't top class. In fact it was on the seedy side. It was used as a cheap stopover, or– Fiona felt slightly ill.

It was used as a place for a quick lay.

So – right – that didn't mean that Richard had taken some woman there. Of course he hadn't. For a start, he wouldn't be so stupid as to leave incriminating evidence like this in his pocket and then ask her to take the jacket to the cleaner's. And it wasn't a bill, after all. Just a coaster. But what a strange thing to slip in to his pocket!

There had to be a reasonable explanation. It nagged at her for the rest of the day. Several times she decided that she would simply ask Richard how it came to be there. Much later, when she was beginning to expect him home, he rang her.

'Hello,' she said, warily.

'Hello darling.' He didn't appear to notice her less than ecstatic greeting.

There was noise in the background. She couldn't quite make out what it was. 'Where are you?'

'Some bar – look, darling, there's been a slight hitch, I might be a bit later than I thought.'

'I see.' She tried to keep it light, but the ice in her voice should have turned her hands blue.

'I'm sorry, darling. I'll be back as soon as I can.'

Was it a bar, or was he on the train? She couldn't hear voices, but he might have his phone clamped to his ear. Or he might have gone outside.

'Just as long as you're enjoying yourself.'

'Hey, what is this?' Richard sounded irritated. 'It's business, darling. You know – what pays the bills.'

'Of course.'

'Look, I haven't got time to argue the point now. I'll see you later. Bye.'

Bastard! Fiona slammed the phone down. She took several deep breaths and tried to control the shake in her hands. He did have to work late sometimes. She knew that. After all, she did used to work with him. If a job had to be completed, it had to be completed, especially if there are last minute changes. And he did have to do a great deal of socialising – lunches, meeting clients and potential clients in bars, that sort of thing. She did understand how things were done. But it was all so one-sided. She was the one who had to make the concessions. She'd turned down the chance of another party job the other day because she knew how much he disliked her doing them.

'When's daddy coming home?' Freya's small figure appeared at the kitchen door. She and Harry were busy in the garden play area Brad had built for them.

'He's going to be late, darling.'

Freya's face creased with disappointment. 'Ooh – we wanted to show him our camp we made.'

'You can show me. I'd love to see it.'

All the time she was admiring the children's handiwork she was seething. How could their father do anything to endanger their happiness, their security? He who always insisted that they must have the perfect childhood?

Her seesawing emotions settled into cold anger. He wasn't having it all his own way. She wouldn't let him dictate her entire life. She had to have something that was entirely hers. With purpose in her step she walked back to the house, consulted a notebook, lifted the phone.

'Hello, Jennifer? Fiona Meredith. Yes, very well, thank you. Listen Jennifer, I think I might be able to help you after all. Yes, the party. Well, I hate to let a friend down, so I've done some reorganisation, and I think I could take it on after all. If you haven't already asked someone else, that is.'

She held her breath. 'You haven't? Oh splendid. Yes, I'm sure I can dream up something really spectacular for you. if you could just let me have a rough idea of numbers and the amount you want to spend ... yes, yes, right ... oh yes, that would be quite sufficient ... perhaps we can agree a date, and I'll come round and talk you through some ideas? Thursday ... ah, yes, fine. No, it's not too soon. I've already had a few thoughts. That's fixed, then. I'll look forward to seeing you ... thank, you, bye.'

Fiona replaced the phone, made a note in her diary, sat back in the chair. 'Right,' she said out loud. 'Just you watch out, Richard Meredith. You're not the only person in this family who can run a successful business.'

The horrible feeling of having events running out of her control receded. She was taking charge of her own life, and if Richard didn't like that, then tough.

It was a lovely summer's evening in the untidy little garden behind Cathy's house. She felt happiest out here, grubbing around in the vegetable patch. The house was too constricting these days. The rooms closed in on her, filled as they were with her and Mike's joint belongings. The scattered CDs, the pictures, the souvenirs of past holidays all vibrated with too much importance. Symbols of togetherness. Out here was her space.

Mike wasn't much of a gardener, he preferred pottering around in his shed, repairing things.

She pulled up a few weeds and tossed them at the bucket. They missed, landing on Goldie the spaniel instead as he lay asleep amongst the lettuces. Goldie didn't stir, and Cathy left them wilting on his age-spotted belly. The sun brought out the comforting smells of warm soil and greenery, along with that of old dog. Cathy looked at her grubby hands.

She'd not had time, yesterday, to shape her nails and slosh on the polish before sneaking out to meet Richard. She'd been ashamed of them, hiding them under the table or sitting on them in the car. Fiona was always so perfectly manicured. But he'd got hold of them and turned them over in his own hands.

'Dear little paws,' he'd said, 'so natural, like a convent schoolgirl's. Who would guess that the owner of hands like these could be such a wild little animal?'

Wild had been the word for it. Cathy shivered with pure luxurious lust as she remembered the tempestuous sex they'd enjoyed. The Oasis. How she adored that place. The very word made her insides churn with excitement. What had happened to that coaster? Had Richard found it and hidden it, or, oh please not, binned it? Had Fiona found it, and demanded to know how it came to be there? Nothing had been said yesterday and she hadn't dared ask. It wasn't the sort of thing she usually did, planting evidence, deliberately stirring things, but she was getting desperate. Something had to be done, something drastic, to push Richard into action. Because she couldn't go on like this, only seeing him for odd evenings. She wanted all of him, all the time.

'There you are. How's it all growing? It's looking good.'

Cathy jumped. For a moment she was disorientated, finding herself squatting amongst the salads with her husband talking to her, instead of her lover. 'Oh, hello. I didn't hear you.'

She stood up and dusted the dirt off her knees.

'No, you were miles away.' Mike stepped over the wobbly rows of vegetables to give her a kiss. Cathy stood stiffly. Once they would have hugged noisily, glad to see each other after the day's work, happy in the comfort of each other's arms. Now Mike put nervous hands on her shoulders as if she might bite him, and gave her a brief peck on the cheek.

'Good day?' he asked, brightly.

'OK.'

His eyes searched her face for clues to her mood. 'Animals all right?'

'Yeah, they're fine.' She couldn't be bothered to tell him about every funny little thing they'd done. She no longer wanted to share it with him.

'Good, well – like a cuppa?'

'Yeah, OK.'

He plodded back into the house. Cathy watched him go, his shoulders slumped under the weight of her rejection. Part of her felt guilty, for he meant well, he was kind, it wasn't his fault. But another part of her wanted to scream with irritation. Go away. Leave me alone.

He came back out a few minutes later with two mugs of tea. Carefully, he brushed the bird poo off the bench seat that he had made under the apple tree, and sat down. 'It's ready.'

Cathy sighed. She didn't really want tea. She sat at the far end of the bench.

'You've got some costumes hanging up in the sitting room,' Mike said.

She'd been sorting them out. After a lot of discussion, it had been agreed that for the last dance of their performance at the summer festival, those who wanted to would wear two-pieces. Cathy had got out her sparkly bra-top and matching belt with the flame coloured layers of skirts. The one she'd worn to the Christmas party, when Richard and she first met.

'They're what I'm wearing for the midsummer festival.'

'You're wearing that red thing?' He didn't

sound happy.

'That's right.' She took a sip of tea and stared at the kittens. They were tumbling over and over at her feet.

'In public?'

'Yes. You got a problem with that?' she asked, aggressively, just like Shauna.

'As matter of fact, I have.'

She knew that tone of voice. It was Mike on a moral crusade. She stole a sideways glance at him. The cuddly teddy bear was bristling.

'Cathy, I really don't think it's quite the thing for my wife to be seen in that sort of an outfit in the middle of the day in a public park.'

He really did sound stupid when he was being pompous. 'Oh for God's sake! What century are you in?'

Mike went red. 'There are going to be people I know at that festival. I don't want them seeing my wife got up like a – a night club act!'

Cathy stood up and put her hands on her hips. 'Really? And just what are you going to do about it?'

Mike took a long breath, very obviously trying to keep control of the situation. 'What you do in a church hall with a bunch of other women is one thing, but to go out and make a fool of yourself in public is quite another. Now I am asking you, Catherine, to listen to what I am saying and for once to do what I ask.'

He asks. He asks. *But what about me?* 'Why should I, when you won't do what I ask of you?'

'I'm always doing things for you. Look at those kittens. You wanted to keep them and I didn't mind.'

He was being deliberately dense, refusing to even look at what really mattered. 'That's not what I mean!' she cried.

Mike closed his eyes briefly. 'Oh,' he said. His voice was flat and dead. 'So that's what it's all about, is it?'

Yes. No. Not entirely. She still desperately wanted a baby, but now there was more to it than that. The trouble was, when he sat there like that, looking so unhappy and frustrated, she felt almost sorry for him. 'Yes,' she said, quietly.

'But darling, can't we just–' he raised his arms and dropped them again, helplessly. 'Can't we just be happy with what we've got? There's the animals, and – and our friends. I mean, we have a good time, don't we? And we've got each other. We still love each other, don't we?'

Did they? Cathy wasn't sure of anything any more, except for one thing. 'It's not enough.'

'Not enough! But it's got to be. What more–?'

That was it. 'You *know* what more!' she

screamed at him. 'That's what all this stupid possessive husband bit over the dance costume is all about, isn't it? You have to get all macho about that because you can't give me a baby and that's the only way you can prove you're a man!'

'That's not fair!' Mike jumped up. Behind his thick glasses his eyes were hot with hurt and anger. 'That's not fair and it's not true!'

'It is true, and what's more, I can't take any more of it!'

Cathy listened to the words coming out of her mouth with amazement. 'I'm leaving, Mike. I'm leaving and I'm not coming back.'

Carried along on a stormwave of resentment, she marched into the house and snatched up her bag from the kitchen worktop.

'Cathy!' Mike yelled. 'Cathy, wait! You can't—'

'Watch me.'

She sailed through the hall and wrenched open the front door. 'And don't forget to feed the animals,' she shouted, and slammed the door behind her.

Mike came running down the front path as she fiddled with the lock on the car. 'Cathy, darling, don't go—'

Bloody car. Open, open, will you! The key turned, she leapt in. Mike had hold of the doorhandle.

'Cathy, please—'

Her hands were shaking so much she could hardly get the key in the ignition. She twisted it round and the car coughed into life. She gunned the engine to drown Mike's voice, and let the clutch in. The car lurched away from the kerb and roared off down the road, miraculously missing the parked vehicles on either side.

It was only as she was heading out of Mellingford that Cathy realised she did not have any idea where she was going. Still she kept on, because at least then she had something to occupy her hands, feet and some part of her brain. Driving gave the illusion of doing something meaningful. Gradually the anger that had fuelled her exit began to die down. She started seeing signs for the M25. Decision time. She either went under it, and into London, where she always got lost, or onto it – and then what? Round and round, wondering whether to go north, south, east or west?

She came to a large village. People were outside in their gardens, children were zooming around on bikes and skateboards, there was a waft of barbecue smoke on the air. Ordinary life, going on.

Cathy felt very alone. Richard, she wanted Richard. She pulled over and scrabbled in her bag for her new mobile. It flashed a low battery warning at her and turned itself off. Cathy banged her head against the steering wheel. Then she drove on, with a purpose now, until at last, welcome as a pub in a desert, a phone box loomed up on the side of the road. A miracle! It wasn't vandalised. It must be an omen. Her heart thudding, she listened to the rings, automatically counting them. Three – four – five–

'Richard Meredith.' Oh, his gorgeous voice. She couldn't speak. 'Hello? Who is it?'

'R – Richard?' she squeaked.

'Ca–? What the–?' The chocolate tones switched to an outraged whisper. 'Wait!'

A few moments' pause, then he spoke again. Low. Urgent. Not happy. 'What the hell are you doing ringing me at this time? I'm at home.'

Cathy felt as if she had been slapped in the face. 'I'm sorry, I didn't think – it's just – oh Richard, I've done it! I've walked out. I've left Mike.'

Now. Now he would have to do something. 'You've done *what?* Are you *mad?*'

He can't be saying this. He can't. He's supposed to be pleased. 'I thought you'd be pleased,' she said, miserably.

'Why the fuck should I be pleased?'

A shrill voice sounded in the background. 'Daddy! Come and watch me!'

Richard's voice, slightly muffled. 'Just a minute, sweetheart. Daddy's on the phone.'

Then he was speaking to her again. 'Look, I don't know what your problem is, but just go back and sort it out, right? And don't under any circumstances ring me again. Is that clear?'

'But–'

'Is that clear?'

'Yes, I suppose–'

'Good.' And the connection went dead.

'Richard? Darling?' Cathy was left clutching the smelly receiver.

Slowly she replaced it. Her body felt unbearably heavy. She could only just open the phone box door. Like a zombie she plodded to the car and flopped down. Around her, amazingly, people were still mowing their lawns, children were still skating and cycling. The world had come to an end and they didn't even know it. Cathy leaned her head on her arms on the steering wheel and cried and cried.

Some time later, exhausted, hollow with spent tears, she tried to consider what to do. Go home? Impossible. Go to her parents? No way. They would only tell her to go back to Mike. Go to one of her friends? But all the long-standing ones were joint friends. They might take Mike's side.

The dancing lot. Judy would take her in. Judy was nice and kind and motherly. But Judy had that awful Alan and those two teenage boys. She couldn't face them. Shauna? She couldn't face her noisy family either. Maggie? She had space in her house and was anti-men and would have her fixed up with a divorce solicitor in a flash, but no. No way.

Naz. Yes. Naz was nice and she wasn't nosy. She wouldn't try to persuade her to do anything. More through luck than judgement, Cathy made her way back to Mellingford and navigated to Naz's house. She stumbled wearily up the front path and rang the bell.

Naz looked shocked. 'Cathy! What's the matter? What's happened?'

The tears were very near to the surface again. 'Oh Naz, I'm sorry but – can I stay the night?'

There was no hesitation. Naz took her arm and helped her into the hall. 'Of course. You can stay as long as you like.'

CHAPTER 19

Maggie tried to simply dismiss the day from her mind. With the inspection just next week, another member of her department had been signed off with stress and supply staff of any kind, let alone people of any competence whatsoever, were totally un-available. Not that she could blame them. Who in their right mind would agree to attempting to teach physics to brain-dead fourteen-year-olds whose names they didn't know in front of the baleful gaze of Ofsted? On top of that John Lang, the erstwhile object of her attentions, and his bloody Emma, had announced that they were to be parents. At his age! He was fifty-two if he was a day. And there he was, smirking as if he'd just invented sex while she was all pink and satisfied, lapping up the attention and flapping her hand around ostentatiously if anyone lit up a cigarette. Well, he wouldn't be looking so pleased with himself when the brat arrived and kept them both awake all night, that was for sure.

Forget it, forget it. They weren't worth wasting energy on. There were better things to focus on, like her visit to Naz.

She whizzed home, dumped her piles of folders and files, said hello to Ben and Shauna in passing as they sat slumped on the sofa watching some ghastly Australian soap and rushed upstairs. Quick change, brushing of teeth and redoing of make-up. There. Not bad. Not bad at all.

'Just off round to give young Karis a helping hand,' she said, breezily.

She failed to notice the look exchanged by Ben and Shauna.

Into the car again, and off to Naz's. She felt renewed, energised, optimistic. There was nothing like getting to people through their children. Trevor had been grateful on both

Karis's and Naz's behalf when she explained Karis's teacher's attitude and offered to carry on coaching her. The thing was, would he come in this week? She thought she might ask his advice about garages. Her car was making an odd noise and she was sure the garage she went to wasn't very good. He might be pleased to recommend one.

The parking in Naz's road was dreadful, as usual. There was a rather elderly Metro outside her house. It looked vaguely familiar, but Maggie couldn't place it. She left her car a few doors down.

Karis came running to the door, which was a good sign. 'We've got a visitor!'

Maggie's heart gave a real skip of excitement. Trevor? She hadn't seen his car outside. 'Have you? Who is it?'

'Come and see!'

Karis took hold of her hand and dragged her across the tiny hallway. She really was a very attractive child. A step-grandchild. It took a bit of getting used to, seeing herself as an honorary grandparent, but it might be rather nice. The sort of thing she could pass off with a little laugh, so that people could say that she really didn't look old enough to be a granny.

Karis flung open the living room door. 'Look!'

Maggie did look. With a droop of disappointment, she saw Cathy sitting on the sofa with Jasmine the cat on her knee.

'Hello, Maggie.' Cathy sounded partly apologetic, partly defiant.

'She's staying with us. She sleeps on the airbed. She's looking after me today while Mummy works late at the college,' Karis told her. 'She's nice, she's called Cathy and she made Jasmine better when she had to have her operation to stop her having kittens.'

'Yes,' Maggie said, taking in this information, pulling herself together. 'Yes, Cathy and I do know each other, Karis. We go dancing together.'

'You're a dancing lady?' Karis stared at her, her eyes brimming laughter. 'Teachers don't do dancing!'

'This one does.' Karis went off into fits of giggles.

'I'm just staying here until I get myself together.'

Well. She'd always thought Cathy and Mike far too dull and boring to do anything like splitting up. 'Am I supposed to congratulate or commiserate?'

'Oh – it was my choice. I wanted to leave.'

She was definitely defiant now. Was Mike a wife-beater beneath that cosy exterior?

'In that case, well done. Us women are far better off on our own,' she said.

Would Trevor call in if Naz wasn't here?

'Ah, well–'

Karis was tugging at her hand again. 'I've

done my homework.'

'Oh – splendid.' If she wanted to get finished by the time Trevor might come back from the shop, she had better get started straight away. Cathy shooed the cat off her knee and stood up.

'I'll go and get the meal started while you're busy. I promised Naz I would,' she said, and drifted off into the kitchen.

Maggie and Karis sat down at the dining table. Maggie went over the homework she had set and was pleasantly surprised. The child did seem to pick things up quickly enough. They worked on some maths, then settled down to some English.

'Now, we need to get some of this punctuation a bit more accurate,' Maggie said. 'You know what full stops are?'

'Easy!' Karis said, and explained.

Maggie nodded. 'Yes, good. But you do need to actually use them, Karis. At the end of every sentence. What about commas? Have you heard of commas?'

'Yes. 'Course. They're like full stops with tails and they go where you want a little rest in a sentence, like when you run out of breath. I know *that*. My great-aunt Judy told me.'

'You've got a great-aunt, have you?'

'Yes. I wanted her to be my grandma, but she said she couldn't because she's not my mummy's mummy, but she could be a great-aunt instead. A special great-aunt.'

Alarm bells began to ring. It's all right. She's probably got the wrong end of the stick. Children this age often do. 'You see a lot of this special great-aunt, do you?'

'Oh yes, she reads me a story every Friday, when she comes to babysit me with my granddad, and sometimes she comes Wednesdays as well. She's nice.'

My God. A girlfriend. Trevor had a girlfriend. 'Oh, good,' she said automatically.

How long had this been going on? Why hadn't Naz said anything? Great-aunt Judy. Oh my *God*. *Judy?*

Karis was chattering on. With a horrible neatness, things began to slot into place. Shauna's suspicions – Judy's improved appearance and confidence – her crying off gym sessions on Wednesdays – Trevor's reluctance. Clearly, like a video rolling in her head, she saw him in the changing room after the charity concert. He was standing next to Judy. Standing very close to Judy. They stood together the whole time she was speaking to him. Like a – like a couple.

Why hadn't she seen it at the time? Because she wasn't looking. She saw him as a single man.

Fury and humiliation consumed her. How could he? How could he do that? Be so underhand? He made her think he was a lonely widower when all along he – it was

John Lang all over again. She'd thought better of Trevor – but why? He was a man. Men would do anything to get their own way. They were selfish, totally selfish and devious to the core.

But *Judy!* She switched targets, and it was worse, much worse. You could expect grief from men, but Judy was a woman. Judy was her friend, or so she had believed. She had tried to help her. She had confided in her. Oh God, what had she said about Trevor? Had she sat there going on about him while Judy just nodded and agreed?

She burnt with horror. How Judy must have been laughing at her!

And the others – did they know? Naz did. Naz let her come along here and give free lessons to her daughter when all along she knew that her father was having it off with someone else. The bitch! Who had Judy told? Who was sniggering about her behind her back? Who–?

'Mrs Stafford. Mrs Stafford!'

'Uh? What?' Karis was shaking her arm.

'Stop it!' She snatched her arm away. One thing was for sure, she wasn't staying here a moment longer. She stood up.

'Where are you going?' Karis looked bewildered. Maggie didn't care.

'Home.' She gathered up her things and headed for the hallway.

'Are you off already?'

Cathy. She'd forgotten all about Cathy. She took a threatening step towards her.

'Did you know about Judy and – and Naz's father?' she demanded.

Part of her, the small part that remained sane, knew that she was making a complete fool of herself. But she couldn't stop it.

'Er, well, yes. Naz told–'

Naz told her! How many others had Naz told? 'I see. So I'm the last person to know anything round here, am I? Well thank you very much.'

She slammed out of the door. All the way home she stewed on the unfairness of life. Fiona had everything and a lover, Cathy – Cathy of all people! – could walk out of a marriage and have a man waiting for her, and Judy, fat stupid spineless Judy, had snatched a genuinely single man from under her nose. It made her so *sick*. She wrenched the car into the driveway and stamped on the brakes.

'Hello, Mum. Back already?' Ben and Shauna were still slumped on the sofa.

'Haven't you two got to get to work?' she demanded.

'Yeah yeah. In a minute.'

Maggie lit a cigarette from the stub of the last one. It didn't do any good at all. She went to the drinks cabinet and poured herself a straight whisky. Ben and Shauna were both gazing at her with open curiosity.

'Well?' she said. 'Is something the matter?' She stood over them, waiting for them to go. They didn't take the hint.

'Nope,' said Ben.

'What's up?' asked Shauna.

She couldn't keep it in any longer. 'I suppose you know all about Judy and Trevor?'

'Oh, it's Trevor, is it? I *thought* she had something going. Well she'll be all right with Trevor. He's a nice old git. Cuddly. He won't give her the run-around.'

Either she was a good actress or she really hadn't known. 'I thought you didn't approve of people having affairs.'

Shauna shrugged. 'I don't but – well – with Judy you gotta laugh, ain't you? I mean, when that arsehole Alan finds out, he's going to be well gutted, ain't he? Serve him bleeding well right, I say. Good on you, Jude!'

In any other circumstances, Maggie might have agreed. But not now. 'I'm shocked,' she said. 'I'm shocked by Judy and I'm shocked by your attitude, Shauna. I really would have thought–'

Ben unfolded himself from the sofa and stood up. 'Give it a rest, Ma,' he said. And, holding out a hand to Shauna, 'Come on, Babe. We gotta mosey on down to the ranch.'

Shauna stood up. She was wearing skin-tight black jeans, high-heeled strappy sandals and a bright pink crop top. Her long hair was drawn up into a ponytail, which fountained down round her shoulders in unruly red locks. She looked down at Maggie.

'See ya, Mags,' she grinned.

The pair of them sauntered out of the house. It was ten minutes before Maggie could even sit down.

Well that had cheered the day up a tad. Shauna needed it. Luckily, it was a busy evening. Shauna rushed about taking orders and serving and clearing, but even flirting with the customers and getting the money right didn't quite take her mind off her continuing career failure.

She checked the messages on her mobile. One from Fiona – *Call me ASAP*. They weren't supposed to make calls in working time, but sod it, she got in twice as much custom as the other girls. The management owed her. She tapped Fiona's number.

'Oh Shauna, I'm so glad you've rung. I had to phone right away, I've got some really exciting news for you.'

'Yeah?'

'I had a meeting with some new clients today, and they had their neighbour there too because – wait for it, Shauna – he's a theatrical agent and they wanted me to liaise with him over the bands.'

Shauna felt a stirring of excitement.

'Well anyway, we got on really well and I

agreed to come to him whenever I wanted to book someone, and then I asked him if he represented dancers, and he said he did! But this is the really good bit, Shauna. I knew by then that he had a youngish family, so I asked if he was going to take them to the midsummer festival, and he said yes, as long as it wasn't raining! Isn't that fantastic? So of course I told him that he must watch the Queens of the Nile because one of the dancers was absolutely terrific and he would really want her on his books–'

Shauna felt breathless. 'An agent is coming to watch us dance?'

'As long as it doesn't rain, yes. So what I thought was, we'll scrap that duo. I don't care what Cheryl says, it's for a good cause. It's no good you having me in the way when you're trying to impress. You do a solo, and then you can really knock him out.'

Tears pricked at the back of Shauna's eyes. She blinked them back. 'You'd do that? Give up the duo?'

'Of course! I'm not the one who wants to be a dancer. This could be your big break.'

'Oh Fiona, you're a superstar, you are. I don't know what to say.'

A laugh tinkled over the air. 'That's a first! I'm just glad to be able to help in some small way. So get out there and give it all you've got, all right?'

'You betcha!' Shauna agreed. 'And thanks

a million, Fee.'

A chance to get herself on an agent's books! This could be it, the start of her career. She wasn't quite sure how she got through the rest of the evening.

CHAPTER 20

'We might as well leave early and have a look round first. The children will enjoy it,' Richard said.

'Yes,' Fiona said vaguely.

They were standing in the bedroom while she sorted out her costumes for the mid-summer festival.

'This one, Mummy. It's all jingly,' Freya cried, holding up a necklace. The coins on it quivered and tinkled.

The phone rang. Fiona ignored it, continuing to riffle through the pile of fake jewellery she wore with her dance costumes. Flashy, jangly and enormous, it was the complete opposite to the stuff she usually wore. She loved it as much as Freya did. They both tried on various pieces and admired each other.

'You realise that this is Saturday and therefore not office hours,' Richard was saying.

For him, then. Though he wasn't generally

so short with clients. 'It's for you,' he said, waving the receiver at her. He was not happy.

Surprise was followed swiftly by annoyance. How dare he speak to her callers like that? She took the receiver from him. It was a minor point over one of the parties. Fiona scribbled a note, gave assurances of close attention, and went downstairs to add the latest requirement to a list in her files.

Richard followed her down into the study and shut the door behind him. 'This is getting beyond a joke.'

'What is?' Fiona asked, playing for time. She stood with her back to him, the file open in her hands. The words blurred and jumbled on the page.

'This ridiculous party thing. Now our weekends are being ruined by it.'

'It's not ridiculous and our weekends are not being ruined by one brief call. You often take business calls at the weekends,' she said, keeping her voice low and reasonable.

'The agency is our bread and butter.'

'The party business is going to be the jam,' Fiona conveniently ignored the fact that the agency provided a good helping of jam as well.

'The party so-called business is taking over our lives.'

'Oh what utter rubbish!' Fiona shut the file and put it away to prove that she was now free for the rest of the day.

Richard's mobile rang. He looked at the number, frowned, switched it off and thrust it back into his pocket.

'There – you do have business calls at the weekend.'

'It wasn't business, it was – nothing important.'

The phone on the desk rang. 'Oh for fuck's sake!' Richard growled.

'Don't swear at me,' Fiona warned, and picked it up.

'Hiya Fiona. How's it going?' Shauna. Thank goodness.

'Oh – fine, fine.'

'Look Fiona, do you think he'll be coming? It's not very nice out there. I watched the weather on the telly and I checked it on the teletext and they both said sunshine and possibility of showers. Do you think that'll put him off?'

Put who off? Oh yes, the agent. Fiona looked out of the study window. Brad's young garden was beginning to bloom. Sunshine danced on the roses and clematis. Above them, white clouds sailed in a blue sky. Perhaps the Watfield estate attracted raincloud.

'Looks lovely out there to me,' she said. 'Don't you worry, Shauna, he's sure to come. All you've got to do is be there yourself. He'll be falling over himself to sign you up.'

'Christ, I hope so. I really do. I tell you, I'm wetting myself with nerves.'

'You'll be wonderful,' Fiona assured her. In contrast to the weather, Richard was looking thunderous. 'Look, I have to go, Shauna. See you there!'

'What did that tart want?' he demanded.

'She's nervous about this performance. I've arranged for a theatrical agent to come and see her dance,' Fiona said. 'And she's not a tart.'

'Oh come on!' Richard scoffed. 'She's sex on legs.'

Suspicion shimmered through her mind. Shauna? Surely not. Shauna was her friend. But other people's husbands had gone off with friends. 'That's what you think of her, is it?' she asked.

'It's obvious.'

'And I'm not? Sex on legs?'

'You're my wife, for God's sake, though there are times when I wonder these days. All you can ever think of is what colour accessories to buy for the next party. It's a wonder the children get fed.'

'That is just so ridiculous! The children haven't suffered one iota because of the parties. In fact, they've probably benefited from having a mother who's busy and focussed.'

Where were they now? The house was very quiet. Freya must still be playing with her dance costume jewellery. Her maternal antennae picked up the faint jangle of music. Harry was at his computer. Again. For the moment, though, it served a purpose. They weren't so likely to be interrupted.

'And that is pure psychobabble,' Richard accused. 'What they need is someone who can keep her mind on them for more than two seconds at a time.'

That was just so unfair. 'They always come first, and you know it.'

'That's not the impression I'm getting at the moment. The children and I come way down the list of your priorities.'

So that was it. 'Oh – *you're* feeling neglected, are you? Just because I've got an outside interest?'

'I think I am entitled to some consideration, yes. I am your husband, in case you've forgotten.'

And did her having an outside interest justify his having one as well? All at once, this seemed like the right moment. She had to find out. Now. She opened the Victorian cabinet in which she kept her files, and fished out the coaster from beneath the pile.

'Does this look familiar?'

He frowned, thrown by the change of subject. 'Should it?' he said, throwing it a casual glance.

'Take it.' She thrust it at him, so that he had to take the horrible thing from her and look at it properly. She watched his reaction like a hunting panther. Was that a flicker of alarm in his eyes as he read the name emblazoned on it?

'It's a coaster.'

'Yes,' she agreed, with the same exaggerated patience that he sometimes used on her. 'Right. Well observed. And do you know how it came to be in your jacket pocket?'

'In my jacket pocket?' He sounded incredulous. 'I have absolutely no idea.'

'Really?' She stood very still, looking at him, letting the one sceptical word drop in.

'Yes really. What would I be doing in a place like the Oasis?'

'Exactly. What would you be doing?'

'You don't think–?' Richard gave a short incredulous laugh. 'You're not seriously accusing me of taking someone to that place?'

It didn't seem very funny to Fiona. 'How else did it get in your pocket?'

'I tell you, I don't know. Perhaps someone's playing a rather unpleasant practical joke. If so, they must be delighted at how well it's working.'

Her brain pounced on this explanation, simultaneously dying to believe and rejecting it. 'What?'

Freya's voice came wailing down the stairs. 'Mummy! Mummeee!'

Automatically Fiona made for the door.

'All right, darling.'

The study was quivering with unfinished business.

'Mum*meeee!*'

'Coming, darling.'

Fiona ran up the stairs two at a time, and dealt with the finger that Freya had pricked on an open brooch pin. 'There, all better. You're just like the Sleeping Beauty. Do you think you'll go to sleep for a hundred years?'

Was that alarm she read in Richard's face? Had he been to the Oasis? Was her marriage in real danger? Somehow, before the end of the day, she had to find out.

At least that week was over. It was the one positive thought that Maggie could raise as she swam into consciousness. The sun was shining through the curtains. She looked at the bedside clock. Eleven-fifty-five! Good grief, she must have passed out last night. All the staff had been for a massive booze-up to celebrate the end of the inspection. After the tension of the lead-up and then the stress of the week itself, they had all been in need of an evening of total irresponsibility. As far as Maggie could remember it had led to general hilarity, tears from some and anger from others, for there had been plenty of criticism from the inspectors from the beginning of day one. Herself, she had been able to just enjoy its all being over, for her department had come out pretty well. Better than practically any other, in fact. And she had been singled out for her efficient management of funds as well as for her good teaching.

'So put that in your pipe and smoke it, John Lang,' she said out loud. But somehow, that didn't make today any better.

Should she even turn up for this performance? Was Trevor going to be there? Before, she would have been counting on it, now she couldn't bear the thought of meeting him, of having to be polite. It was Saturday, the busiest day at the shop. Maybe that would keep him away. On the other hand, he was a devoted father to Naz. He might well take some time off to go and watch her. Even if he wasn't there, how many of the others knew about him and Judy? Had Naz told everyone except her? Had they all been sniggering for weeks?

Judy. The traitor. The very thought of her filled Maggie with murderous rage. Maybe she should–

There was a tap on her bedroom door. 'Mum?'

'Yes?' she said. Her voice came out slightly croaky. But then she had drunk an awful lot last night.

'Cup of tea?'

Pleasant surprise flooded through her. 'Yes. Thank you, darling. Come in, come in.'

Ben padded in and put her favourite mug down on the bedside table. He loomed over her bed, his fair hair flopping forward over his kindly blue eyes. Her son.

'There you go. Heavy night last night? Need the paracetamol?'

For the first time in months and months, Maggie knew what it was to be cared for. It brought a rush of tears to her eyes. How kind. How sweet. He was far too good for that tart Shauna. She sat up carefully. To her surprise she felt all right, physically. Emotionally was another matter.

'No thanks, dear. I'm OK. Tea's lovely.'

'I'm just off to pick up Shauna. She's shitting bricks with nerves. If she can make a good impression on this agent, it could be her big break.'

Pray God it was. Anything to get her away from Ben. 'Yes.'

A short silence developed in which she knew she was expected to say something nice about Shauna.

'Well, I'll be off then,' Ben said eventually, realising that no such support was to be forthcoming from her. 'See you later.'

'Right. And thanks for the tea. It was just what I needed.'

'No big deal.'

He ran down the stairs and out of the front door. A moment later Maggie heard his newly acquired car coughing reluctantly into life. And then he was gone, and the house was quiet.

Her thoughts homed back to their most painful spot. Judy. Judy and Trevor. Lovers. The knowledge throbbed like a bad tooth. All that time, and she had confided in Judy, she had tried to help her, and then fat stupid Judy had snatched the man she wanted from under her nose, and her a married woman.

Big and black and beckoning, temptation reared up. Someone ought to tell Alan. Hot on its heels, a secondary consideration. Someone ought to tell Richard about Fiona. Maggie got out of bed and headed for the shower. Perhaps she should go to this performance. After all, she didn't want to let the others down.

'Where did I put that scarf? I'm sure I brought it. Karis dear, have you seen a yellow scarf with beads on it? Oh here it is, silly me. Now where did I put my bag?'

How did Cathy manage to work as a veterinary nurse? She couldn't organise her way out of a paper bag.

'It's under the table.' Naz picked it up and gave it to her. She had got herself and Karis ready half an hour ago, and put a load of washing in, and run the Hoover round. What she hadn't done was open a book, and she really needed to do a bit more last-minute revision.

'Oh thanks, Naz. Now, make-up – did I fetch that? I thought I did.'

'You can use mine,' Naz offered, though her colours weren't really going to work on Cathy.

'Thanks, but I'm sure I did fetch some.'

Cathy had been home when she was sure that Mike was at work, and come back to Naz's with armfuls of polythene carriers overflowing with personal possessions. Now they were stacked up in the cupboard under the stairs, or scattered over the living room. The flat really wasn't big enough for three people.

All of a sudden Cathy gave up the search, flopped onto her knees and gazed at Naz, biting her lip. 'Oh Naz, I'm so nervous about today.'

'About seeing Mike, do you mean?'

'Well, yes.'

He had phoned the flat several times, begging Cathy to speak to him. He did seem desperate to have her back.

'You've got to see him sometime, Cath,' Naz pointed out. 'And it might be the best place, with lots of people around. Sort of defuses it. I mean, he's not the sort to have a major row in public, is he?'

'No he's not. Well, that was what it was all about, wasn't it? Me making a so-called ex-hibition of myself in front of all his friends.

So stupid. Your Brad likes to watch you perform, doesn't he?'

'Yes,' Naz looked at her watch. Brad would be here in a few minutes. They were going to look round the stalls and the rides with Karis before the performance.

'That's what I mean. But it isn't just Mike.' She twisted a headband round and round in her hands.

'What is it, then?'

'It's – *him*. He's going to be there too.'

The mysterious boyfriend. So he really did exist. 'Oh – am I going to get to meet him?'

Cathy looked cornered. 'I, well, it's not as easy as that. He'll be there with his family.'

'*Cathy!*'

'I know, I know – we're both married. But he's no happier than I am with Mike. If he'd only see that it would be so wonderful if we could be together–'

'They might say they'll leave, but they rarely do,' Naz said. 'Believe me, I know. I've been there. That's why I'd given up on men. You can't trust any of them.'

Except Brad, a small voice whispered. He's rock solid. She pushed the thought aside. He was a man. Enough said.

'It's different for us,' Cathy said. 'When I'm with him, it's like – like I'm a different person.'

Oh yes, been there, done that. But it doesn't last. Then it struck Naz that it wasn't like that with Brad. Cathy was rambling on, but Naz hardly heard her. With Brad, she didn't feel like a different person, she was herself but – more. More confident, more complete, more – happy. He brought out the best in her.

'Got to get to speak to him,' Cathy was saying.

'Crunch time, eh?' Naz said.

'Yes,' Cathy looked drawn with anxiety. 'Yes, it is. Oh dear!'

'Better make sure you're ready, then.'

She often felt like the older one with Cathy. She could hear herself speaking with her mother's voice when talking to her.

'He's here! He's here!' Karis shrieked, jumping around on the table in front of the window.

'Who?' gasped Cathy. She went white, then red, as she realised that it was not who she thought it was.

'My Brad! My nice Brad! I'll let him in!'

Karis scrambled down, rushed to the door and down the front path in her bare feet to wait at the gate. Naz busied herself checking the pile of things for the day out.

'Hello, gorgeous.'

Brad stepped into the hall with Karis wrapped with delight round his neck. His big frame filled the small space. Naz's insides turned to jelly. Her cool collapsed. She wound herself round the bits of him not claimed by her daughter and put her face up to be kissed. Bliss. His lips devoured hers. She wanted to drag him to the floor then and there.

'Me! Kiss for me!' Karis demanded.

Brad parted lingeringly from Naz and planted a quick peck on Karis' head as he put her down. 'Ready for the big performance?'

'Yeah, just about.' Naz indicated the living room with a backward motion of her head. 'She's still faffing about, though.'

Brad raised his eyebrows. 'Still here?' he mouthed.

Naz nodded, casting her eyes to the ceiling. She put her head round the living room door.

'I think we'll go on ahead, Cath. See you there, right?'

Naz picked up her things and followed Brad and Karis out to the truck, where Karis and Lady the dog greeted each other ecstatically.

'She's a lost cause, isn't she?' Brad said, as they rumbled up the road.

'Who, Cathy? She's OK really, and she's going through a tough time,' Naz said loyally. God knows, she'd been through a few tough times herself and needed the support of friends. 'It's just that it's so cramped in the flat with her there. If I had a guest room it'd be all right.'

Brad steered expertly round a double parked van and avoided two kids on bikes.

'There's a cottage out at Eastlea going cheap. I went to have a look at it this morning,' he said, carefully casual.

Naz caught her breath with something between fear and excitement. 'Oh yes?' she said, equally cool.

'It needs a lot doing to it, but it's lovely. Lots of character, and plenty of ground round it and a couple of outbuildings. Ideal for the business.'

'Yes.'

They both looked steadily at the oncoming traffic. Between them, Karis was fondling Lady's head and murmuring endearments, while Lady gazed up at her in adoration.

'It's quite spacious inside, too, though the kitchen's just a lean-to on the back, and there isn't a bathroom at all, just an outside loo, but that's all fixable. It just needs someone with a sense of style to get it really nice.'

Like me? 'Mm,' Naz said, non-committally.

But the seed had been sown. Already in her mind's eye she could see a tatty cottage, overgrown with brambles and dark and dingy inside, just crying out to be renovated and loved. And Eastlea was a nice village, quite big, with its own shop and school...

'Would you like to go and see it? You see the thing is, it's a bargain, and if I don't make a move quickly, someone else will grab it.'

'You'd better go ahead and snap it up, then, if you like it that much,' Naz said, deliberately dense.

Brad's fingers tapped on the steering wheel. 'You know what I mean,' he said. 'Look, if you prefer you could just move in. We don't have to get married if you're so scared of the idea.'

'Married?'

Karis's radar tuned into a word that obsessed her. Even more than being a princess, she wanted to be a bride. Or more practically, a bridesmaid. 'Who's getting married? Can I be a bridesmaid?' she asked.

'No one,' said Naz.

'It's not fair! *Everyone's* been a bridesmaid except me!'

'I'm working on it, Karis,' Brad promised.

'Don't hold your breath,' Naz growled.

'At least think about it.'

The house was quiet after the boys went off to their Saturday jobs. Alan was outside polishing his car. Nobody, he claimed, not even the expensive valet service run by a mate of his on the industrial estate, could make as good a job of it as he did.

Judy prowled around, half-heartedly cleaning this and that as an excuse to inspect her territory. She had put a lot of herself into this house. They had moved here when the boys were eight. All those years of cooking, cleaning, caring. Of watching over her chicks, loving them, keeping them from harm, encouraging them in their dreams, seeing them leave the nest. Soon the boys would be gone too. A-levels were almost over. There was only the trauma of the results and then they would be off to university. Toby to Brighton and Ollie to Southampton, if all went well and they got the grades they needed.

And what would she be left with? This house. She flicked a duster over a row of wobbly ornaments. There was the clay horse Claire had made in her pony-mad phase. There were Matt's football shields. There was the pincushion Toby had laboriously stitched at junior school and the coil pot Ollie had made at art class. They had meaning, these things. But the rest of it – the spacious rooms, the furniture, the pictures, what did they matter? Very little, if the people living there barely tolerated each other. It had been she who had held their marriage together all these years. If she stopped trying now it would fall apart.

The phone rang. 'Mum? It's me.'

'Claire! How are you, darling?'

'Fine thanks, Mum.'

Her daughter chattered on about where she had been with her latest boyfriend, what she had been doing at work. A lot of what she said was incomprehensible to Judy. Claire was an IT expert. She was being headhunted by a logistics company. Which appeared to be a good thing, from Claire's enthusiasm for the project.

'That all sounds very exciting,' she said. How amazing, that the little girl who made that clay horse should be an adult, coping with confidence with the new technology.

'It is. But Mum, that wasn't really what I rang about. I suddenly thought – it's your silver wedding in August, isn't it? What are you and Dad planning to do?'

Oh God. Alan hadn't mentioned it. It was quite possible that he genuinely hadn't realised. Either that or he didn't want to face it any more than she did.

'Well, we haven't really discussed it–'

'*Mum!* You've got to plan ahead a bit if you want a big do. The thing is, do you want to have a bash at home with all the family and your friends, or go out to a restaurant with just us, or hold it at the hotel, or what? Or would you like Matt and me and the twins to arrange something for you?'

She was so efficient, was Claire. Judy couldn't think who she had got it from. 'Well, like I said, darling, I really don't know yet. Let me have a little think and I'll get back to you, all right?'

'OK, but don't leave it too long, Mum.'

They talked on for another quarter hour

or so, and Claire finally rang off. She and the boyfriend were going to play softball in the park.

Judy paced round the house, not even pretending to clean now. Silver wedding. Silver wedding. The children were expecting a big celebration. What would it do to them if she walked out, if she went to live with Trevor? They might be grown up now, or almost grown up, but they still needed her as emotional back-up. It would rock them to their foundations if she left their father.

She went outside and patrolled her garden, deadheading and pulling up stray weeds as she went. Snip! A faded flower here. Rip! A chickweed shoot there. The sun was warm on her back. The roses, the lavender, the sweet peas all smelt wonderful. But they failed to work their usual soothing magic. What was she going to do?

'You ready yet?' Alan appeared on the lawn.

'You're coming, are you?'

He looked at her as if she was slightly mad. 'Yes. Did I say I wasn't?'

He hadn't said he was. Judy gathered her things and met him at his car. It gleamed on the driveway, the sunlight reflecting off its waxed surfaces. That car had far more attention paid to it than she did. Alan was already sitting at the wheel.

'Come on, come on,' he said impatiently.

He was fresh from the shower and changed into white trousers with a faint grey pin-stripe and a monochrome tee-shirt emblazoned with the Armani logo. He put on his shades.

'You're looking very trendy,' she said.

'No point in being fuddy-duddy,' Alan replied, leaning on the horn as a skateboarder whizzed up a driveway ahead of him.

'And who are you out to impress, then? Fiona?' Not that she believed any more that there was anything going on there. She was just surprised he was still interested after all this time.

The words came out before she could stop them. They didn't sound bitter. Just curious.

'Don't be so stupid.'

Judy shrugged. 'Me, I'm really not right bothered.' Right bothered, she recalled, was one of Trevor's expressions.

CHAPTER 21

Now where could everybody be? Cathy climbed out of the car with her overflowing bags of dance costumes. What had Maggie said? It had to be Maggie, of course. Cheryl hadn't thought of arranging a meeting point. By the flower tent. She trailed past rides and stalls, heading for the marquees she could see at the other side of the field. The early clouds had dispersed. It was a perfect English summer's day, and the crowds were out in force for the Festival. There was a smell of crushed grass and candy floss and frying onions.

Cathy stopped dead. There just ahead of her were two of the Morris wives. She dived off in a different direction to avoid them, and finally got to the marquees. The first, she realised by the smell, was the beer tent. Beyond that was refreshments and further on, by itself, the flowers. She skirted round a group of men standing guffawing over their plastic glasses of beer.

'Cathy!' Her arm was grasped from behind. She whirled round. Mike was gazing imploringly at her. Her husband, round, cuddly, reliable. The last person she wanted to speak to.

'Mike! Let go.'

'I've got to talk to you, Cathy. Please. Just for a minute.'

Behind him she could see a couple of the Morris men tactfully turning away into the crowd.

'There's nothing to talk about,' she said. 'Let *go*.'

'Not until you promise to listen. Please. Goldie and Sprogs are missing you terribly. And the cats.'

His eyes were as wide and soulful as a lost puppy's. And she had been worrying about the animals. She sighed. 'All right. Just for minute. I've got to go and get changed.'

He began talking, very quickly, in case she took it into her head to run away before he had finished. People washed round them, some looking slightly embarrassed, others openly eavesdropping on what was obviously a desperate and personal conversation.

'It's not only the animals that are missing you, Cath. I can't bear it, without you. It's terrible, it's – it's empty. There's nothing to come home for, I just sort of wander about. And I can't sleep. Cathy, you've got to come back. Look, I know why you went–'

Cathy stared at him. Did he? She'd not left any clues, as far as she knew. 'And it's all my fault,' Mike swept on. 'I didn't realise just how much it meant to you. I thought the animals were enough, you were just making a fuss, but I see now that it's more than that. Much more. It's sort of life and death for you, isn't it? And I thought, well, maybe I was wrong to say no. And I thought it all through and – the thing is, if it means us having a baby, then we'll go through with this sperm donor thing.'

He was breathing heavily, gazing at her, waiting for a reply.

Cathy felt overwhelmingly sad. Why did he have to say that now? Why not a few months ago, before Christmas, when it would have put everything right between them? She could even have been pregnant by now. 'It's too late,' she said.

They were all by the flower tent, as she had suggested.

'Oh, Maggie, you're here!' Cheryl said, too brightly.

The stupid woman didn't like her, Maggie knew. So what? She didn't need the approbation of people like her.

There was an air of excitement amongst the group of women. Some of them were changing behind the flower tent, some were doing make-up, adjusting each other's head-dresses, practising movements. There was the kind of high-pitched chatter and laughter that Maggie would have groaned at if they had been teenagers in her care. It was the noise of emotions running too high. She carried her carefully pressed costumes in their plastic cover to where the others were changing.

Of her own group, everyone was there except Cathy. They all greeted her, smiling, cheerful. There was Judy, who had taken her man, and Naz, who knew and laughed about it with all the others. Fiona, who had everything and still took more. And Shauna, who was stopping her son from being the success he should be.

She changed and hung her ordinary clothes, now in the cover, from a guy rope of the tent, then took her make-up and a mirror out of her bag.

'Shall I hold that for you?' Judy offered, nodding at the mirror.

Maggie hesitated. She could hardly bear to talk to the woman, but couldn't think of a reason to refuse. 'Thanks,' she said gruffly.

Her hands were shaking as she applied eyeshadow. It was difficult to concentrate on her own face when Judy's was behind the mirror, smiling, chatting with not a care in the world. How could he choose a fat, stupid woman like Judy instead of herself? What did he find so wonderful about her? She looked like a grandmother, for God's sake, and she never had anything interesting to say, forever waffling on about her children or her garden. As for sex – she was quite obviously one of those women who had lost interest in it years ago. She could feel pressure building up inside her, like one of those old whistling kettles coming up to the boil.

Shauna came bouncing up in a flurry of coloured skirts and dangling earrings, the scantiest of sequinned bra-tops on under her semi-transparent tunic.

'Want a hand? Oh no – I forgot. You like to do your own, don't you?'

Shauna's eyes were outlined in black and the eyelids filled in with blue and gold. Her wide mouth was glistening with scarlet.

'She looks amazing, doesn't she?' Judy said. 'Like a head from a tomb painting, Tutankhamun or something.'

'He was a king, not a queen,' Maggie snapped.

'I know, but the eyes were very similar, weren't they?'

God, the woman was ignorant.

'She'll look lovely in that two-piece when she takes the tunic off,' Judy was saying. 'It must be nice to be young and slim enough to bare your midriff.'

'If you'd persevered with the gym, you'd be trimmer,' Maggie said.

Judy looked slightly embarrassed. 'Yes, well, it wasn't really my sort of thing.'

The pressure was getting worse and worse. It was throbbing in her head.

'Oh, here's Cathy at last!' someone cried.

'Cathy, we'd almost given up on you.'

'Are you all right?'

That was Naz's voice. Maggie looked round. Cathy was flushed and breathless, her eyes bright with tears.

'Yes, yes, quite all right, really, it's just – oh dear, am I very late? You're all changed.'

'I'll show you where we're changing,' Fiona offered.

'No! I mean, it's all right – I'll find it by myself.' Cathy hurried off behind the marquee.

'Poor girl, she is in a state. I wonder what's wrong?' Judy mused.

'She's just pathologically inefficient. It's about time she got herself organised,' Maggie said, and swore as she poked herself in the eye with her mascara brush.

Judy laughed. 'You're beginning to sound like Shauna.'

The kettle started to boil over. 'Trevor coming to see you dance, is he?'

Judy looked really embarrassed this time. It gave Maggie a backhand sort of satisfaction.

'Ah – well, I believe he's – that is, Naz said he'd get away to see the performance.'

Maggie snorted with derision. 'Naz! Come on, Judy, it's you he's coming to see, isn't it? You've been having an affair with him for ages, haven't you? And you the respectable married woman, too.'

She couldn't stop the words from coming out of her mouth. Judy was staring at her open-mouthed and white-faced. Still she carried on saying all the things that had been keeping bottled up for so long. They just flooded out, spitting and scalding. Someone was at her side, shaking her arm.

'I think you've said enough.' It was Naz, looking furious.

'It's none of your business,' Maggie told her. 'You get your nose out of this.'

Naz's dark eyes were blazing. 'Excuse me,

but it is my business, if Judy makes my dad happy, then she's entitled to be happy too. It's nothing to do with you, you bitter old bag. You're the one who should be keeping her nose out of it.'

Judy placed a hand on Naz's arm. 'It's all right, you don't have to–'

'Yes I do! You're far too soft to stand up to her. What right's she got to tell you what to do?'

There was a rumble of agreement all around them. Fiona came up and put an arm round Judy's shoulders. 'Come on, Judy. You don't have to listen to this.'

How dare she interfere, the whore? All control finally snapped.

'And you're no better!' Maggie yelled, pointing a finger at Fiona. 'It's like bloody musical beds round here, isn't it? Judy's shagging Naz's father while you're shagging Judy's husband. You've the morals of alley cats, the pair of you!'

'I *beg* your pardon,' Fiona said, her voice arctic. 'I think you'd better be a bit more careful before you start making accusations like that.'

'I've seen you,' Maggie told her. 'I've seen the pair of you together, cosy as anything, buying flowers–'

'Buying–?' Fiona began, incredulously.

Maggie cut her off. 'I wonder what your husbands would say if they knew what both of you had been up to?'

Cheryl was flitting around them in a state of agitation. 'Girls, girls, please! We're on in five minutes.'

Maggie ignored her. She glared at Judy. 'What would Alan say, eh, if I told him that you were having sex with another man? Eh? What do you think he would do?'

Judy stared back at her. She was very pale, and her hands were shaking, but she spoke steadily. 'Do you know, Maggie, I really don't care. You can tell him whatever you like.'

A cheer went up. Shauna hugged Judy. 'Yeah! You tell her, Jude! Good on you!'

'That's right Judy. We're with you!'

'Yeah, right beside you!'

Cheryl bobbed up again, shrill with anxiety. 'Girls, please! We've got to go and wait by the arena.'

Maggie turned and marched off, in full costume.

The row charged Shauna up to full voltage. 'You were just magic, Jude!' she said, as they walked in an excited gaggle over to the arena. 'You really gave that silly bitch what for!'

Judy was looking quite fierce. 'Well really, she had no right to throw her weight about like that,' she said.

They walked to the roped-off area next to the arena. Shauna looked at the people gathered round the fencing to watch them, and her stomach contracted. Oh Christ. Oh shit. With all the drama, she'd almost forgotten the main point of the day. Now it all came flooding back. She felt sick. She gripped Fiona's wrist.

'Is he here? Have you seen him?'

'I don't know. I haven't been able to find my clients in all this crowd.'

'Fuck me, Fee, you got a mobile, ain't you? Why didn't you call them?'

'I did, but all I got was unobtainable.'

Shit. 'OK. Sorry. Only it's dead important to me.'

'I know.' Fiona gave her a quick hug. 'You just get out there and knock 'em dead. If he is here, he can't fail to be impressed. You're a brilliant dancer.'

'Yes, you are,' Judy chimed in. 'You deserve your break.'

'Thanks. You're good mates, both of you,' Shauna said. But it didn't stop the sinking feeling inside. What if this agent wasn't here? What if he was but he thought she was crap? What then? Marry Ben? Have his bitch from hell mother as a mother-in-law? She'd rather top herself.

The previous act, a brass band, was marching out of the arena to limited applause. The PA system crackled into life. 'So let's have a big hand, ladies and gentlemen, for the Mellingford Boys' Band. A very fine performance. And now for a complete change. Our next group has been brought to you at great expense all the way from Egypt– No, only joking, folks. They may look exotic, but they're all local-grown beauties–'

'Wanker,' Shauna muttered.

'Here to delight us with their belly-dancing. Ladies and gentlemen, the Queens of the Nile!'

There were whistles and cheers. Their music blasted out from the amps. Fiona pushed Shauna in the small of her back. 'Go on,' she said. 'You first. Right behind Cheryl.'

Shauna took a deep breath, and moved forward. There was a burst of applause and more whistles as they paraded to the centre of the arena and each took up a pose. The audience attention was like a drug. The stage fright faded, the urge to perform took over. Shauna gave a turn and struck a dramatic attitude. Yes. This was it.

The music changed to the intro for the first number. Shauna felt it flow through her muscles, her sinews, her very bones. She became the music. She rippled and flew with it. It wasn't easy, dancing on grass. Out of the corner of her eye, she could see somebody tripping, someone else treading on her hem, Judy turning the wrong way. Christ, if the agent was watching, he'd know them for the amateurs they were.

The music ended. The audience clapped.

They were easily pleased.

The dancers unwrapped their veils from where they had been swathed round and tucked into their hip-scarves. There were whistles of appreciation. They held them up with both hands above their heads so that the fine fabric floated in the breeze, a rainbow of candy colours trimmed with silver and gold. The slow sinuous music of the veil dance filled their ears. Shauna swayed and undulated. She was the essence of graceful sensuality. She knew she was moving as well as she had ever done. She was in control.

Another burst of applause.

Then the other dancers ran back to get out of their tunics, and Shauna was left alone in the middle of the grass arena. She cast her tunic aside with one graceful movement and stood in her skimpy two-piece, one arm raised and one leg forward and bent slightly at the knee. There were cheers and whistles and hoots of appreciation. The sequins on her bra top and belt glittered in the sun, and her layers of skirts moved gently in the breeze. She looked the goods, and she knew it. The music for her solo began.

Shauna danced like one possessed. She used the space, she played to the audience. Somewhere, somewhere out there, the man who could change her life might be watching. She smiled and whirled and shimmered.

She projected her own love of the dance to the watching crowds. And they loved her. They clapped along with the music and when she finished they called for more. Shauna curtseyed in all directions, acknowledging their praise.

The others came back on. The final dance went by in a flash. And then it was over and they were all back in the gathering area by the arena, laughing and panting and congratulating each other.

Fiona hugged her. 'You were brilliant, Shauna, just brilliant!'

'Breathtaking,' said Judy.

'You had them eating out of your hand,' Naz said. 'And panting for more.'

'Always leave 'em wanting,' Shauna joked. She was all hyped up, elated and sick with nerves at the same time. 'Supposing he wasn't there? Supposing it was all for nothing?' she kept repeating.

The others assured her that the agent couldn't possibly not have seen her. But she couldn't be so sure. The next act was in the arena, the one after was assembling ready to go in. The dancers had to go back and change. Shauna was hustled along with the rest. As they went along, passers-by told them how good they were, how original. Where had they learnt to dance like that? Where did they get those beautiful costumes?

Shauna smiled and said thank you and

answered the questions along with all the others. Where was he? Where was this agent? Did he really exist or was it just some stupid dream?

They got back to their encampment by the flower tent, where some of the groupies were already waiting to congratulate them. Ben flung his arms round her and kissed her. 'Hey Babe! You were unreal!'

'Yeah thanks.'

She pushed him away. He was not part of her plans. Oh Christ, what if the agent didn't want to sign her? She would be stuck with Ben. No, she didn't have to be. She could still get rid of him. But then what would that leave her with?

'I'm going to get changed,' she said.

She wiped off the stage make-up and stripped off her finery and climbed back into her red crop top and black capris. So. What now? She looked between the various bodies and saw Ben waiting for her. He caught her eye, grinned and waved. He was wanting to take her round the stalls, buy her hot dogs and have a go on the darts and the tombola and the bat-the-rat. He was easily pleased. He didn't ask much. He'd be happy as a pig in shit living with her in a small flat. But she wanted more out of life.

There was a stir on the edge of their sprawling group. First one, then several people called her name. 'Shauna, where's Shauna?'

'She was here a minute ago.'

'She's over there.' That was Ben. 'I'll fetch her for you.'

Shauna couldn't breathe, couldn't move. Her body felt as heavy as lead.

Ben came striding over, all smiles. 'Hey, move your arse, Babe, there's some Mr Big here to see you.'

Shauna waved two fists in the air. 'Yes!' she cried. 'Yes, yes, yes!'

CHAPTER 22

This was her moment. This was what Cathy had been waiting for, as she trailed Richard and Fiona and their children round the fair. She stuck with them with a dogged determination, watching their every move. The way he leaned towards her to speak. The touch of his hand on her shoulder as he pointed something out to her. The quick laughter. The easy familiarity. It made her sick to the stomach with jealousy. It was all a show, of course. They weren't really the perfect couple. Not that he had told her, in so many words, but she knew it, sensed it. Women could sense things like that.

But now they were parting company. Richard had Freya in his arms, Fiona was holding Harry's hand. Richard was looking at his watch. They were going to take the children to different things. This was her chance.

Cathy waited until Fiona was out of sight, then she darted forward. 'Richard!' She caught him by the arm.

'What the–?'

This was not right. He was glaring at her. 'Richard, I've got to talk to you.'

He put Freya down. 'Not here,' he hissed at Cathy. 'Not now. For God's sake, are you mad? Anyone could see us. Half Mellingford is here.'

'But I've got to. I can't phone you at work, I can't phone you at home and you won't answer your mobile. I've got to talk to you,' she insisted.

'But I don't have to listen,' Richard said, and turned away, pulling Freya after him.

'Please, Richard. I'm desperate.' She had him by the sleeve. He stopped abruptly, so that a couple of people nearly cannoned into him.

'Let go!'

'How can you do this to me, when I left Mike for you?' she cried.

'Shut up!'

He glanced around, evidently did not see anyone he knew, and retreated between the animal refuge stall and the St John's Ambulance. Cathy followed him. His face was dark and cold with anger. It made her heart shiver with fear.

'Now listen to me,' he said, and it was an order. Cathy listened. 'I am not having my marriage and my family's happiness jeopardised by you. What you do with your life is nothing to do with me. You can leave your husband if you like, that's your decision, not mine. Is that clear?'

He was jabbing his finger at her as he talked, emphasising his point. Before, she had thought his way of gesticulating a very Italian and romantic trait of his. Now it seemed threatening.

'But I did it for you. I left Mike so that we could be together,' she wailed.

'There is no "we". It was just a fling, OK? It didn't mean anything.'

Cathy felt as if she had been kicked in the stomach. She was breathless with the pain of it. 'It does to me. I love you!' she cried.

Richard's face was hard. His voice was cold and controlled and utterly forbidding. 'If you are going to make scenes like this, then it's best we don't see each other again,' he said, and turned away.

'No!' Cathy flung herself at him. 'No, don't go! You can't. I – I'm pregnant!'

She didn't know where the lie came from. It surprised her. But once it was past her lips, she stood by it. For she had his full attention.

'You're *what?*'

'I'm pregnant, and it's got to be yours, because Mike's sperm count is almost nil. It must have been that last time at the Oasis, you know, when we–'

'Shut up!' Richard was pale. He was looking at her with loathing. 'You are not going to pin this on me, do you hear? It's your problem. I'm not going to let it hurt my fam–'

He broke off and looked round. 'My family,' he repeated. 'Where's Freya? She was here. Where is she? Did you see her go?'

Cathy shook her head. She hadn't noticed anything outside the two of them. They might have been alone in the world for all she saw of the rest of it.

'Christ but you're useless,' Richard said. 'How long have we been here? How long has she been gone? Freya? Freya!'

His shout rose above the noise of the crowd. People turned to look. He glared down at her. 'This is all your fault. Don't just stand there, start looking.'

He pushed past her and started questioning the St John's first-aiders and the people behind the animal shelter stall. None of them had noticed a six-year-old girl on her own. Richard put his hands to his head. 'We were going to the roundabouts,' he said. 'Quick, she might have found her way there.'

Once again Cathy found herself trailing

him, but running this time, pushing through the crowds, stumbling on her high heels. Freya was not at any of the rides, nor had anyone seen her.

'Oh God, oh God, where can she be? Why didn't I hold on to her?'

He had gone away from her, Cathy realised. She didn't matter. She could be a stranger for all he cared. All he wanted was to find his daughter. He looked at her for a moment.

'You start searching. I've got to find Fio – oh my God, Fiona – what am I going to tell Fiona? She'll be frantic.' He jabbed at the buttons on his mobile. 'Shit! Turned off. What's she turned it off for?' He marched away from her, calling for Freya as he went.

Dissolving with misery, Cathy watched him go.

Fiona and Harry were with Naz, Brad, Karis and Lady the Labrador, watching the birds of prey being flown.

'You see that thing on the end of the string?' Brad said to the children. 'That's called the lure. It's used to attract the bird back to the hand.'

Both children nodded solemnly. Harry asked lots of questions.

'He's very knowledgeable, your Brad, isn't he?' Fiona said softly to Naz.

'Mm.'

Naz wasn't watching the birds, she was looking at Brad talking to the children. 'He's asked me to go and look at a cottage with him. Over at Eastlea.'

It would just be so right. Fiona cast about for the correct thing to say. Naz was so touchy about men. Being over-enthusiastic was not the right approach.

'What's it like? Did he say?'

Interested but not gushy.

'It sounds lovely, but very run-down. No bathroom, no proper kitchen.'

'Plenty of room for improvement, then?'

'Yeah, you could say that.'

Fiona took a breath. 'Are you going to go and see it, then?'

'I don't know.'

Good God, woman, you'd be mad not to. Can't you see he's absolutely the one for you? Lightly, she said, 'You'd be good at doing up an old place. You're very practical and you've got a good eye for design.'

'Yeah, I guess.'

Fiona wanted to shake her. 'Of course, it's a big step to take.'

Naz caught her bottom lip in her teeth. Her face was creased with indecision. 'That's just—'

'Is she here? Is she with you?'

Richard burst into their peaceful little group. Anxiety caught at Fiona's guts. This wasn't the usual Richard, in control of the whole world. He was out of breath and looking distraught, and Freya–

'Where's Freya?' she demanded.

He put his hands to his head, squeezing his skull between his palms.

'I don't know.'

Real fear gripped her then, raw and icy. 'You don't *know?*'

'I hoped she'd run back to you. She knew where you'd be. I was just talking to someone and when I turned round she'd gone.'

'Oh my God!' A dozen possibilities, all of them bad, raced through her head. Her stomach churned.

'What's up?'

It was Brad. Naz filled him in.

'Have you been to the commentary box? They'll put a message out over the PA,' he said.

'No. Right. I was going to do that next.'

Richard was angry that he had to be told such an obvious thing. As if male ego mattered at a moment like this, when her baby was at risk

'We must search now, at once!' Fiona cried. 'Harry, you stay with–'

'No, we need a central point. It's no good if someone finds her and you're not there to receive her. We'll end up chasing each other round in circles,' Brad said. 'Why don't you go back to the meeting point by the flower tent with Harry and Karis, and tell anyone else who's still there to join in the hunt, and then you can co-ordinate the search and we'll all know where to come back to.'

It made sense, even though it went against her instinctive need to start rushing about calling out Freya's name.

'Yes. Right,' she agreed.

'I'll go to the commentary box then I'll look in the car park. She may have gone back to the car,' Richard said. 'I've already been round all the rides.'

'We'll take the side of the fair nearest to the road,' Brad said.

'Right, right,' Fiona repeated. 'Car park, and side nearest the road. Done the rides.'

She had to remember. It was vitally important. Oh God. Freya. Freya. Where are you? Panic rose in her. 'What are you waiting for?' she screamed. 'Find her! Find her!'

Richard's arms came round her, holding her tight, holding her together. 'I will, I will find her, I swear it,' he told her. 'She's probably being taken to the commentary box by someone right now. Just stay calm and wait by the flower tent, and I'll bring her back to you if it's the last thing I do.'

She nodded, not trusting herself to speak. Keep a grip. It was the only thing she could do for Freya. Richard went off on one direction, Naz and Brad in another. Fiona held out her shaking hands to Harry and Karis. 'Come on,' she said. 'Stay close. We don't want to lose you as well.'

Unusually silent, the two of them grasped her hands and trotted alongside her as she hurried to the flower tent. A couple of women from the group and their families were still there. Fighting to keep her voice under control, Fiona explained what had happened. They scattered to join the search and to tell anyone else from the group to look too.

'Sit down. There,' she said fiercely to the children.

They sat, silently. Now what? She couldn't sit herself. She paced up and down. She was sensible, Freya was. She knew not to speak to strangers, not to accept lifts. But why had she run off in the first place? It was so unlike her. She didn't do things like that. Images of kidnaps swam through her head. Someone marking Freya out, following her and Richard, waiting for that one moment of inattention–

'All alone? We can't have that.'

Fiona gasped. Alan. The very last person she wanted to see. He was smiling, moving too close.

'You were wonderful in that performance. The star of the show. Knocked spots off the rest of them. And that green dress really suits you. You should wear green more often, it brings out the lovely colour of your hair–'

Shut up shut up! 'Shut up! Just go away!'

Alan threw his hands up in mock dismay. 'Oh dear oh dear, what is this?'

He laid a hand on her shoulder. She recoiled in revulsion and lashed out at him. 'Just fuck off! It's the same every time we have one of these things. You're always there breathing down my neck. Just fuck off out of my life, you sad loser!'

'All right, all right!' Alan was backing away, shocked.

Behind her, the children were shrieking with delighted laughter and repeating, 'Fuck off! Fuck off!'

'Go back to your poor wife, though if she's any sense she'll leave you for – oh!'

There in front of her were Judy and Trevor, hand in hand. 'Judy!' she gasped, 'I–'

'Granddad!' cried Karis.

'It's all right,' Judy said, putting a motherly arm round her. 'We heard what had happened and came to see what we could do to help. Trevor, can you rustle us up some tea from the refreshment tent? And take the children with you and get them something as well.'

'Right you are. Come on, kids.'

Trevor held his hand out. Karis jumped up and ran to him. Harry hesitated.

'It's all right, Harry. You can go with Karis's granddad,' Fiona told him.

The two children went off with Trevor

towards the refreshment tent. Out of the corner of her eye she could see Alan, staring at them in bewilderment. Judy turned to him. 'What are you waiting for? She told you to go, didn't she? And in no uncertain terms, too.'

'What? But – right, yes, well, right.' And he shambled off.

'Good riddance,' said Judy. She was red in the face, and her eyes were shining. 'What happened? Did she get lost in the crowd? It's so hard to keep an eye on them all the time.'

Thank God. She wasn't asking about Alan. 'She was with Richard.' Fiona explained. 'He was talking to someone, and when he looked round she had–'

Talking to who? She hadn't thought of that before. Who had distracted him so much that he didn't know what had happened to his own daughter? The older worry surfaced again, multiplying the new one.

'She had run off?' Judy prompted.

'What? Yes.'

Had he been talking to *her*, the woman who put the coaster in his pocket, the women he took to the Oasis?

The PA system crackled into life. 'We have a little girl lost. Her name is Freya and she's wearing–'

Fiona went cold. It was real, her child was missing. She listened to the details, each word falling like a stone into her heart.

'Oh my God,' she whispered. 'Oh my God!'

Judy had her arm round her. 'Don't worry, someone will find her now. Poor Richard. He must be blaming himself. But she won't have gone far, truly she won't. It's so easy to get lost in a place like this. And she's a sensible little girl, isn't she? They all know about not talking to strangers these days–'

'Yes, yes, I know.'

But supposing she had been abducted? These things happened. She saw police camped at the house, volunteers out searching the fields, divers in the river, Freya's photo on TV, happy, smiling, herself and Richard making an appeal before the press. Please, whoever you are, bring our baby back to us. 'Bring our baby back,' she whispered. Nothing mattered as much as that. Certainly not the party business, not even the Oasis woman, if she even existed. Nothing mattered at all, just as long as Freya was all right.

Maggie heard the appeal over the PA. Freya? Was that Fiona's Freya? Without realising it, she slowed down from a furious march to a walk. Despite the wild churning of emotion in her guts, the mother in her could not but feel a twinge of concern. A lost child … the nightmare of it...

'Were really good. Where did you learn?' She became aware of a woman talking to her. 'So nice to see women of – you know – our age doing something like that. I'd love to have a go.'

'Oh, yes.' She looked down at herself with something like surprise. She was still wearing her dance costume. She tried to gather her wits, to sound normal. 'I go to a class here in Mellingford.'

Not that she would be going any longer. She didn't want to see that lot again as long as she lived.

'Lovely costumes,' the woman was waffling on. 'Do you make them yourselves?'

The costumes – Naz – Trevor. God, she'd made such a fool of herself! 'Yes,' she lied, then gasped as a small figure cannoned into her and clasped her hips.

'I can't find my daddy!'

She looked down at a pink tearful face. Thin arms clung to her bright dance skirt. 'Freya! What are you–?'

'I want my mummy!'

Maggie knew what she had to do. Freya had to be taken back to the dancers' gathering place.

'All right,' she said. 'It's all right, don't worry. You're safe now. I'll show you where mummy is.'

She took Freya's hand and trailed back through the happy jostling crowd towards the very last place in the world she wanted to go to. As she neared the flower tent, she considered just pointing Freya in the right direction and watching to make sure she got there, but she knew that was cowardly. She was going to have to face them.

She saw a little knot of them standing there, Trevor with his hands full of polystyrene cups and chocolate bars, Judy with her arm round Fiona, Harry and Karis swigging from coke cans. She waved and called to Fiona, who looked up, saw her, then spotted Freya. At exactly the same moment, Freya caught sight of her mother. They ran into each other's arms.

'Oh my darling!' Fiona was laughing and crying at the same time, kissing Freya's head and neck and shoulders until the little girl squealed that she was hurting. Maggie felt tears pricking at her own eyes.

'I'm sorry, darling. I was just so worried,' Fiona was saying.

'Don't cry, Mummy.'

'She was a sensible girl. She saw me in my dance costume and knew I was someone she could trust,' Maggie said.

Fiona looked at her over her daughter's shoulder, still rocking her in her arms. 'Oh Maggie, I can't thank you enough,' she said.

Harry was hanging on to her skirt, looking put out. 'You're in trouble. You know we mustn't run off,' he said to his sister, smugly self-righteous.

'But there was a nasty lady, and she–'

'Hadn't you better call Richard?' Judy said.

'Oh, yes.' Fiona fumbled for her mobile.

Maggie looked at Judy. She took a steadying breath. 'I shouldn't have said what I did. It was out of order,' she admitted.

Judy gave a stiff smile. 'It's all right. Water under the bridge.'

There was an awkward pause. 'Well – I'll get changed then,' Maggie said.

'Right.'

By the time she had got into her ordinary clothes, Richard had returned. He picked Freya up and put his spare arm round Fiona. Harry put his arms round them both.

'Thank God,' Richard said. 'Now we're all back together again. Our family.'

On hearing that Maggie had found Freya he thanked her warmly, kissing her on both cheeks.

Maggie felt embarrassed. 'It's nothing.'

She looked at them, Fiona with Richard, Judy with Trevor, the children hanging about them. Did she really want all that? The domestic bit? The family ties? She'd never really been that good at it. She'd slid into thinking that she wanted it because that was what people did, and because she didn't have it. But when it came down to it, she actually liked being on her own and doing what she wanted when she wanted, not having to make allowances for anyone else. It was stupid to try to be something she wasn't.

'I shan't be coming back to the class,' she announced. 'Ben's more than big enough to look after himself. So I'm a free agent.' A free agent. She could go wherever she liked. 'I might go abroad to teach. Possibly to Africa.'

She only half heard the good wishes for her future. The group was already part of the past. She left her dance costume on the grass in its plastic cover and walked off to find her car, already making mental lists of things to be done.

CHAPTER 23

Judy stood watching the reunion of the Meredith family. They looked so touching together, the two attractive children, and Richard and Fiona such a devoted couple. Tears rose in her eyes.

'She's back, then.' It was Shauna.

Judy gave her a watery smile. 'Yes, thank God. Maggie found her.'

'Jude–?' Shauna was not sounding quite her usual confident self.

'Yes?'

'You know – well – what the Bitch Queen said?'

Judy felt amusement tugging at her. Shauna was trying to be tactful. Now that was something new.

'You mean Maggie?'

'Yeah, who else? I mean, what she said, like–'

'About Alan and Fiona? I never believed it for a minute, not from Fiona's side, that is.'

Shauna grinned, relieved. 'Boot-faced old cow. What a load of bollocks! I mean, Fiona and Alan–'

She stopped short. Judy laughed out loud. Tact hadn't lasted long. 'Exactly. It's hardly likely, is it?'

Something, maybe nearly twenty-five years of married intuition, made her look away to the far side of the touching scene between Fiona and Richard. There by himself was Alan. Watching the reunion too. Coolly, a detached observer, Judy looked at his face as it dawned on him that here was a strong marriage, and that Fiona really wasn't the least bit interested in him. She saw his shoulders slump. A new sensation rose in her, something between pity and contempt. Poor old Alan, the ageing Romeo, wanting something he could never have, and losing something he could have kept forever but didn't value.

Shauna's voice cut through her thoughts. 'You were fucking brilliant with the old bitch. I never thought you had it in you.'

'Oh, I surprise myself sometimes,' Judy said.

And realised that it was true. The last few months she'd found herself doing quite a lot of things that amazed her. Changing her appearance, performing in public, finding a lover. A lover. It was funny to think of Trevor as that. She looked across at him. He was playing Round and Round the Garden with Karis. Bless him.

Shauna followed her gaze. 'He's a dead nice bloke, old Trev.'

Dead nice? Yes. Old? No.

Still looking at him, Judy smiled. 'He's made me feel like a proper woman again.'

For a moment an appalled expression crossed Shauna's face. Judy had seen that before. The realisation that Old People still Do It. Gross. But, miracle of miracles, Shauna didn't comment. Instead, she gave her a big hug.

'Hey, you go for it, you hear?'

'I hear,' Judy agreed, hugging her back

They both looked at Richard and Fiona as they fussed over their children.

'I suppose it gets to you like that, having a kid. Like, Fiona was out of her tree, wasn't she?'

'Your mum'll be pleased when she hears about your new agent,' she said.

'Yeah. She always wanted for at least one of us to make it off the Watfield estate.'

If anyone was going to, it was Shauna. She was young, brash, beautiful and talented. 'You'll make it, Shauna. A long way off the Watfield estate. I'm quite sure of that.'

'Yeah.' Shauna grinned at her. 'Look, I'm going to push off now, right?'

'Right,' said Judy.

Shauna slung her bag with her dance costume over her shoulder and strode off, drawing every man's eyes after her as she went. Soon afterwards Fiona and Richard drifted away too, a child on either side of them.

Karis was getting bored. 'When's Mummy coming back?'

'She's on her way, sweetheart. I told her Freya had been found.'

'*I* wouldn't run off like that. It's very naughty.'

'I know you wouldn't, pet.'

Cathy turned up. She was looking wild and strained. Her eyes were puffy and her mascara streaked across her face.

'Cathy.' Judy went to put an arm round her. She seemed to be having to mother the whole group today. 'What is it? What's the matter?'

'Nothing,' Cathy said, and burst into tears.

Judy caught Trevor's eye. 'More tea,' she mouthed at him.

Trevor cast his eyes to the heavens and took Karis off to the refreshment tent once again.

'It's all my fault,' Cathy was sobbing. 'I've been so stupid.'

'There there,' Judy soothed. 'We all do stupid things sometimes. But it's not too late, you know.'

'It is, it is. I know. He said–'

'But your Mike's such a nice man. I'm sure he loves you really. It's just a question of swallowing your pride. I know it's hard, but it's worth it.' My God, who am I to talk like this?

'But he said he wouldn't leave her.'

Judy failed to follow this. Did Mike have a girlfriend? 'Leave who, Cathy?'

'Fiona. He won't leave Fiona and his family.' She started sobbing again.

Richard?

Something odd that Freya had said flashed through her head. 'There was a nasty lady.'

Cathy? Had she been the person Richard was talking to, the person who so distracted him that he didn't see Freya go? Surely not. And yet she was very upset about something. Bloody men. If it was true then Richard deserved to have his balls cut off. Dear me, she was sounding like Shauna. Only Shauna would have said bollocks.

'Bollocks,' she said out loud.

'What?'

Cathy was staring at her, shocked out of her weeping.

'I mean–' Now then, she must say the

right thing here. No use encouraging Cathy to think of Richard in that way. 'Yes, they do seem right together, don't they? A lovely little family. Poor Fiona was out of her mind with worry over Freya, but they're together again now, so all's well that ends well.'

'Not for me,' wailed Cathy. She broke away from Judy and began searching the heap of bags for her belongings.

'Cathy,' Judy said, hardly knowing what she might say next. 'Cathy, you know–'

Cathy found her bag and straightened up. 'Leave me alone!' she cried. 'You wouldn't understand!' And she stumbled off, wobbling on her high heels.

Judy sighed as she watched her go. 'Oh, I think I do understand,' she said.

Trevor reappeared with more teas in polystyrene cups. 'She gone?' he asked. 'Oh well. All the more for us.'

He was just taking a lid off when Karis jumped up, knocking his arm and spilling tea everywhere.

'Mummy!' She rushed to fling herself into Naz's arms. 'Mum! Freya came back. Mrs Stafford got her. And I've had loads of crisps and coke.'

'Might as well shove off, then, now that the panic's over. We've seen everything here,' Brad said.

'Thanks for looking after her, Dad,' Naz said. 'We thought we'd go over and take a look at this cottage Brad's found. It sounds wonderful. I mean, it needs everything doing to it, but it's got three little bedrooms up in the roof with those dormer windows, you know? And those stairs that you open what you think is a cupboard and there's stairs there, and a great big garden going right round the side so there's lots of room for swings and sandpits and things.'

'Sounds absolutely beautiful,' Judy said.

'Yes, just right,' Trevor agreed.

'It does, doesn't it?'

Naz's face was glowing. She turned to Karis. 'You're going to love it, aren't you?'

'Is Lady coming?' Karis wanted to know.

'Of course she is. Lady goes everywhere with me,' Brad told her.

They walked off, Brad and Naz with their arms round each other, Naz holding Karis's hand, Karis hanging on to Lady's lead.

'That sounds very hopeful,' Judy said.

'It does. Thank goodness she's come to her senses. I thought the silly girl was going to blow him out, when there he is, the best thing that's ever happened to her. He's such a decent bloke, that Brad. I don't know why he puts up with so much nonsense from her.'

'That's love for you. And you're right, he is just right for her. And nice looking too. I could fancy him myself if I was twenty years younger.'

'Watch it. Any more loose talk like that and I'll have to put you in a chastity belt.'

'I'd like to see you try.'

The afternoon was wearing on. From the arena there was the sound of a steel band. The last of the dancers came back to claim their baggage and left with their families.

'No point in hanging round here any longer,' Trevor said. 'I suppose I'd better get off home. What about you?'

Judy took a deep breath. She threaded her arm through his. 'I've decided,' she said. 'I'm coming with you. To stay.'

This Large Print Book, for people
who cannot read normal print,
is published under the auspices of

THE ULVERSCROFT FOUNDATION